D1387860

Rachel Wells is a mother, writer and cat lover. She lives in Devon with her family and her pets and believes in the magic of animals. Rachel grew up in Devon but lived in London in her twenties working in marketing and living in a tiny flat with an elderly rescued cat, Albert. After having a child, she moved back to Devon and decided to take the plunge and juggle motherhood with writing. *Alfie the Christmas Cat* is her seventh book.

Also by Rachel Wells:

Alfie the Doorstep Cat
A Cat Called Alfie
Alfie and George
Alfie the Holiday Cat
Alfie in the Snow
A Friend Called Alfie

RACHEL WELLS

ALFIE

the Christmas Cat

avon.

Published by AVON
A division of HarperCollins*Publishers* Ltd
1 London Bridge Street
London SE1 9GF

www.harpercollins.co.uk

A Paperback Original 2020

First published in Great Britain by HarperCollins*Publishers* 2020

A catalogue copy of this book is available from the British Library.

ISBN: 978-0-00-841197-8

Typeset in Bembo 11.25/15 pt by Palimpsest Book Production Limited,
Falkirk, Stirlingshire
Printed and bound in UK by CPI Group (UK) Ltd, Croydon CR0 4YY

MIX
Paper from
responsible sources
FSC™ C007454

Acknowledgements

For my seventh Alfie book, I think I am running out of people to thank! My 'team' is, as always, amazing: agents, editors, publicists, marketers, copy editors, proof readers, it takes a lot of people to make a book.

Alfie has become such a huge part of my life and my family's life too. Every time I write about him, I am able to bring out someone who has become like a best friend, and all my characters are so important to me as well. I get to write about things that I care about: kindness, friendship, family, love, community and helping people.

I feel so lucky to be able to write these books. But it's only because I have such a wonderful readership. You are all important to the process: you give me inspiration and you made me want to write more with your kind words. When you enjoy my books that makes me very happy. So, thank you all for reading, for being a part of Alfie's journey and for staying with us for seven books! I hope you all keep reading and enjoying, knowing that I appreciate each and every one of you.

To my niece Claire, who loves cats as much as I do.

Chapter One

We prepared for noise and chaos to fill our house on what can only be described as one of my favourite days. It was family lunch day, and we have a big family. What I have learnt, as a doorstep cat, is that family isn't just about blood. As George and I groomed ourselves, ready to greet all our favourite people, we were more than a little bit excited.

I'm Alfie, if you haven't met me before, and George is my kitten, although he's not exactly a kitten anymore. As most parents know, there is a reluctance to acknowledge that our children are growing up, getting older and more independent. I have to admit, looking back, I miss when George was younger and needed me more than he does now. Thinking about how I used to moan about lack of sleep, no time to myself, constantly being on guard for danger . . . But I'd turn the clocks back in a heartbeat. Of course, George still needs me at times, but he is so independent, with his own life and even a girlfriend, Hana. Oh how he's grown into a fine tom. But I digress.

I am a doorstep cat, which means I have more than one home, more than one family that I spend time with. George and I have our main home with Claire, Jonathan, and our children, Toby and Summer. We live on Edgar Road. It's a big street with lots of different types of houses. We often gather at ours as it is one of the bigger houses, and we have a lot of people, pets and children to fit in.

'Hey guys!' Matt, who is one of the most laid back of our

adults, approached the doorstep with his wife Polly, and their children, Henry and Martha. Oh, and on the lead was a very excited Pickles, their pug who spends a lot of time with us. I am not only a cat who looks after humans, but also dogs, it seems.

Pickles tries to eat everything in sight, and likes to lick whatever he can't eat. He's still a puppy, albeit quite a chubby one! I am often charged with Pickles sitting; have been since he was tiny. Now, as I said, he's far from tiny – as the time he got stuck in the cat flap proved – but he's part of the family. He might have taken a bit of getting used to, us cats and dogs aren't natural friends after all, but we love him very much. Although . . . George took longer than me to come around to having him in our lives, and he can still sometimes be a bit cutting with him.

'Meow,' George and I greeted them, along with a friendly nuzzle. As they stepped inside, Pickles licked us both then licked Jonathan's feet. Thankfully, he was wearing slippers. The children shrieked as they all went upstairs to play. Toby, Summer, Henry, and Martha are the best of friends, which is lucky as we all spend so much time together. As Polly and Matt went off to help with drinks and food, we waited to see who our next arrivals would be.

The doorbell rang again and Sylvie, Marcus, their teenager Connie, and their baby Theo were there. They'd also brought their cat, George's girlfriend Hana. They made such a cute couple.

Claire practically trampled us to get hold of Theo, before they even set foot inside. Theo was our latest addition; he was only a few months old and ever so popular. It was the same when George was a kitten and Pickles a puppy. People liked babies.

'Come in out of the cold,' Jonathan said as Claire walked into the living room cuddling Theo.

'I'm just going to pick Dad up,' Marcus said, before leaving to get his dad, Harold, who lived at the end of the street.

It was largely down to George that Harold became part of our group and, in turn, his son Marcus and Sylvie – our next door neighbour – fell in love. We can actually pretty much take credit for baby Theo, thinking about it.

I grinned and raised my whiskers at George and Hana. We could hear the children laughing upstairs, the adults in the kitchen – Jonathan and Claire were cooking, and Polly now had hold of baby Theo. Pickles was running around in circles, Sylvie was enjoying a much-needed sit down and Connie hovered anxiously. We all knew who she was waiting for.

The sound of the doorbell heralded our final guests. As well as Harold, who brought his cat Snowball, my girlfriend and first love – it's a long story so I'll tell you about it later – Tomasz, Franceska, and their teenagers Aleksy and Tommy stood on the doorstep.

There were more hugs and kisses and nuzzles and strokes before we were all finally in one place. Our family lunch was about to start. And I couldn't have been happier.

George, Hana, Snowball and I snuck into the garden. We should have known that Pickles wouldn't like to be left out and watched as he emerged through the cat flap, which was actually a doggy door. He got stuck in the cat flap so it had had to be replaced with a bigger door.

'What are you doing?' Pickles asked. He might not be tiny anymore but he was only a year old, so still a baby. He'd also spent most of the first year of his life trying to be a cat. It's a hard lesson every non-cat has to learn, that not just anyone can be a cat. It takes a lot of skill.

'Just getting a bit of fresh air and a bit of quiet,' I said.

'It is so noisy in there, isn't it?' he said.

'I love it when we're all together but we are a lot aren't we?' George stated. There was no arguing with that. We were a lot.

Lunch was in full swing. We didn't have a dining table big enough for everyone, so the children sat at one table and the grown-ups at another. I, obviously, was with the grown-ups, but I hovered by the chairs – it was frowned upon for cats to be on the table, although sometimes that didn't stop me. George and Hana were with the children and Pickles was under the table, trying to catch any food that had been discarded. He really liked his food. Snowball was curled up in my bed, taking a rest. I noticed that Connie and Aleksy were sat with the adults, but Tommy, Aleksy's younger brother, was at the children's table and he didn't look happy as he pushed his food around his plate. I made a note of that. If people were unhappy, it was my job to sort them out.

I padded over to him and tried to get his attention, but he ignored me. I was put out – I'm not used to being ignored – but then, Tommy really did look thunderous. I made my way back to the safety of the adults.

'We have this school project; it's about homelessness,' Aleksy said.

'God, that's heavy, in my day we just did Geometry,' Jonathan said with a laugh.

'Showing your age, Jon,' Matt teased.

'In my day we wrote with quills not pens,' Harold added, then laughed loudly. I had no idea what he meant but as Harold was quite fond of being grumpy, it was nice he was laughing.

'So, what is the project?' Marcus asked.

'We're learning about awareness campaigns. We have to design a campaign to highlight the problems facing homeless people today and make people aware that it's a problem,' Connie explained.

'Goodness, that sounds very serious,' Claire said.

'We wanted to go to the local shelter and meet people who are actually homeless to find out what it's like,' Aleksy said. 'So that when we do our project we will have direct experience to draw on.'

'And then we thought we might come up with ways to raise money for them,' Connie added with a blush.

'You are very good and kind, Aleksy and Connie,' Franceska said. 'I'm proud of you both.'

'I'll come with you,' Tomasz said. 'We give food from the restaurant to the local place so I know them; I can take you both.'

'Oh that would be great!' Connie's eyes lit up.

'But it will be hard,' Sylvie said. She was very overprotective and I knew she would be worried about Connie.

'Yes, but these two will be fine,' Polly cut in. 'They are

tough and have big hearts. I think it's wonderful that you're learning about these things at school.'

'In my day—' Jonathan started, but then laughed.

'So, we'll visit the shelter and then think of a way to raise money and awareness,' Aleksy said. I nuzzled him. I was very proud of him too.

After lunch, the children all went to play again and Connie and Aleksy snuck away, which just left Tommy.

'Can we go home now?' Tommy – who had barely said two words to anyone – asked.

'No, if you don't want to go and set up games for the little ones, then you can just sit there on your own,' Franceska snapped. It wasn't like her. But then, Tommy wasn't normally so unpleasant either.

'Go into the living room and put the TV on,' Jonathan suggested.

Tommy scowled but he went. I glanced at Snowball; we knew all about teenagers. They could be problematic but Tommy was also fun, and he loved setting up assault courses and competitions for the others. I knew he felt left out when Aleksy and Connie started going out together but he normally invited one of his friends to come to our family events. I wondered why he hadn't today.

'He's been nothing but trouble, lately,' Tomasz said quietly once Tommy was out of earshot.

'He's grounded and I said he couldn't have a friend here today, because of his behaviour,' Franceska added. Ah, that explained it.

'What's he done, Frankie?' Claire asked.

'Being rude, answering back, not doing his homework. He even took money from my purse the other day. It's like my lovely little boy's been taken and replaced by someone else.' She sounded upset so I went to nuzzle her.

'Oh God, teenagers; I am not looking forward to that,' Matt said, shaking his head. 'But it's not like Tommy,' he added.

'Do you want me to have a word with Connie? Ask her if she and Aleksy could be more inclusive?' Sylvie suggested.

'No, thank you. He and Aleksy are at odds all the time – they can barely stand to be in the same room at the moment. Aleksy said that Tommy is acting like a jerk, Tommy says Aleksy is a goody-goody. Honestly, we are hoping it's just a phase, because otherwise . . .'

'I could give him a good whack with my walking stick. That'll soon sort him out,' Harold offered. I wasn't sure if he was joking; he didn't look as if he was.

'Dad, we don't do that anymore,' Marcus replied.

'National service, that's the answer. He should go into the army.'

'Um, he's only fourteen,' Claire pointed out.

'Make a man of him it would,' Harold began one of his favourite tirades, and there would be no stopping him now.

If they really needed to punish Tommy they should make him listen to one of Harold's lectures.

Chapter Two

It was another one of my favourite days of the week – Sunday – and George and I were patrolling Edgar Road. It was freezing, and winter was definitely knocking on the door, but that didn't stop us from popping into homes where the Sunday Lunch Club was in full swing. To explain, the idea of the club was that people opened their homes to someone who would otherwise be on their own, and gave them a lovely Sunday lunch. Simple but brilliant.

And, it was a doorstep cat's dream.

Harold wasn't being grumpy for once and came up with the idea to help ease loneliness by setting up The Sunday Lunch Club. George thinks it was his idea initially, which it probably was. George and I are known for our brilliant ideas – he gets it from me. A chip off the old paws. The club helps lonely people feel less lonely and it also means a lot to those who host the lunches, so it helps the community as a whole. A wonderful idea and one which has now grown beyond Edgar Road. I am very proud of George and Harold. They did have my help, of course, but I'm not one to boast . . . Although they could not have done it without me.

Anyway, I digress. Today we popped in to see all our neighbours who were hosting lunch on our street – and not just to get treats, although both George and I had very happy tummies by the end of it. But most importantly, it warmed our hearts to see people who would otherwise be on their own enjoying food and company. The host families got to meet new people and widen their social group as well. It was a winning situation for all. Harold was at Marcus and Sylvie's house with a couple of other people. Snowball was there and I had popped in to see her briefly. I would love to see more of her, but we are always surrounded by people these days – it's hard to get time alone. We're lucky that we're older and not in that teenage kind of love that George and Hana have where they want to spend every moment together.

'It was such a brilliant idea that me and Harold had, wasn't it?' George said. He said this every time.

'Yes, son, such a wonderful idea and getting to see how happy people are is such a huge credit to you.' I was proud of him, despite the fact that he liked to inflate his little ego at times. But who could blame him? He deserved it. And I had often been accused of the same thing, although I'm pretty sure my ego is fully in check . . . most of the time.

'And Harold and I really are genius, aren't we?'

'You are.'

'And I might be the cleverest cat who ever lived.'

Hang on, that was my title. 'Well, maybe the second cleverest cat,' I purred with a smile. We both grinned. 'Right, son we better head home.'

The days were becoming darker as well as colder. I could feel the chill in my fur, announcing we would soon be facing the coldest part of the year. We had to brace ourselves for it. I loved to go out, and was reluctant to become a fair weather cat like some of the others, but I still preferred the warm.

We went through the cat flap of our house. Today, we had hosted our lunch with Doris, a lady who always knitted, even while eating, and Clive, a very smart ex-teacher who liked to debate politics and scared Jonathan by asking him questions he had no clue how to answer. They were both lonely, and having that in common was enough, but they still bickered with each other. Jonathan said they should just get married, as they were like an old married couple, but Claire told him that wasn't funny. Claire and Jonathan were still young but had been married for ages now, and they did bicker quite a bit, but they also laughed a lot too. We didn't see Clive and Doris laughing, so I was pretty sure even my matchmaking skills would be pushed to the limit trying to get them together. Didn't mean I wouldn't try though! I put that thought on my 'save for later' list.

I had got many couples together in my time, Claire and Jonathan being my biggest and first success. But there was always so much to do keeping my cats and my families under control, I had little time for much else these days. I certainly had my paws full.

'Look,' Summer said when we went into the living room, where all the family, along with Doris and Clive, were sat drinking tea. 'Doris knitted a cat bonnet.'

'Meow?' What on earth is a cat bonnet?

Doris proudly held out a knitted red hat, which she then proceeded to put on George's head. He tried to squirm away but he was too slow. He looked furious – us cats do not like being dressed up, thank you very much; we have lovely fur and that's enough for us. As he tried to pull it off with his paw, the others admired him.

'Oh Doris, it's so cute,' Claire said, beaming.

'Perfect fit,' Clive said.

'It's adorable. Doris, will you teach me to do knitting?' Summer asked.

'Of course I will, my dear.' Doris's cheeks flushed with pleasure.

My eyes widened. I couldn't believe it. It was terrible. It made his head look like a tomato. Thank goodness I didn't have one.

'Don't worry, Alfie, I'll have one for you next time I'm here, but your head is a bit bigger, so I need to get more wool. And thinking about it, green might be your colour.'

I had no words as I slunk off to see if there were any more leftovers.

That night, when George and I took our last steps outside before bed – without his cat hat, I may add – we looked at the dark sky and saw the brightest star blinking at us.

'There's Tiger mum,' George said, lifting his paw.

'Yes.' I gulped. Despite the fact that it had been quite a while since we'd lost Tiger – George's adopted mum and my last partner – it still floored me whenever I thought of her not being here anymore. We have both moved on in many ways, the way life forces you to, but although I am happy and with Snowball now, I will always have a place in my heart reserved for Tiger. She was my best cat friend on Edgar Road before we fell in love.

I've loved and lost a lot in my life, both humans and cats, and you never stop missing them, a lesson I have learnt the hard way. But on the flip side, a heart is a wonderful thing.

It's big and has the capacity to love many people and many cats. I even managed to love Pickles, who is a dog, and I never thought I'd hear myself saying that. Despite the fact I'm now reunited with Snowball — who was my first love, before Tiger — I miss Tiger. And that's fine, because as I said, the heart is a miracle and it's big enough for all it needs to be big enough for. It allows you to miss those you've lost and still love those who are with you.

'She'd be so proud of you, son,' I said, because it was true. She would.

'I know, Dad,' George replied.

I think he gets his modesty from me.

'Right, lad, let's go to bed.' I started to make my way inside, giving the star one last glance. It seemed to blink at me. I blinked back.

We probably had a big week ahead of us, we had a lot of people and cats to check on so there was always a list of things to do. Especially as I worried about Tommy; I had to be on alert.

'Before we go to bed, Dad, what am I going to do with that awful bonnet that Doris gave me?'

'Well the polite thing would be to wear it when she is here, at least for a bit.'

'But it's scratchy. I was thinking I could bury it in the garden, blame it on Pickles.'

'George, that's not nice.'

'But the hat isn't nice.'

'I know, but we do these things to make people happy and if you have to wear it for a short time, every now and then to make Doris smile, is that so terrible?'

He glared at me and then he raised his whiskers.

'I guess not, especially as you'll have one as well next time.' I could hear him laughing as I followed him into the house.

Chapter Three

Humans will never cease to amaze me. In the morning, our house springs to life in a very dramatic way. There's shouting, jostling, arguments, and occasionally tears. Jonathan gets ready for work – normally with maximum fuss as he seems unable to find anything. Claire rouses the children from their beds (the tears are usually theirs), then she feeds us cats and prepares breakfast for everyone before going to get dressed. Toby rushes downstairs as if there's a fire, and Summer sulks as she hates mornings these days. Claire fires questions at everyone: 'Have you got much on at work today? Have you done your homework? Do you need your PE kit? Why won't you eat your toast . . .' You get the idea. George and I eat our breakfast and then attempt to escape before the madness of trying to get everyone out of the house begins. Trust me, it's chaos. Jonathan leaves first, rushing out, often moaning about where his keys are even though they are always in the same place. Summer takes forever getting her shoes on, Claire gets exasperated as she repeats the same thing over and over, and Toby gets cross about being late, because he hates being late. The thing is, this happened every single weekday morning. Every single one. You would think they would learn, but no. Humans! Who'd have them?

If only they could be more like us. George and I get up, have a good stretch and a quick wash before we have our breakfast, then we have a more thorough clean up and we're ready for the day. Totally fuss free.

I know that our house isn't unique. Polly and Matt, with Henry and Martha, have the same situation. George says that our next door neighbours, including Hana, are far more organised than our family, and definitely not as shouty. But Sylvie has just had baby Theo, so she doesn't go to work, and her partner Marcus is actually very calm. As for Connie, she's more sensible than any of the grown-ups put together, so she manages to get herself to school. The main noise is caused by Theo, who basically ensures none of them get enough sleep – I can vouch for that as I remember when Summer was a baby. We were all sleep deprived and grumpy in the mornings as a result. But like Summer, Theo will grow out of it and start sleeping at some point. When George was a tiny kitten it took him a while to learn to sleep at night as well, actually, thinking about it.

Back to ours. George and I gave them a wide berth until they were all safely out of the house. After snatching a few moments' peace and quiet after they were gone, our day could begin.

'I'm going to Hana's,' George said. Since the baby, Hana had been happier to go for walks than normal. Hana was from Japan, and she was a house cat when she moved with Sylvie and Connie next door to us on Edgar Road. After trying for ages, we managed to get her to go outside but she only liked it when it was warm. However, since Theo's arrival, she seemed to prefer the cold to staying at home all day long. I didn't go with George and Hana on their morning walks because it was the cat equivalent of a date for them and who wanted their parents to go on a date with them? No one, that's who.

Despite the fact it was a cold and breezy day, I decided to go and visit Tomasz, Franceska, Aleksy and Tommy. They lived in Edgar Road when I first moved there, but for a few years now, they'd lived next door to one of the restaurants they'd opened. They had come over from Poland, worked hard, and now had a number of popular restaurants, which provided great food. And I should know, as I am sometimes one of their chief tasters.

I assumed that Aleksy and Tommy would be at school, and Tomasz and Franceska would probably be working in the restaurant, so I hoped I might get a snack, and could see my cat friend Dustbin who worked for them. He was a bit of a feral cat, with a big heart and we had been friends for years. He kept the rodent population by the restaurant under control – not a job I would like by the way, but he loved his work. He was totally dedicated. I was still a bit worried about Tommy. He wasn't himself on family day – understatement – and Franceska and Tomasz were obviously upset, so I wanted to see if I could gather as much information as possible about the situation, before I came up with a plan to sort it out.

I felt the wind in my fur as I ran through the back alley to the yard. Dustbin was there, licking his paws – probably after another successful rodent control – with his friend Ally, whom he was loath to call his girlfriend, although she was.

'Hey Alfie,' he said as he spotted me. His whiskers were raised and he sounded pleased to see me.

'Dustbin, Ally,' I said in greeting.

'What brings you here in the cold?' Ally said. She always teased me, calling me a spoilt cat with my warm homes and numerous humans to pamper me. Who was I to argue? I loved my life. But I wasn't that fair weather, as I've already said. I even went out in snow. I felt my fur shiver at the thought of snow, but it might not be too far away now. Snow made me think of Christmas, and Snowball, who was as white as snow – hence her name.

'I thought I'd brave it in order to see my two good friends,' I replied, with a grin. I liked Ally, but she had taken a bit of winning over. She wasn't used to being friends with 'pampered' cats.

'Good to see you, Alfie. Here to catch up on the news?' Dustbin asked. He kept me abreast of the goings on with my third family, as he saw them far more often than I did.

'Is there news about Tommy?' I raised my whiskers.

'Well, yes, I'm afraid there is,' Dustbin said, sounding serious.

'Oh no.' I felt my heart sink. Whereas Aleksy – who happened to be my first ever human child friend – was sensitive, serious, and a hard worker, his younger brother Tommy was the opposite. He was a good kid but he did get into trouble. Once, when George was a kitten, he sneaked him to church with the family, another time he snuck him into the younger children's Nativity play and put him in the manger, replacing the doll that was supposed to be the baby Jesus. That even made the local newspaper. But you get the idea. He was mischievous rather than bad, I liked to think. Although, if family lunch had been anything to go by, he was now transitioning to bad.

'He's still not doing his homework, he's had so many detentions, he's getting bad grades, and being rude to his teachers. He stays up late – we see his light on, playing games and he even fell asleep in class the other day. The school have called in his parents this week to have a serious talk about him, I'm sorry to say,' Dustbin explained.

'Oh dear.' I knew that this would be very stressful for Tomasz and Franceska. And, although I adore Tommy, he can be his own worst enemy. His parents work so hard and are such good people, I wasn't happy at the idea of him worrying them so much. I didn't want him in trouble either, it never ended well. I realised that I would need to get involved.

'Franceska said he's still grounded and he's mad because you know how he likes to go hang out with his friends. Aleksy is trying to keep the peace but he can't really say anything to his brother right now, and Tomasz even said that Tommy was going off the rails and needed taking in hand.'

'What are they going to do?' I asked. I had taught Dustbin well. When we first met he was more interested in rodents than people. Look how far he'd come.

'They don't know. Tomasz has said Tommy has to start working in the restaurant, washing dishes to keep him out of trouble, and Tommy said that is unfair, but I have a feeling it might get worse before it gets better, Alfie.'

'Poor Aleksy is trying,' Ally added. She had also become an asset. 'But he doesn't know how to get through to Tommy either. You hear the two of them arguing quite a lot. Tomasz was supposed to take him and Connie to the homeless shelter yesterday after school, but because they got called in to see Tommy's teacher, Tomasz was late. They went in the end, but Aleksy accused Tommy of ruining things for everyone. Tommy said Aleksy was a "goody-goody" and Aleksy said

Tommy will end up in jail if he carries on this way.' My eyes widened. Surely it couldn't be that bad?

'I'll have to think of something.' I knew it would come down to me to try to find a way to fix this – most things did. I didn't mind, it was my job. Dustbin kept the rodents under control, I kept the humans under control. I have to admit I think his job is easier though, even though I'm not keen on rodents.

'I know you'll come up with something,' Dustbin said. 'I hate to see Franceska so worried, Tomasz helpless . . . They think that if he doesn't shape up he's going to be in real trouble.'

'Hmm. I get it. He's always been a bit wild and he's never liked school work the way Aleksy did . . . I'll think about it, talk it over with Snowball maybe, see what we can come up with.'

'Speaking of Snowball, how is she?'

'Yes, she's good. Harold has had a bad cold so she's stayed in quite a lot to keep him company; she's got such a good heart. I know sometimes she still misses her old family too but she and Harold are pretty close. And of course George is there a lot – and me – so she's never really allowed to be down for long.' Snowball used to live next door to us many years ago. Her family had moved away, which was sad for me, but just last year they had to go overseas and couldn't take her with them, so she moved in with Harold. It was a wonderful surprise.

'Life can throw a lot of changes at us, can't it?' Dustbin asked. He wasn't wrong.

'Goodness, if we went through all of them we'd be here all week. Right, shall we go and scratch at the door and see

if they have any treats for us?' I suggested. I had to think of
a way to sort Tommy out, but before I even thought about
coming up with an idea, I knew that it would be easier to
do so once I had a full tummy.

I always managed to think better after food.

After a little bit more time spent with Dustbin and Ally and
some delicious plump sardines, I headed back to Edgar Road.
As I entered through the cat flap I could tell the house was
empty, and I wondered if George was still next door. After
taking a quick rest, I went to see Snowball, who lived near
the end of the road. Edgar Road is quite a big street, with
different types of houses on it, and that means we have a
lovely mix of people and cats. As I walked past Tiger's old
house – would I ever stop thinking of it like that, I wondered
– I saw Oliver, the Barkers' new cat in the window, though
he was not so new now. I felt a pang and, as if sensing this, he
raised a paw at me. I greeted him and walked on. I was happy
the Barkers had got a cat after Tiger, but I also found it hard
– the dichotomy of life. I knew they gave Oliver a good
home and he was a splendid cat. And, of course, every cat
deserved a loving home, but it was still hard to have a reminder
of Tiger being gone every time I passed.

I walked on, past the recreation ground where us cats met
up, but no one was there. But then, the weather had turned
quite horrible so my sensible cat friends were probably warm
and cosy at home. I would see them soon though, I knew.
We Edgar Road cats were quite the gang. I made it to Harold's
house, went round the back, and let myself in through the
cat flap.

Harold wasn't a fan when he first met us, but George saved his life and now he liked cats more than people. Especially now he had Snowball. It hadn't been easy for us at first, me and Snowball. Not only were we trying to see where our feelings were – she was my first love, after all – but also I had been with Tiger in between and, on top of that, George took against her because he felt she was trying to replace his mum. It took us a while for us all to figure out our relationship but we did, eventually, and we were all happy together now.

This was illustrated by my finding George and Snowball together in the living room at Harold's house. Harold sat in his favourite chair, watching some kind of war programme on the TV. Snowball was sat on one arm of the chair, George on Harold's lap. They all looked so comfortable, I felt a pang. I stood and watched them for a moment, the two cats I loved so much together, and then Harold spotted me.

'Ah Alfie, now I have a full house!' He laughed. I jumped onto the other arm of his chair and lay down. None of us moved for a moment. We were there together and that was enough for now. More than enough, in fact, as we all purred with contentment.

Chapter Four

By the time George and I returned home, the house was full again. I hadn't had the chance to tell Snowball about Tommy yet; George was present, and I didn't want to worry him until I had a chance to think it through a bit more – that was parenting for you. You tried to protect your children, although I had learnt you can't protect them from everything.

We went through the cat flap and into the hallway where Pickles, Polly and Matt's pug, waddled up and licked us both.

'Oh, hey Pickles,' George said, as he used his paw to wipe where Pickles had licked. I followed suit. Pickles licked everything and you could never be sure quite where that tongue had been.

'How are you?' I asked. My role with Pickles was like an uncle; he didn't have dog parents, so I took the responsibility of being the non-human figure of authority very seriously. I'd known him since he was tiny, and often been in charge of looking after him, and I really was very fond of him. As was George, even though he didn't always like to admit it. George saw him as an annoying younger sibling, I think. Pickles got me in a lot of trouble, but then most people and cats in my life did, so I was certainly used to it.

'I'm so good,' Pickles said, snuffling around to see if there was any stray food. I liked my food but I had nothing on Pickles. Polly was always putting him on a diet so he had to come up with more and more ways to sneak food. When it came to eating, there was no stopping him. 'George, the kids are playing upstairs, will you come with me?' Pickles asked, waggling his bottom with excitement. We could hear Toby, Summer, Henry, and Martha, laughing and shrieking.

'OK.' George tried to sound reluctant. He was so grown up now that he said the games they played with the younger kids were beneath him! However, I knew he secretly still loved it. I watched them both rush off then went into the living room where, to my delight, Polly, Franceska, Claire, and Sylvie were. Claire was clutching baby Theo, who seemed to be asleep.

'I can't believe he's sleeping,' Sylvie said, as if reading my mind. 'He's been terrible lately; I think it's a growth spurt. Feeding all the time, not sleeping, it's exhausting. If I knew that having a baby at my age would be so tough . . .'

'You wouldn't be without him though, would you?' Polly asked.

'No, of course not – I adore him. But Connie's so much older, so I really had forgotten what it was like to have a newborn. Thankfully Marcus is great and supportive, but I'm conscious that he has to work.'

'It's a tough time, the first year,' Claire said. 'But also amazing. I sometimes look at Toby, who feels as if he's been with us forever, and I feel guilty that I wasn't the one to comfort him when he was this age.' Claire sounded emotional. Toby was adopted by us when he was five. We don't talk about his life before and neither does he anymore. Now he's been with us, such a huge part of our family for years, it's as if he was always here. I kind of know what Claire means though.

'Theo's only three months old, remember,' Franceska said.

'Soon enough he will find his routine; babies do it in their own time. Goodness, not that I remember, my two are so growing fast.' I glanced at Franceska and jumped onto her lap. She got her words a little bit mixed up when she was worried. Perhaps I would hear more about the Tommy situation now. Franceska sighed.

'Things still bad with Tommy?' Polly asked.

'Ah, yes. He's always been such a naughty boy but mostly harmless. You know, so physical, unlike Aleksy, but sports seemed to keep him under control. But now he's really playing up at school and we don't know why. He doesn't do his homework, he's been in detention so many times and his head of year even called me and Tomasz in. He said he is not doing well in lessons and he's becoming known as a trouble maker by the teachers. He has broken so many rules, I don't think there's many he hasn't broken. Thankfully he hasn't been fighting, but that seems to be the only thing he hasn't done.'

'Oh Frankie,' Claire said. 'Tommy's a bright boy but he's always been a little bit of a live wire. Do you think this might just be a phase?'

'I hope so, but as Tomasz said, if he starts being in trouble all the time, how do we stop it? It's hard, you know? Tommy's always been a leader and he is being seen as the bad influence on his friends now; Aleksy told me this. He didn't want to say too much because it would betray his brother. He also said he would try to talk to Tommy but I don't think it's done any good. They just argue about it all. Tommy says Aleksy is a "suck up" and Aleksy gets quite upset by him.'

'You've already grounded him?' Sylvie said.

'Yes, and we took his phone and his iPad, and now he just says he hates us! I just don't want my lovely boy to go off the rails.'

'I'm sure he won't – he's got a good heart at the end of the day – but you know, maybe he still feels a little bit out of place . . . with us. He's older than our lot, and Aleksy has Connie . . .' Polly pointed out. This was true. Poor Tommy was a little bit on his own. We noticed this and I somehow managed to draw attention to it. He sometimes had a friend come with him, when we had family day, but not now, not when he was in trouble. He wasn't allowed.

'That is why we told him to invite a friend, but now he is grounded we said he had to improve his behaviour before his friends can visit again,' Franceska said. 'We really don't know what to do for the best.'

'Keep an eye on the situation, that's all you can do. And if you need any help, we're all here,' Claire said.

'Meow.' I seconded that.

'I know. I'm hoping that the next family day we have, maybe Jonathan can have a word. For some reason he seems to take to Jonathan.' Yeah, I didn't know why either.

'I think it's because they're similar.' Claire laughed. 'But I have an idea. Tommy said he wants to work in the city, which he can only do if he does well at school. Maybe Jonathan could say that if he improves his grades he can do some work experience for him.'

'That's a genius idea, Claire,' Franceska said. 'I would be so grateful.'

You see, I had taught my humans well. Claire had almost as many good ideas as I did. Although, knowing Jonathan as I did, I wasn't sure he'd be thrilled. He often found himself having to do things that he had no say in. But, I also knew that even if he objected there would be no point. When Claire made up her mind there was absolutely no changing it.

Tommy being in trouble was something I would have to ponder. He was a good boy. He was fun as well, always laughing and joking, and yes he didn't love school the way Aleksy did and he didn't find lessons easy either, but he had great potential. And I would not let Tommy ruin his life – not that he was going to, but if Franceska and his school were right, he was in danger of going down the wrong path and it would take a cat like me to get him back on the right one. Oh, don't get me wrong, I was pretty sure I wouldn't be able to do it alone, but I had my family, my cat friends, and I was determined. All I needed now was a plan, and I was very, very experienced when it came to making plans.

Theo woke up with a quite startling cry soon after, and Sylvie took him home in order to make Connie's tea. Franceska reluctantly left us to go and deal with her family. I could see in the way her shoulders were slumped that she was seriously worried about her younger son. I nuzzled into her, giving her a bit of extra fuss so she knew that I was here for her.

'Shall I do tea for the kids here?' Claire offered.

'Oh that would be fantastic. I'll pour us a glass of wine shall I?' Polly replied. The kids all got on pretty well most of the time. There was the odd squabble, but that was only to be expected. They all had tea together a few times a week, especially as Claire looked after Henry and Martha when

Polly had to work late, and Matt couldn't get home either. I loved how lively the house was, but it was also quite exhausting.

As George and Pickles and the children descended on the kitchen I watched my family with a mixture of love, pride and worry. We never stopped worrying about those we loved, that was for sure. As the children ate their tea with all the usual chatter and laughter, George and I sat in our basket in the kitchen, enjoying our family. Pickles lurked under the kitchen table, trying to pick up any scraps that were dropped, and Polly and Claire sipped glasses of wine. I wished I could press pause on our lives. Keep this snapshot for a bit longer, because it was truly lovely. And because sometimes life moved far too quickly.

George and the children were growing up fast, the adults trying to keep everything balanced – and I include myself in that by the way – and even Pickles wasn't technically a baby anymore. At least we had baby Theo to keep us young, I guessed, but then we'd blink and he'd be a teenager. Oh listen to me, getting all maudlin. It was only because I was worried about Tommy, and once I started fretting I generally started worrying about everyone I loved.

That was the sort of cat I was.

I went out the front to take a bit of thinking time in the fresh, albeit damp and cold, air. I saw Aleksy and Connie standing at Connie's front gate. I went to greet them.

'Ah Alfie, I was just going home. I don't want to give my parents any more grief,' Aleksy said, petting me.

'No, your brother's doing quite enough,' Connie added.

'Meow.' I've heard, I said.

'At least we did get to the homeless shelter. Oh Alfie, it was so sad, so many people without homes,' Aleksy said, still stroking my fur. I nuzzled. I had been homeless once, which seems like another life now, but, I understood.

'Yes, we want to raise money for it. Not because of the school project but because Christmas is coming up and it's tough enough being homeless at any time but imagine at Christmas,' Connie added, sounding passionate.

'Mew, mew, mew.' I thought that sounded like a very good idea. Not that I had experience of raising money.

'I knew you'd agree. Now we just have to think of an idea, because we don't have one yet. But I better go. As I said, I don't want Mum to worry about anything else.' Aleksy bid me and Connie goodbye. He was a good kid, as was Connie. And they wanted an idea.

Well, they had come to the right cat.

Chapter
Five

It was another family day, an unscheduled one actually. Sylvie wanted to host a lunch, which she hadn't done since Theo was born, to sort of officially welcome Theo into our extended family. As far as I was concerned we already had, but if it kept Sylvie happy . . . Hana told George that Sylvie felt as if she had received so much support from us all since Theo was born, she wanted to thank everyone, so a Japanese feast it was. And I wasn't too upset about that because the Japanese were huge fans of fish, just like me.

Sylvie's house, which used to be very minimalistic, was full of baby stuff now. By the way, for something so small, babies seemed to need a lot of stuff. Not like kittens, kittens were easy by comparison. We cats are so self-sufficient, it's a shame that humans can't learn from us; believe me, I have tried to teach them. Dogs can't learn that much either by the way. Trust me, we tried with Pickles.

I was hoping I might get a bit more information about the Tommy situation. Having reviewed all I knew so far, I had a number of conclusions. Tommy was a teenager and he was misbehaving at school and home. I loved Tommy as I loved all my children, and therefore I could not allow that to happen. However, at this point in time I had no idea what to do. The problem was I could feel trouble brewing. I could feel it in my fur.

Hana, George and I stand poised by the front door of Hana's house to greet the families. George and I snuck over early, entering through the cat flap, because we were so excited. Hana's house used to be a quiet and immaculate place but hurricane Theo had changed things somewhat. Now, there was baby paraphernalia all over the place, and it was also pretty noisy. Theo was a beautiful baby but he had a strong set of lungs on him.

On the upside, it was also a happier home now. They had had challenges when they first moved in. Sylvie and Connie arrived from Japan after an upsetting time – divorce. Connie struggled to settle in England, and worried about her mum, but then Sylvie met Marcus, and now they're a family, which baby Theo helped to complete.

Hana took a bit of time to get used to life in Edgar Road too. In Japan her life was very ordered but in Edgar Road, well, let's just say order isn't something that we do very well.

Claire, Jonathan, Toby and Summer arrived first as they only had to come from next door. Claire made a beeline for baby Theo, practically grabbing him out of Sylvie's arms, and Summer, who was fascinated by babies, and played with dolls a lot, attached herself to her mum's side, begging for a hold. Sylvie, who is usually quite uptight, sat Summer on the sofa and said she could give Theo his bottle. Polly, Matt, Henry and Martha arrived next with Pickles, who was allowed to join us as long as he behaved himself. He never behaved himself, though, as he set about licking everyone. Martha immediately wanted a turn with Theo; this baby was in demand. Just as a row threatened to break out, Sylvie said there would be enough time for everyone to hold Theo. Poor thing, he was going to spend the day getting passed around like a parcel. It reminded me of when George was a tiny kitten. Everyone wanted him then, too. They lose interest when you get bigger. It's a fact of life; I can tell you that from personal experience. Not a terrible one, I might add. There are benefits to not being manhandled all the time. Theo could look forward to learning that when he got a bit bigger.

'Where's my grandson?' Harold boomed as he arrived with Marcus, carrying Snowball. I raised my whiskers at her, I was pleased to see her but we would wait to greet each other properly when she was on the floor. Harold treated Snowball as if she was his baby sometimes, even though she was a fully grown cat, like me.

Years ago now, Snowball and I had a rocky start to our relationship – for some reason she was immune to my charms – but I won her round eventually. And yes, I do have a few charms, I'll have you know.

Harold put Snowball on the floor, and we rubbed noses.

'Here, Dad, sit down and I'll pass Theo to you,' Marcus said. See, just like a parcel.

The doorbell went again and Franceska, Tomasz, Aleksy and Tommy were on the doorstep.

'Sorry we're late,' Franceska sounded stressed.

'It was this one's fault.' Tomasz gave Tommy a gentle push into the house.

'I wanted to hang out with my friends, not be here,' Tommy said, sounding surly.

'Yowl!' I chastised him. He rolled his eyes at me. Where was my fun Tommy? He went into the living room, sat in the corner and folded his arms. Goodness, he looked sulky, even worse than Summer did when she didn't get her own way, and that was saying something.

'I am so sorry,' Franceska said to the other adults as they made their way into the kitchen. 'But he's impossible. He wanted his phone back but we had to stand our ground, so he won't be good company today.'

Even the kids knew to give Tommy a wide berth as they looked at him suspiciously. Aleksy and Connie shrugged, but didn't even try to speak to him. Only Pickles seemed oblivious as he went up and licked him. Tommy didn't even acknowledge the poor dog, as he sat with a scowl on his face. Eventually Pickles got the hint and slunk away.

I noticed Franceska nudge Aleksy.

'Tommy, why don't you come with us, Connie's got a new Xbox game.' Aleksy was trying. He was being kind, just how I'd taught him.

'Nah.'

Aleksy rolled his eyes at his mum and he and Connie went upstairs.

Apart from Tommy, it was a lovely, busy, cheerful family day. The kids played nicely, baby Theo seemed to enjoy the noise and the chaos, which was lucky as he would have to get used to it. The food was certainly delicious; Snowball, Hana, George and I had a feast. Poor Pickles was rationed though because, as usual, he was on a diet.

'You know, it's time to start thinking about Christmas,' Claire said, as lunch finished and the kids went off to play. My ears pricked up at the word Christmas – it really was a wonderful time of the year.

'Oh God, Claire, not yet, surely we get a few weeks more

of normality before we mention the C-word,' Jonathan retorted.

'Bah humbug,' Claire shot back. 'And it's practically November, or it will be next week.'

'Claire is right, we need to be organised. Last year, there were lots of us, and this year there are even more to invite, because we have our Sunday Lunch Club,' Franceska pointed out.

'And, that's a lot to cater for, so we need to plan it,' Polly agreed. 'Not just the food, but transport, presents . . . Wow, we do have a lot to think about.'

'We can open up the restaurant for a big lunch,' Tomasz offered.

'But we should divide tasks, so that there's not too much for anyone,' Matt said, being sensible.

'And as I'm at home at the moment, I'm happy to pitch in,' Sylvie said. 'Theo and I can do some baking or something like that.'

'Right, so it's settled,' Marcus said. 'We'll have a big Edgar Road Christmas again, and as it's Theo's first Christmas, we'll make it perfect.'

'If we're having it at the restaurant it won't be on Edgar Road,' Harold pointed out. Normally Harold didn't like Christmas, but since meeting us, and having Snowball, he actually seemed to be changing his tune. If only Jonathan would do the same. 'I can be in charge of the guest list, if you'd like. To make sure that no one we know is on their own on Christmas Day,' he offered, a little bashfully. Harold wasn't used to being helpful – even Marcus, his own son, said that, so this was new for him. I believed George could take credit for that change in him. With my help of course.

'Great, so if we can only sort out that son of mine, we'll be all good,' Tomasz said, scratching his head. I felt sorry for him. Tommy and he had always been so close, both being into the same things, and having similar personalities. Aleksy was more like his mum, sensitive and serious.

'I'll have a word,' Jonathan offered. 'I'm not an expert at teenagers but it's worth a go.' I purred and rubbed his legs to show him I approved, although we all know that he was doing it because Claire had told him to.

I sneaked out to find Jonathan and Tommy in the back garden. Jonathan was clutching a bottle of beer, Tommy looked sulky.

'Listen, mate, I don't know what's up with you but trust me, if you keep getting in trouble at school there won't be a job in finance for you when you leave.'

'I just don't like school. They tell us what to do all the time and don't even give us a chance to have any thoughts of our own,' Tommy replied, looking at the ground. The most he'd said all day.

'Mate, that's life sometimes. If you want things you have to play the game.'

'But why?' Tommy asked.

'You want a job like mine, right?' Jonathan asked.

'Yeah, I want to make loads of money and I really like the idea of working with stocks and shares, I even read about it,' he mumbled.

'So why the hell are you behaving like a jerk then?' Jonathan

46

asked. Not one to mince words was Jonathan, but in this instance I agreed with him.

'I dunno,' Tommy looked at the ground. 'I guess I just get fed up with everyone telling me what to do like I'm some dumb kid.'

'You're behaving like a dumb kid,' Jonathan pointed out. 'Sort out your grades, sort out school and get your parents back onside and maybe, just maybe, I'll get you some work experience in my office.'

Tommy's eyes lit up. He looked really pleased and he even almost smiled.

'Really?'

'But you need to sort your act out first. Because I'm not going to help you until you start behaving yourself. Deal?'

'Deal,' Tommy said.

'And if there's more to it than just being a bit fed up with school or being a teenager, then you tell me. Don't mess up your future, Tommy; honestly, it's not worth it.' Jonathan ruffled Tommy's hair and then went back into the house. He looked relieved as he did so.

I felt, perhaps, that Tommy needed some support, rather than more telling off, so I went up to him, gently pawing him.

'Ah, Alfie, sorry I didn't make a fuss of you. I'm just so annoyed all the time. I don't know why half the time either.'

'Meow.' I rubbed his legs. He was still my Tommy, but he was also a teenager and I knew, from experience, how terrible being a teenager could be. Not only for humans, by the way. When George had his teenage phase I despaired as he refused to tell me anything. Thankfully, it passed eventually, and I hoped that with Tommy it would do the same.

'I just feel so angry and then I feel sad that I'm angry. I don't like to push everyone away but I don't know how to stop. Does it make sense?'

'Meow.' I let him scratch my head – I do love a head scratch. I understood poor Tommy didn't mean to be horrible, but that was a teenage thing too. It might even be a medical condition – 'being a teenager' – but I didn't know for sure. I'm a cat not a doctor after all.

'I promise I'll try harder,' Tommy said, but his shoulders were slumped and he sounded sad. I cuddled into him as much as I could. He needed me, and I would be there for him. I tried to convey to him that he wasn't alone because I could feel his loneliness. It might not have made any sense as he had lovely family and friends surrounding him, but then, life didn't always make sense and feelings certainly didn't either.

Chapter
Six

Snowball and I were enjoying a bit of alone time in her back garden. It was quite rare, because Harold was a very needy human. He was quite old and had suffered ill health in the past, so it was understandable, and also George would often be around, or one of our other friends. But today Harold was at his senior centre, playing chess or cards, and George was with Hana, so we took advantage of a bit of time and space for ourselves. We appreciated it more because it was so unusual, I guessed.

'Isn't life funny?' Snowball asked as she played with a pile of leaves. Like me, she was quite a philosophical cat. I think becoming a parent to George had made me think about things more deeply, for sure.

'I know. When you left and moved away I thought I'd never see you again. And yet, here you are and I see you every day.'

'Exactly. And although I will always miss my family a bit, I have grown very fond of Harold – even his snoring doesn't bother me anymore – and I adore George. It's also nice to be back with my other cat friends.'

'It is. We never stop missing those we love,' I added. I was speaking from experience here.

'I know.' We were both silent. 'Hey, let's be more cheerful. Race you to the rec ground,' she shouted as she bounded off.

I chased after her, and was pleased to see our other friends there as we approached, slightly out of breath from our run. Nellie was playing in a bush, Elvis was licking his paws and Rocky was lying in a very rare sunny spot. We cats of Edgar Road tried to catch up regularly but with winter and the frequent rain, we didn't always see each other as much as we'd have liked. No one liked having damp fur.

'Snowball, Alfie,' they greeted us.

'What's going on?' I asked as I caught my breath.

'Nothing much, it's been so cold lately I feel that I've barely been out,' Rocky said.

'But, I have news. There's a new woman moved in to one of the flats at the end of the road. I think where your families used to live,' Elvis said, stretching his legs out.

When I first moved to Edgar Road, Tomasz and Franceska lived in the upstairs flat of one of the houses and Polly and Matt lived in the downstairs. They had separate front doors but it was a house split in two.

'Does she have a cat?' Always my first question.

'No, it's just her on her own. I thought I might take an interest as she would possibly be a candidate for your lonely club,' Elvis explained.

'It's the Sunday Lunch Club,' Snowball corrected.

'Well, anyway, she looks about the right age, although maybe a bit younger than your Harold, I would guess, and she's definitely on her own.' Goodness, Elvis had done his homework.

'Has Salmon's family met her yet?' I asked. Salmon was the neighbourhood watch cat, he knew everything that was going on. As did his family. Heather and Vic Goodwin ruled Edgar Road in many ways. They wore matching jumpers and were the busybodies (Jonathan's word) of the street. Salmon used to be our nemesis but we had all softened towards each other and found a way to be cordial nowadays.

'Probably,' Nellie said. 'But I haven't seen Salmon for a few days. If I do, I'll see what I can find out, and you do the same,' she suggested.

Salmon was useful for knowing all the comings and goings of Edgar Road – nothing seemed to escape his notice. We sometimes had to butter him up a bit to get the real gossip but I wasn't averse to that.

We all spent some companionable time together, watching the world of Edgar Road go by. Snowball climbed a tree, Nellie chatting to her from the safety of the ground as she did so. Rocky closed his eyes and Elvis and I watched people go about their business. It was a pleasant time, but of course, it was soon time to leave. We had to before our fur froze. We spotted Sylvie pushing Theo in his pram up the road towards her house and I knew that was probably a sign that the humans would be returning from school, or work, or their chores, soon. Snowball and I took some privacy to say goodbye, because she wanted to make sure she was home to greet Harold when he got back, and then we took our leave.

When I first met Snowball I used to hate it when I wasn't with her but then I was a very young cat in love. Now I'm grown up. I've lived through losing her, becoming a parent, falling for Tiger, losing Tiger, finding Snowball again . . . I'm far more realistic these days, steady and sensible in our relationship, because when I first met her it was all about the two of us – and the humans, of course – but now it's about so many more people and cats, and we know that is part of our relationship. It's funny how you change and evolve as you grow up.

I headed home and arrived to see George at the front door. He was waiting for the children to come home from school. They loved it when we greeted them on the doorstep for some reason. Today, Claire arrived with Pickles – Toby holding his lead, and Martha, Henry and Summer trailing him. It was one of Polly's busy work days and Claire often picked the children up from school. She also dog sat Pickles a lot. In fairness, I had to dog sit quite a lot too. Dogs aren't like cats; they hate to be on their own, and if left alone for too long Pickles managed to get up to all sorts. Only the other day Claire had to leave him here when she went to the supermarket and because George and I were out, he managed to chew one of Jonathan's favourite loafers. Claire hid it at the back of the wardrobe, so I'm not sure Jonathan has noticed yet, but the rule now was that either a responsible adult or a responsible cat has to be with Pickles at all times.

'George, can we play?' Pickles asked as he was let off the lead once inside the house. The children, having made a fuss of us, had moved on to getting snacks.

'OK, you hide.' George loved playing hide and seek with Pickles, because he always won, which I don't believe is in the spirit of the game, but there was no telling George that. I tried to suggest he let Pickles win sometimes but he refused, saying that Pickles needed to learn. It's been over a year and he hasn't got it yet so I'm not sure he ever will, but George is resolute. Hide and seek hasn't always been a success – in fact, it has been quite treacherous in the past. Pickles once got stuck on the top bunk of Toby's bed with no idea how to get down and he's also been trapped in a cereal box, the cat flap, and once he even almost buried himself in the garden. But as long as he's supervised when playing it's normally OK.

Pickles went to hide behind the armchair (his favourite place), and George humoured him by looking everywhere else before he finally found him. George, when it was his turn, hid behind the living room curtain. I could barely watch as Pickles ran around the room trying to find him, and failed. George hid there nearly every time they played, but the poor dog just couldn't get it. I never knew whether to laugh or cry. Instead, I gave up and went in search of adult company.

'Hi Alfie,' Claire said, picking me up and giving me a cuddle. 'I've started making lists for Christmas. We both love Christmas don't we?' She set me down.

We do both love Christmas, the most wonderful time of the year. It's a time for family, friends, happiness, and good food. I am partial to a bit of Christmas dinner, I cannot lie. I could feel Claire's excitement, which was contagious. It wouldn't be too long before the children were writing letters to Santa, the man who delivered presents, asking for whatever it was they would want this year. George and I were happy enough with the food but we always got a few cat toys and treats as well. But the fact we were all together as a family, the fact that we had each other, always struck me as the most important thing about Christmas. It was a time of year when I would definitely count my lucky stars – and there were a lot.

It was always welcome when we could start planning for

Christmas. Normally it was December when the excitement really got going with trees, decorations, advent calendars, and events at school, but I was happy to get a bit of early Christmas spirit. What cat wouldn't be?

Polly arrived after tea, taking her two reluctant children and an exhausted Pickles with her. I went to find George.

'I heard that a new woman moved onto Edgar Road,' I told him now we were alone. I didn't want to mention it in front of Pickles, because I was going to suggest that George and I go and check her out and as Pickles absolutely couldn't come with us, it didn't seem fair to talk about it in front of him. Also, he had been known to follow us out and get us into trouble so possibly a good idea to avoid that.

But, I was suddenly nostalgic for the days when I visited Franceska and Polly's flats, it seemed so long ago now. 'Apparently she doesn't have a cat, so maybe we should go and introduce ourselves?' I was curious and, being a doorstep cat, I couldn't help but be excited every time someone new moved onto the street. The first thing I would need to know was if they had a cat, and if they didn't I would go and charm them. You never knew if they would have need of a cat or not. Most people did though.

'Dad, it's been a long day and I'm tired, but if you can wait I promise I'll come with you in the morning, even before I go to see Hana.'

'OK, it's a deal.' I tried to hide the disappointment I felt. But then George had pretty much always lived in this one house, and although he visited the others with me, he didn't quite have the doorstep cat gene, so I tried to be under-standing. And the morning would be fine because he was right, it had been a long day and we were all tired. But I was still feeling a little bit disappointed. I wasn't known for my patience.

Later that evening, Claire and I were catching a few minutes' peace and quiet and I was trying not to be too impatient, waiting for the following day. Jonathan was working late, the children were upstairs, ready but not in bed, and George was with them.

The doorbell went, startling me, and I ran to wait by it, because as far as I knew we weren't expecting anyone. Claire opened it and Aleksy and Connie stood on the doorstep. I immediately jumped into Aleksy's arms; it was just what I needed, another cuddle from someone who loved me. He also gave me a very nice head scratch.

'Come in you two. Did I ask you to babysit?' Claire asked, sounding confused. Aleksy and Connie were now old enough to babysit for Summer and Toby when Claire and Jonathan went out. They also did the same for Polly, and it was quite the money maker, according to Aleksy.

'No,' Aleksy said. 'We wanted to talk to you about some-thing.'

Claire led them into the kitchen, and I for one was eager to hear what they had to say.

'So,' Connie started. 'We were wondering if we could ask your advice?'

'Of course, on what?' Claire's eyes darted between the two of them.

'So, you know how we were doing our school project on homelessness and we went to the local shelter? It gave us a real wake-up call about how bad the homeless situation in London is.'

'It's terrible, Aleksy, you're right,' Claire said.

'And with Christmas coming up they need even more help,' Connie said. 'I mean now, even, as it's winter. But Christmas makes having a home so much more important and not having one seem even more cruel. We wanted to get warm clothes, blankets, food, anything we could to help, you see.'

'That's so great of you. Homelessness is a huge problem in this country, not just in London.' Claire looked concerned. It was hard enough being homeless as a cat, at least we have some survival skills, but imagine being a homeless human? I shuddered; it was a terrible thought.

'But we can do something more to help as well, I think,' Aleksy said. 'We want to raise money.'

'Like a big Christmas fundraiser to do something for the local shelter,' Connie added.

'That's a wonderful idea. Where do I come in?' Claire asked.

'Meow.' Where do I come in, I added.

'Well out of all the adults you have the most time on your hands . . .' Aleksy started. Claire narrowed her eyes. Oh boy. Because Claire didn't technically have a job, a paying job, sometimes she felt undervalued. But she looked after two children, a house, two cats, a husband, Polly and Matt's children part-time, and Pickles. She also shopped and made lunch for Harold some days, she coordinated most of the Sunday

Lunch Club . . . She was incredibly busy and she worked very hard.

'What Aleksy meant was that you used to work in marketing so we thought you might have the right expertise to help us.' Connie managed to rescue things, phew. I noticed that she kicked Aleksy under the table. He turned a little bit red.

'Yes, but Aleksy I don't have much spare time, I'm so busy with the Sunday Lunch Club, the family, Pickles even, and we've got Christmas to organise . . . Anyway, of course I'll help, it's a great cause. What were you thinking?'

'That's the problem, we don't have a good idea yet,' Aleksy said. 'We thought we could do a sponsored thing, maybe a sleep out, but then our parents wouldn't like that.'

'My mum would worry,' Connie said.

'Yes, she would,' Claire agreed. Sylvie could be very over-protective.

'Then we thought we could do something at school, but what?' Aleksy added.

'Yes, you see, we want to involve the community, really,' Connie said. 'But we don't have many ideas that seem good enough.'

So, their big idea was that they needed a big idea, it seemed.

'Meow,' I said. They had come to the right place. Only I needed a bit of time to think about it. Although I had heard them talking about this the other day, with all that was going on, I'd forgotten, so now I needed to put my thinking cap on. Not literally. Not unless Doris knitted me one, anyway.

'OK, why don't you let me think about it for a bit, because I think it'd be great if you could do something,' Claire offered.

'The project at school was to raise awareness but we thought what if we do something that raises both awareness and money,' Connie said.

'I know, we really want to come up with something amazing,' Aleksy said. I was so proud of these two, I purred at him to show him that.

'Let's brainstorm,' Claire said, grabbing a pad and pen. She did love making lists.

'Our first idea was doing something sponsored,' Connie suggested.

'But that's not exactly exciting or different is it?' Aleksy said. 'I mean it's not really very original.'

'Meow.' I didn't exactly know what sponsored something was but it certainly didn't sound as if it was quite good enough.

'People do love a charity song,' Claire said. 'Remember Band Aid?'

We all shook our heads.

'No of course not, before your time. But pop stars made this amazing song to raise money for famine in Africa. I'm sure there've been others, but that's the one that springs to mind.'

'Like the Children in Need songs,' Aleksy said.

'Yes, we could do a song.' Claire nodded.

'I actually can't sing, or write music,' Connie said. 'I did learn the piano in Japan but I gave it up after coming here.'

'No, I'm not exactly Beethoven either,' Claire said.

'And if we did a song, then how would we make it into a record and get people to buy it?' Aleksy asked.

'Yowl.' I knew they weren't quite on the right track. But

it did get me thinking. Raising money for charity, the homeless, Christmas. There had to be something that would do all they wanted to do.

'It's impossible, we'll never think of something that's good enough,' Aleksy said.

'We will if we think about Christmas, how to raise money, and something we can all get involved in,' Connie summed it up.

'Of course we will,' Claire reassured. 'Look, let's mull it over tonight and then get together after school tomorrow to see what we've come up with.'

'Meow.' That was fine, I had twenty-four hours to come up with the best idea ever.

While George and I paid our pre-bed visit to the garden I filled him in.

'So, they want to raise money for charity?' he asked.

'Yes and it's Christmas so I think we should have a Christmas theme,' I explained.

'And involve the community, like the Sunday Lunch Club has done?' he said.

'Yes. Oh what about we have homeless people come to lunch as well as our regulars?'

'But Dad, you said that they're raising money for the local shelter, which already feeds people,' George pointed out. I was glad he'd been paying attention. 'And they all go there for help already so we need to give them the money we raise.'

'Oh yes, of course. Um, right, it's harder than I thought.'

'I know, Dad, but you'll come up with something, you always do.'

'Thanks son.' I was so touched he had faith in me and I was determined not to let him down. I hoped that I would have a very good night's sleep and then wake up full of inspiration. I was going to come up with the best ever idea, of that I was determined.

Chapter
Seven

I woke early with excitement rippling through my fur, and as I opened my eyes and stretched, I remembered that we had a new friend to meet. I hoped that she had good taste in food, and also, as she was on her own, I hoped she wasn't too lonely. But if she was she had come to the right road. We specialised in helping lonely people. I had been thinking about Aleksy and Connie and their idea for raising money, but I had to put it aside to make a new friend. I told myself I would go back to it later.

George actually saw it as his job. Last year I caught him visiting Harold when he was ill in hospital, and it turned out that whilst there he had managed to cheer up people who didn't have any visitors and were feeling very down. He said it was his career. I managed to get him fired, with Pickles' help — accidentally of course, as I was just worried about him, but that's another story. The point was that George, who was very much my son, liked to reach out a helping paw to those who needed it and this woman, newly moved into our street and on her own, would probably be one of those people.

I was impatient as I waited for George to get up. He slept in Toby's room, something he'd established when Toby first came to live with us and didn't sleep well. Now, although Toby slept better than anyone else in the family, George still always slept in there, curled up at the end of his bed. It was very sweet.

I did my ablutions as I waited, tempted to wake George, but knowing it was too early for us to go anyway. You see, I might be a grown-up but I still got overexcited at times. There was a kitten in all of us, I believed. Finally, George emerged with Toby, who was rubbing his eyes. The house was about to spring to life, and the morning routine would begin.

'Why can't I find any socks?' Jonathan shouted as he emerged from the shower.

'They are all in your sock drawer,' Claire replied, far more patiently than he deserved.

'Mummy, I don't feel well I think I better stay home from school,' Summer groaned, as she did most mornings.

'If you have all your limbs then you're going to school,' Claire replied. 'Now both of you get dressed and then come down for breakfast.'

'I can't find my pants,' Toby said.

'They're where they always are, Tobe,' Claire replied. I honestly don't know how she managed to keep so calm.

George and I headed downstairs for breakfast.

'Right, can we go now?' I asked after we'd eaten. I was bouncing around like a kitten. Not only did I want to avoid the chaos of the morning, which seemed to be ramped up today for some reason, but I was eager to go and check this new person out. I could barely contain myself.

'She might not be up yet, it's still early. Look, it's even dark outside, Dad,' George said. For once he was trying to contain me, rather than vice versa.

'But we can stake the flat out, and then at least we'll be

ready for when she does emerge.' I was pretty much an expert on people and knew that if, for example, the curtains were open or a light was on, she would be up. And even if she didn't have a job, she would have to go out at some point. I was happy to wait for as long as it took.

'Fine, but don't expect me to hang around all day waiting for someone we don't even know,' George said. He was grumpy this morning, but I hoped he'd cheer up when we set off.

'George, everyone is someone we don't know until we meet them,' I pointed out, but he just flicked his tail at me and stalked over to the cat flap.

It didn't help matters that it was a particularly cold day as we made our way along Edgar Road. The cold wind was whipping our fur, and it was damp and dark. I couldn't exactly use the weather as a good reason for us to be out this early. Even I was having trouble keeping my spirits up. I just hoped this new woman was worth it, otherwise I was pretty sure George would sulk with me for at least the rest of the day, if not the week.

'If this woman turns out to be anything but wonderful, you know I'll blame you,' George said, echoing my thoughts.

The street was deserted, and although I could see lights on in some houses, people hadn't yet emerged. Maybe I should have been a little more patient, I thought, as we reached the flat in question. I felt a pang of nostalgia as I always did when I saw it, thinking back to when I first met Franceska, and Aleksy, who was just a small child then, younger than Summer is now, and Tommy, who was still a toddler. And then Polly and Matt with Henry, who was a baby, not much older than Theo is now, I don't think. Goodness, so much had happened between then and now, it struck me how full and wonderful my life had been and still was. In fact with each year it seemed to get fuller and more wonderful. I wasn't a young cat anymore but there was plenty more lives left in me. Just look at Elvis; he was much older than me and still going strong.

'What are you thinking about?' George asked, clearly bored of sulking.

'Just how much has happened since I first visited this flat, when Franceska and family lived here.'

'Are you getting all soppy?' George asked.

'You know me so well, son. I know I always tell you stories about the past and you say that I go on and on, but it's such a part of me, of all of us, and that's probably why I do it so much.'

'I understand. Now I'm a big cat I do, anyway. I remember when I first came to live with you and how much I loved it, and then when Toby came, and going on holiday and meeting Hana, Harold and the others. There is a lot in our lives to be grateful for . . .'

'But?' I asked, I could sense the sadness behind his words.

'I still miss Tiger mum and I always will. When Harold was ill last year and I thought I would lose him too, I didn't know how I would bear it. I was so happy when he got better. I'm so happy we have each other, you know – all of us – but I miss Tiger mum with every beat of my heart.'

'Oh George, so do I. But we were so lucky to have had her in our lives.'

'I know, but it doesn't make missing her any easier, does it?'

'No, I'm afraid it doesn't.' As much as we could say the right things about loss – you know, how it's better to have loved and lost than never loved at all and that sort of stuff people always say – it doesn't make it any better for the ones left behind. There are people and cats that I have had to say goodbye to in my life that I will never stop missing. I felt quite emotional as I gave George a nuzzle.

'On a more cheerful note, we are here,' George said, as we found a bush in the front garden of the flat to shelter in.

We staked the flat out for quite a while, before George nudged me and we looked at the front door opening. I sat up straight as a woman with short grey hair walked out. The evaluation of her seemed about right. She was fairly old, but not quite as old as Harold, it seemed, and she was wearing a big jumper, and trousers. She was also carrying a bin bag, which explained why she had emerged. George and I looked at each other. It was our cue.

'Meow,' I said approaching her.

'What on earth?' She spun round, almost bashing me with the bin bag. Lucky I ducked out of the way. I felt bad, I had obviously startled her.

'Meow,' George said, joining us, turning on his charm.

She looked at us as if she wasn't quite sure what we were. George and I exchanged glances as the woman stood still, staring at us. What was going on?

'Get out of my garden,' she shouted, eventually, putting the bin bag down on the ground, precariously close to my tail. George took a step back but I stayed where I was. When George first met Harold he kept telling him to go away, but

George won him round in the end, so I wasn't too worried. Instead of moving, I purred at her.

'You horrible stray cats, what are you doing here, clawing around my bins? I'm going to call animal control and have you taken away.' She didn't look or sound very friendly. The opposite, in fact.

'Yowl!' I objected. How on earth could she mistake us for strays? Me with my fine grey fur and George with his lovely, bright ginger-ish coat? We were absolutely nothing like stray cats. Not that I have anything against strays, I might add – I was homeless myself for a while, if you remember. However, I certainly didn't look my best then, and the point was that I was affronted by this woman. How dare she criticise us like that.

'Meow,' George said, putting his head to one side, and looking his cutest. Surely she couldn't resist us now?

She picked the bin bag up and before we knew what was happening, she started swinging it at us.

'Yowl!' I said as it caught my tail. I looked at George, telling him, with my eyes, to run. He didn't need to be told twice.

We both turned to escape. The woman was chasing us, swinging the bag at us and shouting. We got to the kerb, where would we go now? She was gaining on us, looming over us. All I could see was a big shadow. I was terrified of what might happen if she caught us.

'We have to try to cross the road,' I managed to say, my breath shallow. We looked – there was a car not far away – and I hoped we could make it. We had no choice. 'As fast as you can,' I added.

'I'll get you for trespassing,' the woman screeched and we both took off across the road. I let George go ahead, I was his father, so I had to protect him, but as George ran as fast as he could, I stayed pretty much on his tail. A horn beeped as the car swerved, narrowly avoiding us. I could hear the roar of the engine and the pitch of the beep in my ears as we kept going.

Finally, we made it to the safety of the pavement on the other side of the road. I stopped and looked back across. She was waving her fist angrily at us, but thankfully she didn't attempt to follow as there were more cars around.

We both lay on the pavement, panting. I couldn't get the sound of the car out of my head, or the sound of her shouting. George lay still for quite a while. It had been a very close call.

'Not a cat fan then?' George said, when he finally got his breath back.

'Seems not. Home?' I said, dejectedly. I was filled with disappointment. I was pretty annoyed about being chased with a bin bag, and almost being hit by a car, but I didn't want to upset George anymore, so I thought I would play the incident down.

'I think I'll go and see Hana, if that's OK?' George said. 'After being attacked by a mad woman, then almost getting run over, I need cheering up.'

''Course.' I felt guilty, it was my fault that that had happened at all. I tried to keep George away from danger but I had unwittingly led him to it yet again. 'And remember when we're walking down the street to give that flat a wide berth,' I added seriously.

'So you don't think it's worth trying to win her round?' George asked. I wasn't sure if he was being sarcastic or not. I wasn't taking any chances though.

'George, when Harold was telling you to go away he never threatened you with the cat warden or a bin bag did he?'

'No.'

'Right, so let's not try to win her round, we might not come out of it in one piece. It's not worth the risk, son.'

I was a very persistent cat, but, I had enough people in my life not to need one like that. I wasn't going to take any risks with that woman. Oh no, she was definitely off my Christmas card list. Not that I had one, of course.

Chapter
Eight

I was still fretting about our encounter when I got home, leaving George to go next door. I felt a bit unsettled still – one of those moods where you don't exactly know what to do with yourself. Do you go visit friends who might cheer you up, do you spend the time pondering why it is you feel so fed up? Or do you take a nap? I stretched. I decided to take a nap. I had been up very early after all. A nap it was.

I was shaken from my nap some time later with an almighty thud. I opened my eyes to find Pickles had jumped into my basket and was almost squishing me. He was quite a weight, let me tell you.

'Pickles, it's lovely to see you but please get off,' I asked, as nicely as I could. He shuffled a bit so he was no longer crushing me but we were both still squashed up. He licked me.

'Claire's going shopping and she said you were in charge of me.'

'Oh I must have been sound asleep because I didn't hear her leave, or you arrive,' I said.

'You were snoring,' Pickles said.

'I don't snore,' I replied.

'Well it sounded like it. Anyway, where's George?'

'I think he's with Hana.'

'Boring. So you'll have to play with me.'

'Right.' I tried not to sigh. 'So what are we playing?'

'Ball.'

I was pleased with this. One of Pickles' easiest activities – by that I mean one where he can rarely get into trouble – was ball. I would push a ball with my paw in the hallway, he would run after it, fetch it, and bring it back to me. He could play this for hours and although it was a little boring for me, I didn't mind. It would give me time to think about the horrible lady at the end of the street, to think about Tommy, and to think about what I was going to do about it all. At the moment, I had nothing. Just hope that the talk Tommy had with Jonathan the other day would have an effect. That the woman at the end of the street wouldn't be a problem if we kept out of her way. That Pickles would get fed up with playing ball before my paw really began to ache . . . Why on earth didn't I hold out much hope for any of that? While Pickles was distracted with the ball, I jumped up onto the hall table, for a break. I noticed that there were various flyers with pictures of food on, and one which I knew was for a Christmas pantomime because Claire had put it there, saying that she needed to book. I wasn't sure exactly what it was, but I did know it was some kind of show that happened every Christmas and the kids loved it. I wished for a moment we could go, but we were never invited.

'Alfie, ball,' Pickles said. And I jumped down. Sore paw or no sore paw, Pickles wasn't going to let me off the hook for long.

Claire took Pickles out for a walk, and Snowball came to surprise me. Clearly I wasn't going to get much rest today, not that I minded one bit.

'I wasn't expecting you,' I said, nuzzling her.

'Harold had some appointment and Sylvie's taking him so I thought I'd visit.'

I filled her in about our near miss and also about Aleksy and Connie's idea.

'You need to keep away from that woman,' she said.

'I will and also when I have some energy I'll warn everyone else about her,' I added. 'But let's focus on Aleksy and Connie. They're coming over later and they'll probably be expecting an idea.'

'Think about it, Alfie. Christmas, what does it mean to you?'

'Ah, you are doing that thing Claire does. You know, brainstorming,' I said.

'Yes, I certainly am,' she replied.

'OK. It means nice food, family, friends, happiness, keeping George and Pickles away from the Christmas tree and the tinsel, presents, Santa, and everyone being together.' I think I'd done a pretty good job of summing it up.

'Right, so let's try to get those into an idea. Being together is a good one.'

'Oh I see, like if you get loads of people into one place to raise money.' I suddenly felt excited as the ideas began to trickle into my brain. Everyone together. The community as a whole. Of course, that was what was needed. 'Do you mean an event?' I asked.

'Oh yes, an event. Like the Christmas Nativity at school – everyone goes to that. In fact, the children love it and the adults do too,' Snowball pointed out. 'Although it's usually done by the younger children isn't it?'

How she was an expert on the Nativity, I didn't know.

'George told me about how the other year Tommy put him in a manger at the kids' school Nativity and how he and you have been banned from going since,' she explained.

Ah, that was how. But she was right, it was for younger children. But it didn't have to be, did it? It wouldn't even have to be at the school at all.

'I've got it,' I said. 'How about a Christmas show for the community to raise money for the homeless shelter? What a brilliant idea.' If I did say so myself. Although my fur fizzed with excitement at the idea, I was unsure how we would actually do it.

'Wow, it is, although we might need a few more details,' Snowball said.

'No, what we need is to pass this idea to the humans and once we've done that they can come up with details. I mean, details are not what this cat should be concerned with. Gosh I still have it! I'm still an ideas genius.' I did a little spin, I was pretty pleased with myself.

'And as modest as ever,' Snowball replied. 'But you have to convey the idea to the humans now and you know that's a whole other problem.'

'Leave it with me, I'll come up with something.' I wasn't going to tell her that I didn't have a clue how to do that. I had got a bit carried away with talk of the show, and Christmas songs and someone being Santa and a part for me and George and even Pickles, Hana, and Snowball . . .

Now for the logistics. I needed to give them the idea of putting on a show but how? I started thinking, then had a flash of inspiration. I remembered seeing the flyer for the

Christmas pantomime on the hall table, when I was playing with Pickles. And although I didn't know what it was, I did know it was a show that happened at Christmas. So if I could somehow get her to link that to an idea for a show, it might just work. All I had to do was push the leaflet under Claire, Aleksy and Connie's noses somehow. I hoped they didn't think I meant for them to do an actual pantomime, because clearly someone was already doing that.

'Aha, I've got an idea.' I explained it. It didn't sound like my strongest one when I said it out loud but, again, it was all I had.

'It might work but it's a long shot,' Snowball said.

'Honestly, you have no faith in me. I will make it work. It's the best idea I've got anyway.'

'Alfie, it's the only one you've got,' Snowball pointed out.

Ready to put my plan into action, I jumped up onto the hall table and meowed loudly, hoping that Claire would come to see what was going on. But when she finally came into the hall she was on the phone and she shushed me, walked into the living room and closed the door. I knew from experience that getting the attention of humans, when you wanted to show them something they needed to see, wasn't always easy. I pushed it with my paw onto the floor and decided to stay with it, one paw on the bottom of the leaflet until she reappeared and noticed. But when she came out of the living room, she barely gave me a second glance before she dashed out of the house, saying she was late for Harold. So, was I going to wait there with the leaflet until she came back? No, I was not. I needed a new idea.

I was lying in my basket in the kitchen when George appeared. I told him of my plan.

'I love the idea of the Christmas show but do you think if you shove the flyer in front of her she'll get it?'

''Course, Claire's clever.' I began to have doubts, but still, I had nothing better.

'Well, you said that Aleksy and Connie are coming over after tea to come up with ideas, wouldn't it be better if you got them all to see it?' George said. 'Then it's more likely that one of them might understand.'

'Clever, just like your dad. Yes, of course, if they all see it someone will definitely get it. But how? I'll have to pounce as soon as they come in.'

'Or you could find a way to get the leaflet to them – you know, when they sit around the kitchen table,' George suggested. He was examining his paws. I got the feeling that he was trying to teach this old cat new tricks.

'But how? Pushing it all the way from here to the kitchen with my paw will be quite exhausting.' I had done this before, but it wasn't easy. You see we cats did have our limitations. 'And how would I even pick it up?' My mind was whirring, trying to figure out the logistics.

'Can't you try carrying it in your mouth the way Pickles carries his ball, or Dustbin carries a mouse?'

I considered it. I had once carried some of Polly's best flowers in my mouth when trying to woo Snowball. That hadn't gone well, but I had managed and for a lot further than the hall to the kitchen. It wasn't the worst idea, I decided, but then . . .

'How will I pick it up from the floor?' I asked George. I felt as if I should have all the answers but I didn't. My kitten, it seemed, did.

'Slide your paw under it like this.' He demonstrated. His paw lifted up a bit of the piece of paper, and he bent down and picked it up in his mouth.

'I'd have figured it out eventually,' I muttered.

''Course you would have, Dad,' he said. 'But I do have youth on my side.'

I tried not to take offence. I also tried to copy what he'd done, but it wasn't anywhere near as easy as he made it look. I was getting frustrated and George was trying not to laugh at me. First the flyer kept sliding away from me, and then when I did manage to elevate it slightly I couldn't grip with my mouth. I even managed to bang my head on the floor, which hurt.

'I just can't seem to do it,' I said.

'Dad, you never give up. Look, I'll talk you through it.'

After a bit more (annoying) coaching from George, I used my tongue and ta dah! I did it. The leaflet was a little bit soggy from all my attempts, and my head was a bit sore, but I felt confident that when the time came I would be able to do this again.

'Teamwork,' I said to George. Although I wasn't sure that it was, actually. More of an old cat struggling to learn new tricks. But if it worked, it would be worth it, I kept having to tell myself that.

'Teamwork, Dad,' he replied. 'And now I'm going to see if I can get a snack. Trying to teach you has made me very hungry. And after I've eaten, I'm going to see Harold.' I lay down on top of the leaflet. I was exhausted, too tired to try to get to my basket, so I just shut my eyes.

I heard the door open, which woke me, and I sat up to see Claire come in alone.

'Hi Alfie,' she said. 'Polly and Matt are taking the kids out for tea tonight, to give me a bit of a break, and also as a treat for them.' She smiled. I could see sometimes that Claire got tired, and as she worked at home, she didn't have much time to herself. Claire might be the only one who didn't have an official 'job' but she worked harder than anyone, as far as I could see.

'Meow.' You deserve it.

'And Connie and Aleksy will be over soon to talk about their fundraiser. I hope they've come up with some ideas, because I have to admit I haven't really got any. Goodness, there's so much to do, but I really don't want to let them down.'

'Meow.' Don't worry, I had it all in paw.

My plan now ready, I stayed in the hall to wait for the right time. It felt like ages, but then I was impatient, so it probably wasn't. I really wanted to get going with this, not only because I was a little nervous about making it work, but also because the more I thought about it the better it sounded to my ears. I shuffled around, unable to sit still, willing them to hurry up.

Eventually, the doorbell rang and I started to get ready. Aleksy and Connie walked in, gave me a quick fuss before following Claire into the kitchen. It was my cue. I managed to get the leaflet into my mouth on the third try – definite improvement – and I walked slowly to the kitchen with it in my mouth. I had to be careful not to drop it, and although it was a bit bigger than I would have liked and meant I could barely see over it, I finally made it. As I approached the table, I misjudged and banged into the table leg, and I nearly dropped the leaflet, but managed to keep hold of it. My poor head would have two bumps on it, possibly.

'So, you haven't got any ideas?' Claire was asking, as I turned myself and got ready to jump up.

'No, we've been thinking and thinking. We don't want to do anything sponsored, as that's normal, and we want to get people involved. Our aim is to raise money so they can have a nice Christmas dinner and get some warm clothes and sleeping bags maybe . . . We need something good to raise enough money and get many people involved.' Poor Aleksy sounded dejected.

'Yes, we want everyone at the shelter to have proper treats at Christmas, to give them something to look forward to, or as much as they can when they're homeless,' Connie added. 'Also, we thought we could help raise awareness at the same time.'

'Of course, it's such a lovely idea. I feel terrible that I haven't got a good idea for you, but I'll keep thinking about it.' Claire sounded a little upset now. It was my cue. I steadied myself and jumped on the table, nearly but not quite dropping the leaflet. When I reached the middle of the table, I let the leaflet go and it fluttered down looking a bit worse for wear. I hoped it would still work. The best thing was that finally I could feel my tongue again as I licked my lips, and rubbed my head with my paw.

'What is this?' Claire asked, picking it up. 'The flyer for the pantomime? Why on earth have you brought this here, Alfie?'

'Oh, maybe Alfie is trying to tell us something,' Aleksy said, stroking me.

'Meow.' Of course I am. Even after all these years my humans could be a little slow on the uptake.

'You want to go to the pantomime?' Claire asked. See what I mean?

'Yowl.' No.

'You want us to do a panto?' Aleksy asked. I tried to move my head a bit, but it still smarted.

'It would be far too hard,' Connie said. 'And anyway there's loads of them around, so why would anyone come to ours?'

'Meow, meow, meow.' Honestly, I couldn't spell it out any more than this. I did a spin on the table, not sure why but I was frustrated.

'What about a show?' Claire said.

'Purr. Purr.' Yes!

'You mean a Christmas show?' Aleksy said.

'Purr.' Now we were talking.

'For the local community, with everyone involved?' Connie added.

'MEOW.' Finally.

'Oh what a fabulous idea,' Claire said. 'We could have Christmas songs . . .'

'And what about a grown-up Nativity, that could be a good idea?' Aleksy chipped in.

'And maybe carols, and all the children can be involved, and we can ask at school . . .' Connie sounded excited.

'We could sell tickets, and make posters advertising it.'

'I think it's a brilliant idea. Of course it should be a Christmas show.' Claire sounded excited. 'It's perfect, in fact.'

'But where would we have it?' Aleksy asked. 'And what about the cost?'

'Leave that to me,' Claire said. I lay down, relieved. They had got the idea, they liked it and now it was going to hopefully come to life. I wondered what part I would play, and George and Snowball, too, of course. And maybe Hana would be involved. It would be a real family affair and I loved the idea that we'd get to all work together on it. After all, we were a big part of this community. I could see it bringing everyone together in the most wonderful way.

I listened with one ear open as they chatted around some ideas, it seemed they were really getting it now.

'Yes there's a lot to do,' Aleksy said, after they'd chatted for a while. 'But maybe if we make a list we can do it.'

'How about you and Connie be the directors?' Claire suggested. 'And if you want to do the Nativity you could even write a script so it will be new and original?'

'Good idea,' Connie said.

'We could ask the school to support us as well,' Aleksy suggested.

'Now that is a good idea,' Claire said. I agreed.

'And we could hold auditions, which would be really fun!' Connie added, excitement audible in her voice.

I loved the way they were all thinking and coming up with ideas, and I was so proud of Aleksy and Connie. Teenagers get a bad rap (and yes I am guilty of that), but Aleksy and Connie were doing something good, rather than just worrying about themselves. They were being so unselfish, helping others. I had taught them well.

'We'll need to do lots of social media,' Connie said. I climbed onto Aleksy and nuzzled into his neck. As they continued to chat away about the show, I could see it in my mind. I lay down in Aleksy's lap. My work was done and yet another plan was now underway.

Chapter Nine

The next few days proved a whirlwind for my humans and me. As the show was my idea, I felt as if I had to be involved in everything. And as Claire pointed out, we didn't have any time to lose. As it was a Christmas show, it really only gave us just less than a month to hold auditions, build sets, and get everything ready. If we were able to pull it off, it would mean a lot of hard work for everyone involved. And of course, that meant very hard work for me.

It seemed that there were a lot of issues we needed to address. Firstly, my idea might have seemed simple, but it was not. As soon as they understood my vision, they then began questioning everything, which in turn made me question everything.

'Do you think we have enough time?' Claire said, when she told Jonathan. 'It's nearly November, and we'll need the show to be on just before Christmas so that doesn't give us a lot of time to find a hall, write the show, rehearse, sell tickets . . .' She chewed her lip anxiously.

'It is ambitious. But there are a lot of us,' Jonathan said supportively, which I was pleased about. He wasn't always so keen to take on our projects. 'We can all muck in and help. Write a list – you're really good at them – and we can take it from there.'

Claire made a list, which she talked about to me a lot. The first thing we needed to do was to find a venue. We needed a hall which could accommodate a lot of people, had a stage, and was free, because we couldn't spend money when the aim was to raise it. I didn't understand everything but as Connie, Claire, Aleksy and I sat around our kitchen table trying to come up with something, I had to admit it made me a bit nervous.

Claire called a number of people, but there was always a problem. Aleksy asked at school but they weren't allowed to let him use their hall for anything which wasn't related to school. There were insurance problems, apparently.

Franceska offered the use of the restaurant but then realised that it was busy so how would they rehearse there, even if they closed it off for the show. Tomasz asked everyone who came to dine at the restaurant but it seemed there was nowhere we could use. I had a terrible feeling in my fur that the show might be over before it even began. I hated the thought that one of my ideas might fail. They never did. Or almost never, anyway.

We were all feeling a bit dejected when Matt turned up at our house with Pickles and started babbling.

'Slow down, Matt,' Claire said. 'I can't understand a word you are saying.'

'There's a hall, I just found it. Edgar Road Parish Hall, it's tucked behind the end of the road not far from here. It's a bit neglected but come on, come look.' He was breathless but excited. Could this be it?

'How did you find it?' Claire asked as she grabbed a coat and left the house, shouting to Jonathan to mind the kids. Of course I followed her.

'Polly is making me take Pickles for longer walks to try to get him to lose some weight, and I was just doing that really. I managed to look through one of the windows and it's a bit dusty but it looks as if it might fit the bill.'

'Oh Matt, if you're right then you're the hero of the hour.'

I wondered how I had never noticed the hall before; it wasn't a long walk to get there, and it was tucked away past the park we used to go to a lot when the children were younger. And George too actually. We went there sometimes still, but to be honest, not as much as we used to. I remember when Summer was a baby we would go with Henry and Martha, hauling prams and pushchairs, and have picnics with Claire and Polly. Those were the days before George of course, and goodness how it felt like a long time ago. George was right, I was a pretty nostalgic cat these days. In my early days in Edgar Road I had even fallen into the pond at the park – I was admiring my reflection – and Matt had to save me. Goodness, I'd almost forgotten about that.

The building was near the church and Matt said that as it was a parish hall it probably belonged to the church, which was a good thing, as churches were known for charity.

We had a good look around and I was able to jump onto one of the lower window sills and look through a very big window. It was dirty, though, as Matt had said, so we were limited in what we could see. Inside was big, there were chairs stacked up and I thought I could make out a stage. It was dark as well, and clearly needed a good clean.

Claire had gone from despondent about the show to buoyed up, as had I. She said she didn't want to speak about it to Aleksy and Connie though until she had tracked down the vicar. That necessitated a trip to the church the following day, but if he agreed it looked as if the show might be a go after all. I had my paws firmly crossed.

Being an optimistic cat, I decided to get George, Hana and Snowball on board now. Although they knew about my idea, and had agreed to be part of it in theory, they, like everyone else, weren't sure it would actually happen. Our other Edgar Road friends were shyer than us and didn't want to be part of a show, and of course Dustbin and Ally would rather be in the yard, but the four of us were willing to take centre stage. I knew we wouldn't have talking parts — I did accept I was a cat after all — but we could definitely be very important members of the cast. However, first we needed to secure that venue.

I woke up feeling tense the following day. Claire was going to find the vicar after she dropped the children off at school, and I didn't go with her because it was pouring with rain, which meant she had to take the car. All I could do was wait and pace the floor until she returned.

It felt like hours before I heard the key in the lock. Claire rushed in, picked me up and spun me around.

'We can use the hall! Matt is a genius, and you're a genius, Alfie, and I can't wait to tell Aleksy and Connie.'

I purred my delight. This was turning out to be a very good day.

Claire arranged to visit the hall with Aleksy and Connie after school. It did have a stage, as I suspected, but it wasn't really used much nowadays. Ralph, the local vicar, told Claire that with dwindling congregation numbers and lack of funds, the hall was used less and less. But, not only was he keen for the hall to be used for something big like this, he also was a keen supporter of the shelter. Claire said that, in a way, us having a show there might put it back on the map, and make it a very valuable community asset. Not that I quite knew what that was. Ralph and Claire agreed to work together to make the show a possibility. And Ralph said he would not only ask for volunteers to help clean the hall up – after all, it desperately needed it – but also he and his church goers would get involved in the show.

Today we were going to have a look at the hall. When I say we, I mean Claire, Connie, Aleksy and myself. I invited George and Snowball along but it was cold, so they passed and said they would be just as happy with me telling them about it. Honestly, it was lucky that I wasn't a fair weather cat like them, we would never get anything done.

We met Ralph, who wore a collar around his neck – a bit like a cat collar. I recognised this as a sign he was a vicar. I had seen one before, after all, having been to church for Claire and Jonathan's wedding, a long time ago.

'Hi, this is Aleksy and Connie,' Claire said.

'Meow.'

'Oh yes, and Alfie.'

Ralph didn't seem to notice me.

'We don't get many requests for the hall these days, as I said,' he explained. 'It's a shame that it's going to waste. We used to have some local groups come here and the school used to use it but now they've got a new school hall, they don't anymore.'

'It's amazing,' Claire said. 'Such a waste of a great space, maybe after the show there'll be more events on here.'

'That would be great,' Ralph said. We were still standing at the door, freezing and getting wet.

Claire shivered. 'Can we go in?'

'But that's a cat,' he said, pointing at me.

'Yes, that's Alfie, he likes to come with us.' Aleksy said it as if it was perfectly normal, which it was, of course.

'I don't think we normally have cats in here,' Ralph said, narrowing his eyes at me. 'But OK, then, come on in.' He bent down to give me a stroke, so I decided I did like Ralph the vicar.

As he opened the door we all gasped. The big hall was still a bit dusty and gloomy, but we could see where they had started cleaning it and the stage at the front would be perfect.

'Wow, this will be perfect,' Aleksy said, echoing my thoughts.

'Look at all the chairs stacked,' Connie pointed them out. 'We can have loads of people come and watch.'

It was much bigger than it looked from outside as Ralph gave us a tour. There was a small kitchen where Claire said they could sell mince pies and mulled wine, which would also raise money. I snuck behind the stage where there was an enormous cupboard layered with dust and cobwebs, which held all sorts of things. I started to explore and startled as I came eye to eye with a person lying on the ground. I stopped, and backed away as quietly as possible.

'Yowl!' Something fell on me. It wasn't heavy but as I wriggled out from under it, I could taste dust in my mouth. It wasn't the nicest taste ever.

'Meow!' I shouted, and Aleksy and Connie came running.

'Oh God, Alfie, you are covered in cobwebs and dust,' they said, as I tried desperately to get the worst of it off me with my paw.

'Oh look, it's a dummy,' Connie said, picking up the 'person' who scared me. Well, obviously now I could see it wasn't real.

'Look Claire,' Aleksy shouted and Claire came to join us.

'Amazing' she said. 'It looks like there might be things we can use for the sets here. Would that be OK, Ralph?'

'As far as I'm concerned, you can use anything here. So this show, what exactly is it about?' he asked.

'We don't know just yet but we thought we'd have Christmas songs, maybe the Nativity – but with adults – and carols of course. As long as it fits the Christmas theme we could have a variety of acts; a real family show,' Connie said, looking at her feet and blushing. She could be shy around people she didn't know.

'And who's going to be in it?' Ralph asked.

'Meow.' Me, of course.

'Um, well, we are going to hold auditions,' Aleksy said. 'If you're interested?'

'I might well be. We have a small but pretty good choir at our church, I'm sure they would all love to get involved.'

'Great, when we've got the posters and the date for the audition we'll let you know,' Claire said.

'We'd love that. And here's two sets of keys for you. You can use the hall whenever you like, as no one else uses it at the moment.'

'We'd love you to be involved,' Claire added. 'We're so grateful for this, by the way. Thank you again.'

There was still no mention of what I would be doing but I knew it was only a matter of time.

After we'd finished at the hall I went home with Connie to see George and Hana, and fill them in on the day's events.

'I'll be in the show,' Hana said. 'I said no at first because I'm a bit shy but as it is Connie's show, I feel that I should get involved.'

'Great, I'm sure the four of us will get some kind of starring role,' I said. 'I don't know what, but we are bound to steal the show.'

'Well, Hana, Dad, remember I have the only stage experience among us.'

'What?' I asked.

'I was the baby Jesus in the school Nativity a few years ago so I can give you advice on stage presence and how to get over stage fright. I am something of an expert after all.'

'Wow, that's impressive George,' Hana said.

I shook my tail. Tommy put George in the manger of the school Nativity where he fell asleep and woke up, forgetting where he was, and jumped out, making a racket. That was the sum of his experience. It hardly made him Oscar-worthy but, then, I wasn't going to tell him that. I would let him have his moment as Hana was hanging on his every word.

'I guess I'm too old to be baby Jesus this time?' George said, sounding disappointed.

'They'll probably use Theo, seeing as he's a real baby,' I pointed out.

'Yes, I'll have a more grown-up part then. But, don't worry Hana and Dad. As I said, I'll help you both.'

'Thanks son,' I said. Honestly, was he ever going to let up with this stage business? Knowing George, probably not.

Theo let out a loud cry just then and Sylvie brought him to where we were chatting.

'Ah, all the cats. Right, well, guys I am going to take Theo round to Claire's. Being at home all day is sending me crazy.'

'We might as well stay here then,' George said, after she'd gone. 'Our house will be really noisy now,' he finished.

'I better go,' I said. 'I promised Snowball I'd let her know how we got on today.' As much as I was disappointed to miss George's acting lesson . . .

'Don't worry, Hana, I can give you plenty of acting tips.'

I got soaked to the skin again as I made my way to Snowball's house. Honestly, the things I did for love. But thankfully, when I got to Harold and Snowball, the living room was warm and cosy so I lay by the fire and soon dried out. We waited until Harold nodded off and then made for the kitchen to chat.

'I've already heard about the venue. Claire popped in to see Harold and told him all about it. He said he was even going to audition for it! As Connie is his granddaughter now, he felt it only fair he support her.'

'How wonderful, although not sure what talent Harold has?' Harold was much softer now but he was still a bit of a grumpy old man.

'Claire said they could get him to be Santa,' Snowball said.

'But he'd have to smile and be nice,' I said and laughed. Imagine Harold dressing up as Santa. It would be almost as bad as Jonathan.

'He is so much more cheerful now he's got his family around him, especially me and baby Theo, so maybe he could do it.'

'Yeah, perhaps.' Snowball always saw the best in people. 'I'm more concerned with what parts we'll have. George thinks he's some kind of acting expert but I think we'll probably have to dress up as other animals for the Nativity.'

'That will stretch our acting abilities,' Snowball pointed out. Us cats were superior to all other animals, so I knew exactly what she meant.

Chapter Ten

Something rained on our parade, both literally and figuratively, and the excitement of the show, and having found the perfect venue, was suddenly overshadowed. Our families were incredibly tight knit, so when something happened we all heard about it, we all felt a part of it. The good and the bad. And this was bad.

Tommy had been excluded from school for a week for cheating on an exam. He had written some answers on his arm and of course, because it was possibly the most stupid thing in the world, he got caught. Honestly, where did that boy get it from? Aleksy told Connie, and Connie told Sylvie, and Hana overheard so she came round to tell me and George. At the same time, Claire was on the phone to Franceska who, by the sounds of it, was crying. Then Matt, who had been to see Tomasz, told Polly and everyone ended up at our house to discuss it and what they were going to do about it. Everyone apart from Tommy, of course, and Aleksy, who had been asked to keep an eye on his troublesome brother. I didn't envy him that job.

They had called a meeting of the adults, and I sat along with Claire, Jonathan, Matt, Polly, Sylvie, Marcus and Tomasz and Franceska in our living room. Connie was babysitting Theo, who would probably be much easier to look after than Tommy.

'We don't know what to do,' Tomasz said. 'I'm so angry.'

'You had to go to the headmaster's office again?' Matt asked.

'Yes, I felt like I was in trouble too as their headmaster is quite scary. Tommy had been warned already about his behaviour and now here he was, acting up again, and he wouldn't say anything. Just kept mumbling. They even asked if there were problems at home,' Franceska was tearful as she explained. Tomasz put his arm around her.

'What did Tommy say when you left the school?' Polly asked.

'He actually was upset and said he was sorry. He said he was trying to do better, but he was worried he'd fail the test and he wanted to work with Jonathan, so he needed to make sure he did well in the exam.'

'Oh God, I told him he had to get good grades if he wanted work experience. I hope it's not my fault.' Even Jonathan sounded upset.

'No, of course not,' Tomasz said. 'I think he's just a bit lost as he's at that age where it can go either way. But of course, now he's been excluded, we need to get him on the straight and narrow. We thought rather than keep shouting at him we'd come and ask for advice.'

'He's been grounded for so long, he'll be fifty before he can go out at this rate,' Franceska added with a sad smile.

'Rather than punish him, maybe give him tasks to do, to keep him busy,' Claire said.

'Look, I meant what I said,' Jonathan added. 'He can do some work experience with me, at some point, but let's make sure he gets his act together first, as it would seem like too much of a reward for bad behaviour now.'

'Hey what about this Christmas show?' Marcus said suddenly.

'We can't talk about that now, we need to focus on Tommy,' Sylvie pointed out.

'No, I mean get him involved with that. It's such a great thing that Aleksy and Connie are doing. It will keep him busy, and because we're all involved we can all keep an eye on him,' Marcus explained.

'He doesn't like being on stage, he refuses to be in any school plays,' Franceska said.

'But we need so much more than just people to be in it. Posters, for starters, then help building props. Tomasz, you said you'd be in charge of that so he could help you!' Claire sounded excited.

'He loves social media and making videos,' Franceska added helpfully.

'Yes and we'll need all that to help raise awareness,' Polly added.

'So we tell him he has to help with the show to prove to us that he really is trying to change things around?' Franceska still sounded doubtful.

'I think it's great. It also means that he can work with Aleksy, which would help re-build their relationship. We can all do our bit to help him, great idea, Marcus,' Matt sounded excited.

'Yes, nice one, Marcus,' Jonathan said. 'Can we also get him to work with the little ones? He used to be so good with them.'

'Great idea,' Claire replied. 'I know Toby and Summer miss playing with him. He can make posters with them.'

'That's sort of a punishment,' Jonathan said with a laugh.

'Jonathan, our kids are great, so of course it's not a punishment,' Claire chastised, but with a giggle.

'Well, it might be. I mean, Summer will probably try to boss him around something chronic.' Jonathan laughed.

'So we keep him busy, we get him involved with the good cause, he's forced to spend time with the family, and it's sort of a punishment but not a terrible one?' Franceska summed it up.

'Exactly.'

I beamed with pride at my humans. Look, they had come up with this all by themselves and they were all going to play their part. I couldn't have come up with a better plan myself. Well, I possibly could have done, but not much better, in any case.

I didn't get to see how Tommy took the news because Tomasz and Franceska went home and it really was too cold and too late for me to follow them, so instead I filled George in. George and I both decided to visit Dustbin the following day to see if he'd heard anything and also it meant we could check on Tommy ourselves as he wasn't allowed to go to school. I'd heard about him from the adults but I wanted to see him for myself. After all, he was my responsibility too.

With this in mind I went to bed early, and tried to ensure I got a good night's sleep. Of course I was worried about Tommy and thinking about the Christmas show – I had a lot on my mind still – so I was slightly restless. But in the morning I was raring to go again and hurried George along.

'What's the rush? It's not like Tommy will be going anywhere.'

'I'm just impatient to see what's going on,' I said. 'If you don't want to come with me, you don't have to.'

'No, I do. I want to see Dustbin and of course Tommy. Just hate being rushed in the morning. I wish you'd chill out a bit.'

Goodness, my son could be cheeky. I tried to 'chill out' by examining my paws but I really wanted to go. I wasn't a 'chill out' kind of cat.

It seemed like hours before George declared himself ready and we set off. Thankfully it wasn't raining but it was cold. The streets were quite busy as we took our usual route, people going to work, school, or shopping. We strode with purpose ourselves, as we had much to do; I set the pace and George was happy to keep up.

'Goodness I feel like I've seen loads of you lately,' Dustbin said in greeting.

'I know. Where's Ally?' I asked as we made it into the yard.

'She's off having a bit of a stalk today. Felt like a change of scene and you know me, I hate leaving the yard except for emergencies.'

I grinned. Dustbin had left the yard to help us over the years, but that was about the only time he did.

'So, Dustbin, have you seen or heard anything about Tommy?' George asked.

'Oh yes, there was a bit of a row last night as it happens. Franceska and Tomasz told Tommy he had to be involved in Aleksy's Christmas show and both Tommy and Aleksy objected to that.'

'Really? Why?' I asked, I thought it was a good idea.

'Well Tommy said it was dumb, but you know what he's like lately, and Aleksy said that it was so important he didn't want Tommy to mess it up. So Tomasz got really angry, more than I've ever heard him and he said that Tommy better get involved and do a great job or he could forget Christmas, and Aleksy should support his brother by giving him a fair chance. No one, not even Franceska, spoke for a while after that.'

Tomasz was a big man but so, so gentle, so it took a lot to make him lose his temper. This was a lot.

'So Tommy's still not really behaving himself?' I had hoped Jonathan's talk, along with the exclusion from school, would be enough to get him to turn things around. But no. My only hope now was that the Christmas show would do the trick.

'I really think this Christmas show is going to bring everyone closer together again,' I said, optimistically.

'You know it was Dad's idea, don't you?' George said, puffing his chest out and sounding proud of me. I was touched.

'I know. It has Alfie written all over it,' Dustbin said. We all grinned.

Tommy came downstairs with Franceska and they fussed over us.

'Nice to see you here, Alfie, George,' Franceska said.

'Mum, do I have to come to the restaurant? Can't I stay at home?' Tommy asked as he gave George a cuddle.

'No. You have school work and I need to make sure you're doing it.'

'It's not fair,' Tommy whined.

'I think it's very fair. You've put me and your dad through a lot and the school said you are not going to pass any exams if you go on the way you are doing.'

'Not another lecture,' he said, rolling his eyes.

'Meow.' He was being really rude. And poor Franceska looked as if she didn't know whether to shout at him or cry. I nuzzled her and ignored Tommy. He really was being a brat but I knew, deep down, my Tommy was there somewhere. I just had to figure out a way to get him out.

George and I hung out with Dustbin for a while, enjoying our snacks, and then took our leave. I hoped Tommy being part of the show would finally bring him back to us. I thought that if everyone got involved it would be the best show ever and as Dustbin said, a way of bringing everyone I loved together. Thinking about it, it might have been one of my best ideas yet.

George left to go and see Hana and I made my way to the recreation ground, hoping that some of our other cat friends would be around. I was buoyed up from a good morning's work and I felt confident that although Tommy had got into a lot of trouble, it was the wake-up call he needed to start being better. He had even been doing his school work when we left, so that was definitely a good sign. Nellie and Elvis were there as I approached and I filled them in on my latest news. Just as I finished, Salmon joined us.

'Ah, glad you're here, Alfie, I thought you might like to know that I have news.'

'What news?' I asked. Damn Salmon; that cat knew I couldn't resist gossip but he was circling around, taking his time with it.

'That woman who was horrible to you, the new one? She came to visit us last evening. Her name is Barbara and my humans went to see her the other day but she wasn't in, so they left a card with our address and neighbourhood watch details on . . .' He stopped to examine his paw.

'Get on with it, Salmon,' Nellie said. She didn't have any patience with Salmon at all and so said what the rest of us were thinking.

'All in good time. Her husband died, so she's on her own and she said that she was forced to sell her house and move here, into the flat which is smaller than she's used to. She also said she was very lonely.'

Ah, that was interesting. As you know, I'm an expert in lonely people, and I had thought that that might be the case when she was horrible to George and I. But then, I didn't understand – if she was lonely, why she was so horrible to us and polite to the Goodwins?

'She didn't pay me any attention though,' Salmon added. 'So I still don't think she's a fan of cats, but she told my owners that she would be happy to help out with any neighbourhood watch businesses, so that's interesting.'

'Thanks for telling us,' I said kindly. I knew the way to keep getting information was to ensure Salmon was onside. 'I really appreciate it.'

Nellie shot me a look, maybe I was overdoing it a bit.

'Anyway, that's all I have to say about that. So I'll be on my way.'

Salmon was really a strange cat but I was actually very fond of him, in my own way.

I was mulling over what he'd told me when George arrived.

'Oh George,' Nellie said, immediately fussing over him. She was like an aunt to him and had taken a more maternal role with him since Tiger's death.

'Nellie, let's go climb the tree,' he said, jumping around. Nellie also climbed with him, something I was unable to do, due to a fear of heights.

'I thought you were with Hana,' I said.

'She's not feeling too good. She was sick earlier, she thinks it was something she ate.'

'Oh no, I hope she's OK. Is Sylvie or Marcus going to take her to the vet?' I asked.

'Nah, she says she's better now, just tired. I think she must have had a bit of dodgy fish or something and you know how busy they are with Theo. She doesn't like to make a fuss.'

'But you will go and check on her later, make sure she's OK?' I didn't like vets, they weren't bad people but it's just not nice being prodded and poked, to be honest. However, even I knew they were valuable if you were ill. And I was a cat who liked to make a fuss.

''Course I will, but she's fine. Honestly, you are so dramatic.' George bounded off to the tree with Nellie right behind him. I took umbrage with his remark; after all, I was just being concerned for her. I was the sort of cat who wanted to make sure everyone was alright.

Elvis and I both lay shaded by the bush, watching George and Nellie enjoy the tree climbing, and savouring a few minutes of peace and quiet.

'Do you think I'm a drama cat?' I asked Elvis.

'Oh Alfie, you know you are. But we wouldn't have you any other way.'

'Don't go too high,' I shouted to George who waved his paw at me dismissively.

'I rest my case,' Elvis said as he raised his whiskers.

Chapter Eleven

Even I thought it was a bit of a harsh punishment as Tommy sat around our kitchen table with Summer, Toby, Henry, and Martha, and an array of colouring pens, charged with making the audition posters for the Christmas show.

'Right,' Aleksy said, in his stern voice. 'I need at least ten posters, because we can photocopy if we need more, and I've written out what each one needs to say. Tommy, you are in charge of writing – maybe do capital letters as you are neater with those. The rest of you, I want you to draw Christmas things around the writing so it looks enticing.'

'What does enticing mean?' Martha asked.

'You know, really good so people will want to join in,' Aleksy said. 'I'm going out, to look again at the hall, so I'll be back in an hour to check your progress.' He was taking being in charge very seriously.

Tommy groaned and I saw Claire, who was babysitting baby Theo, stifle a giggle. Aleksy left, and Claire went to the living room with Theo. Pickles followed her, and George said he was going to go next door because Theo was here, so it would probably be nice and quiet. That left me as really the only adult left supervising the poster making.

'Right, let's get on with this because the sooner it's done the better,' Tommy moaned.

'What should I draw?' Henry asked.

'Whatever,' Tommy replied with a sigh.

'Why are you so mean now? You used to be our friend,' Henry said, sounding sad.

'Yeah,' Toby agreed. 'You used to be fun.'

'Oh, boys, he's still our friend, he's just going through some stuff,' Summer said. We all turned to look at her, including Tommy.

'What stuff?' Martha asked.

'You know, teenage stuff. We'll be like that one day, although I don't think I will, because I am far too nice to become like him,' Summer explained. I jumped on the table, and nuzzled Summer. I mean, she was a genius sometimes. Even Tommy's lips twitched.

'And how do you know I am "going through some stuff"?' he asked, but more kindly.

'I heard Mummy and Daddy talk and they said you were a good kid underneath it all, so it would probably be OK. Although Daddy said if it wasn't then we'd have to visit you in jail.'

Tommy burst out laughing. The others looked at him a little hesitantly and then they joined in. I'm not sure they understood why they were laughing. Neither did I. I had heard about jail and it didn't sound fun. You were kept in cages, like cats were when they were in the shelter, but at least in a shelter lovely caring people looked after you; in jail they did not.

'OK guys, you're right. I am your friend and I have been a bit unhappy lately but I'm fine. I know, let's make these the best posters ever and then Aleksy will be so pleased with us he'll stop bossing us around.'

'He won't,' Martha said. 'Because we are going to audition

and he said he and Connie are in charge of choosing the talent.'

'Does that mean he might not choose us?' Toby sounded worried.

'Of course he will,' Henry reassured him.

'Yes, because we're brilliant,' Summer finished.

'What are you going to do?'

'The four of us are going to sing "Rudolph the Red-Nosed Reindeer",' Toby said. 'We wanted to do something cooler, like rapping, but Mum said it had to be Christmas songs.'

'You could write a rap to go in the song,' Tommy suggested.

'But we don't exactly know how to write a rap,' Henry pointed out.

'OK, how about we do the posters and then before the audition I can help you write a rap for the song? Are you all going to dress as reindeers?'

'If we have to,' Henry muttered.

'We do,' Summer declared.

'And Pickles is going to be Rudolph, we have to figure out how to make his nose red and I've got antlers to put on him, but Mum's worried he'll eat them,' Martha said.

'He probably will,' Tommy said with a laugh. Every time he laughed I saw my old Tommy again. I went to give him a fuss, to reward him. He was still there, I was right.

'So you'll really help us?' Toby asked, still not convinced. Toby wasn't as easily persuaded as the others.

'Yeah, we can write a rap, like "Rudolph's nose was so red, he couldn't play with others, had to go to bed, but one night it was dark and stormy and Rudolph was the hero of the story." Wow, I just did that off the top of my head, I'm pretty good at this.' Tommy laughed again.

'It's brilliant,' Martha said, sweetly. 'The boys can do the rap and we can all do the singing.'

'And Pickles will be so cute as Rudolph,' Summer finished. That was all well and good but what about me, George, Snowball and Hana? No one had given any hint as to what our parts would be yet.

Aleksy was amazed when he came back and found a neat pile of posters all stacked.

'We've done twenty for you,' Tommy said, but he'd gone back to using his sulky voice.

'Wow, and they are really good.' The children all beamed at him.

CHARITY CHRISTMAS SHOW

AUDITION FOR A CHARITY
CHRISTMAS SHOW
IN AID OF HELEN STREET SHELTER – A
BRILLIANT AND WORTHWHILE CAUSE

ALL WELCOME – SINGERS, DANCERS,
ACTORS

JOIN US ON SATURDAY 1ST NOVEMBER AT
EDGAR COMMUNITY HALL

*SUPPORT A GREAT CAUSE BY HELPING US
TO PUT TOGETHER A GREAT
COMMUNITY EVENT*

*BRINGING CHRISTMAS SPIRIT TO ALL AND
HELPING PEOPLE WHO AREN'T LUCKY
ENOUGH TO HAVE HOMES THIS CHRISTMAS*

*WHAT ARE YOU WAITING FOR?
YOU WILL NOT WANT TO MISS OUT!!*

There were drawings of stars, Christmas trees, and even Santa on the posters. Aleksy was right, they were really good.

'And we've been practising for our audition too,' Toby informed him.

'Nice one, Tommy,' Aleksy said, patting him on the back. Tommy scowled. 'The hall is looking good now, but we need to hold the auditions and then cast the show before we can start rehearsing and then we need to look at sets and selling tickets and wow, there's so much to do.' He sounded a bit dejected.

'Where's Connie?' Martha asked.

'She had to go out with her mum. Because of the baby taking up so much time, Sylvie wanted to spend some time alone with Connie while Claire babysat.'

'It'll be fine, Aleksy,' Summer said, sweetly.

'Tommy, will you come and help me put the posters up?' Aleksy asked.

'If I say no you'll tell Mum, won't you?'

'Yup, but because I need help, not because I'm a snitch. Anyway, it'll keep you out of trouble,' Aleksy said.

'Meow,' I said. Tommy could always get into trouble, there were no two ways about it.

I followed Aleksy and Tommy as they went to put some of the posters up. Tommy was dragging his feet and acting as if he didn't want to be there but Aleksy persisted. They had put the posters in plastic sleeves that Claire had pinched from Jonathan. They put a couple on lamp posts on Edgar Road, which brought back memories. A few years ago there was a spate of catnapping going on around here and posters kept going up on lamp posts looking for cats. I foiled the plan, but not without danger – I put my son George at risk and I have never quite forgiven myself for that. That was another story, and thankfully had a happy ending, but I had to say it was nice to see good news going up on the lamp posts for once.

'We should put one in the restaurant, and some up in school, although I'll have to do that as you're excluded,' Aleksy said.

'Thanks for reminding me. I never thought I would say I miss school, but I do,' Tommy said.

'Really?'

'I miss my mates, I miss football and, yeah, it's a bit boring being on my own working at home all day. Plus I have to do a load of washing up in the restaurant. That sucks.'

'You should tell Mum that, it'll make her very happy.'

'Whatever.' Ah, there he was again.

'Maybe I will. How about we take a poster to the neighbourhood watch people? The ones who wear matching jumpers and always carry binoculars wherever they go?' Aleksy suggested. I meowed my approval, it was a very good idea. The Goodwins knew everyone and would soon spread the word.

I stood on the doorstep between Aleksy and Tommy as they rang the bell. Heather and Vic Goodwin came to the door at the same time. I don't think they ever did anything without each other. I had never seen either of them on their own, in all my years on Edgar Road. Salmon was behind them. We raised our whiskers at each other.

'Hello, are you here to report a crime?' Vic Goodwin asked.

'Please don't tell me you're here to commit one? I mean, you don't look like criminals,' Heather added.

'You know us. We're Aleksy and Tommy . . . from the restaurant?' Aleksy explained, looking confused. They had seen the boys a lot, especially as they watched the street nearly all the time, and they had met them when we had the big Edgar Road power cut a couple of years ago and we all had to have Christmas lunch at the restaurant.

'Well I know that, but that doesn't exclude you from criminal behaviour,' Heather said. I shook my tail. Honestly, these people!

'We are trying to put on a show for charity,' Aleksy said. 'And we made posters to ask people to audition.'

Tommy stared at his feet.

'And as you are so important on the street we thought if we gave you a poster you might . . .' Aleksy said, cleverly. Flattery would get him what he wanted.

'Audition ourselves? Oh yes, and we could also spread the word to everyone else on the street. In fact, we could rally the troops, so to speak.'

Tommy and Aleksy exchanged glances.

'That would be amazing,' Aleksy said. They were being very polite, but I could sense they were both trying not to laugh a bit.

'What do you think you might audition with?' Tommy asked.

'As you can see from the poster, it's a Christmas show,' Aleksy added quickly.

'Well, we could maybe try to form an Edgar Road singing group? And do some Christmas songs?' Vic suggested.

'We both have lovely voices, if I do say so myself,' Heather added.

'That would be awesome,' Aleksy said. 'The vicar said the church choir would probably audition but they are probably more into carols. We are also going to do a grown-up Nativity play, which we thought would be fun, and then the children want to sing, but it would be great to have your group involved.'

'It sounds like a terribly good idea.' Vic took the poster that Aleksy was holding. 'Leave it with us, young men, and as I said, we'll rally the troops.'

'Thank you.'

'Meow,' I bid Salmon goodbye. It seemed my idea for a Christmas show was coming together really very nicely.

Chapter Twelve

I went to find George at Hana's and saw that all hell had broken loose. Marcus was jiggling around Theo, who was screaming, his poor face all red, Sylvie was on the phone and Connie was hovering around, trying to help but without knowing what to do.

'What's wrong?' I was immediately worried.

'Oh, it's fine,' George said. 'He's growing teeth and it hurts him a lot, hence all the screaming. Sylvie is asking Claire what to do to help him, and Polly's going to the pharmacy for them because Theo's been screaming for a long time and no one in this house can think straight. Not even me and Hana.'

'So, it's nothing to worry about?' I was concerned. Poor Theo sounded as if he was definitely in pain.

'No, apparently this is a normal baby occurrence,' Hana said. She looked tired, but then, listening to that noise would make anyone tired.

'It was good you didn't both leave,' I said, whilst wondering why they hadn't. After all, they were only a cat flap away from freedom and peace and quiet.

'I wanted to be here, just in case,' Hana said.

'And I couldn't leave her here alone,' George added.

'No, of course not.' I wondered if I could leave but before I could, the door opened and in walked Polly, Harold and Snowball.

'Oh Dad, sorry, I forgot about supper. It's just . . . Theo's

123

been screaming for an hour straight.' Marcus sounded harassed. He was the calmest man I knew, apart from Matt actually, but he was definitely stressed out now.

'Don't worry. Give Theo to me, I got these powders, they worked wonders with mine and Claire's. Also got you some gel in case that doesn't help.' Polly took Theo and then she gave Sylvie the bag. Sylvie got the powder out and Polly rubbed it on Theo's gums. It was very interesting to watch, despite the ear splitting noise. After a while, Theo stopped crying and the adults were all relieved as he closed his eyes, having exhausted himself as well as everyone else.

'I'll put the kettle on,' Polly said as Sylvie and Marcus slumped onto the sofa. Harold was cuddling Theo in the chair.

'I don't have to stay, if it's a bad time,' Harold said.

'Don't be silly, you're not going anywhere,' Marcus said. 'After all, you have the magic touch with Theo.'

'He's the spit of your mum you know. I thought he looked like you, which he does, but then you looked like her when you were a baby.' Harold sounded emotional. His wife died a long time ago but he was still sad about it. I understood that only too well.

'She'd be so proud of what a wonderful granddad you are,' Marcus said. We were all emotional. Maybe we'd caught it from Theo.

Now that things had calmed down, Connie went to do her homework and I greeted Snowball properly.

'I'm going home,' George announced. 'It's probably supper time.'

'I'll be along in a bit,' I said. I was thinking how nice it would be to spend a bit of time with Snowball. Calm, quiet time. Goodness knows I'd earned it.

I filled her in on the latest news, and I was surprised to realise there was so much. We were rushing towards the Christmas show now, everyone was preoccupied with it. I just hoped it didn't stop anyone from remembering to order the turkey and our treats.

'No word on what us cats are going to do in the show?' Snowball asked. She had also been treated to a lesson from George on stage craft. We tried not to laugh about it but honestly, he really took the (cat) biscuit.

'No, the auditions are next week and then they'll allocate our parts. I am expecting we will be central to the show, of course.'

'Do we have to audition?'

'No, I don't suppose so,' I said. 'I mean, they all know how talented and important we are so I'm pretty sure we'll just get given our roles. But we'll all go to the auditions anyway, because we need to keep an eye on things. We can't trust these guys not to need help after all.'

'Too true, Alfie. We'll all make sure we're there – us, George, and Hana. Are the others sure they don't want to be in it?'

'No, they don't fancy it. You know how some cats will just be cats.'

'Never mind, we'll have such a ball. I'm actually looking forward to it, we need some excitement.'

'Don't say that, Snowball. Our lives often have far too much excitement in them!' I wasn't joking.

★　★　★

When I finally tore myself away from Snowball, leaving her with Hana – Snowball was like an aunt to her, as she spent so much time at her house – I went home to find it was bedlam there too. Honestly, calm had barely been restored at Sylvie's house; it was as if it was catching.

Summer and Toby were fighting over the Rudolph song. 'Why can't I sing a bit on my own?' Summer was asking.

'Because it's a team effort,' Toby replied.

'But you and Henry get to do your rap yourselves.'

'But only because you didn't want to.'

'That's not the point.'

I wondered why Claire wasn't intervening but then I heard raised voices from the bedroom. Claire and Jonathan always went to their room when they argued, but of course we could all hear them.

I told George to keep an eye on the kids while I went to sort out the grown-ups.

'I am not auditioning and that's final,' Jonathan said.

'But you have to. It's important to Aleksy, Connie, Tommy now, and me. We all need to be involved,' Claire pushed.

'Claire I can't sing, dance, or act. I certainly don't want to be in a grown-up Nativity play. It's not my thing, and it's just not happening.'

'But you have to.'

'No, I don't.'

Honestly they were as bad as the children sometimes. I jumped on the bed and tried to stare at them to tell them to stop, but they were too far into the silly argument to pay me any attention.

'This is for such a good cause, and you know it's not easy.

I'm helping them as much as I can but there's so much to do, and that's why I need you involved. We've to do the auditions, then the running list for the show, sort out the props and get rehearsals underway and we have to sell tickets, organise refreshments . . . We have to make this a success because they are doing this for such a good cause. If it's anything but a huge success it'll be heartbreaking.' Claire sounded upset and I knew why. There was such a lot to do and hearing Claire say it out loud, it really struck me just how much. My idea might have been genius but it also meant a huge amount of work.

'I'll do anything to help, Claire, but I can't audition, please.' Jonathan was softening but I knew that being on stage wasn't his thing.

'Oh God, I don't know, there's just so much. Maybe I've taken on a bit *too* much because I also have Christmas to organise . . . But I promised Aleksy and I have to make sure it's a great show. And we need to find some money to put the show on as well. I forgot to put that on the list.' Claire ran her hands through her hair. I looked at her and then I looked at Jonathan. Surely that was what Jonathan could do. His job was about making money as far as I could tell, so couldn't they give some to the show?

'Meow, Meow, Meow, Meow,' I said at the top of my voice.

'Even Alfie thinks you should audition,' Claire said.

'Yowl.' No, that wasn't what I meant. I tried again. 'Mew, mew, mew, mew.' I said this directly to Jonathan, then I did a few circles in order to try to get him to fully understand.

'He's trying to say something, but not that. Alfie wouldn't betray me like that.'

'Purr,' I had to let him know he was right.

'Oh Claire, why didn't we think of it sooner, how about I get my company to sponsor the show? We have a charity pot and they're always looking to help local charities out as well as national ones. So we can sponsor the show, get our name on posters and the tickets and we'll ensure you have enough money to put the show on and hopefully a big donation at the end of it too.'

I lay down, a little worn out. Thank you, you've got it. Honestly, at times I did wish my humans were a bit quicker on the uptake.

'Can you ask them tomorrow?' Claire said, excited.

'Of course, don't say anything to Aleksy just yet, but I'm pretty sure I can persuade them. This is right up their street and such a good cause. But there is a condition.'

'OK, let's hear it.'

'I don't have to audition.'

'Fine.'

It seemed we had all got what we wanted, although not quite me because now I wanted my supper.

'Did the children sort it out?' I asked George as we were about to tuck in.

'Yes, with a bit of help from me. Summer and Martha are going to do the opening bit where they list all the reindeer and Toby and Henry will rap, the rest of the song they will all do.'

'Honestly, George, what would these humans do without us?'

We both shuddered. It wasn't worth thinking about.

Chapter Thirteen

The day of the auditions was here. I was both excited and relieved. Excited because we cats would find out what our part in the show was – besides being the masterminds behind it, of course. Relieved because Aleksy, Connie, and Claire had all been quite uptight for the last few days. They were driving me round the bend.

'What if no one comes?' they all said – more than once, I might add. But we knew that loads of people had said they were going to come, so it was just nerves. We arrived at the hall and found Ralph waiting for us at the door. He was looking pretty pleased with himself as he opened the door and let us in. As he put on the lights, I marvelled at how much cleaner it was than when we were last here.

'Wow, you've done a great job,' Claire said. It even smelt clean. To get us in the mood, Ralph had also put Christmas music on. I swayed along to 'White Christmas' as they inspected the hall.

'It's such a good cause, and I had a few parishioners help. We're auditioning – the choir, that is – and everyone's quite excited. We needed a new lease of life and it seems that this might do the trick.' He smiled. I wasn't sure how old Ralph was – older than Claire and Jonathan but much younger than Harold. He had grey hair, glasses, and was very well turned out. I nuzzled him, he was being supportive and needed rewarding for that.

'Great!' Aleksy sounded relieved.

'Shall we set up a table for us to sit behind, like on *Britain's Got Talent*?' Connie suggested.

'Ha, it will be like Edgar Road Church Hall's got Christmas talent!' Aleksy laughed.

'Right, let's do it,' Claire said as she set about moving a table to the centre of the room.

It was only us here for now. Jonathan was looking after Summer and Toby, but would be bringing them, along with Matt, Polly, Henry, and Martha later. Even Sylvie and Marcus were coming with Harold and Theo. I didn't like to point out that Theo was probably going to be the star of the Nativity show, because I wasn't sure if they hadn't come up with that idea yet. George was going to come with them, along with Hana and Snowball. And the Goodwins had been true to their word and had rallied lots of other people who would be joining us. Oliver, the cat who lived in Tiger's old house, told me that even his owners, the Barkers, were joining Vic and Heather's singing group. Franceska, Tomasz, and Tommy were coming along with his friend, Charlie, who was helping him with social media. Tommy still wasn't keen but had reluctantly accepted that his involvement in the show was his punishment. I was hoping they would take videos of us, because cats were the most popular thing on social media, I was pretty sure. It seemed there was no end to our usefulness.

The audition panel – as Claire called it – was set up. They all had notepads and pens and I was going to sit on the table, so I could watch too, as they clearly needed my help. Ralph had left us so he could go and get changed into his 'audition outfit' and also meet his choir mates, so we were alone for a bit to reflect before the madness started.

'What if no one comes?' Connie asked for the millionth time.

'Meow.' They will, I reassured her. But I could feel their nerves as the reality began to get closer and closer. I was relieved when Jonathan, Polly, and Matt arrived with the children.

'We nearly got mobbed for queue jumping,' he said. 'Thankfully Vic, Heather and their band of merry followers said I was one of the organisers.'

'So there are people here to audition?' Aleksy asked.

'Quite a few, actually,' Summer said as she climbed onto the stage and started spinning.

'Right, well we better get started soon,' Claire said. 'Jonathan, can you keep the kids in order while we begin?'

I very much doubted it. As Summer started dancing across the stage with Martha, and Toby climbed on some stacked chairs with Henry, Polly took charge. I hoped George, Snowball, and Hana would arrive soon so they could help them out. 'We can't start without Tommy, he needs to set up to do some filming and he's going to post on Instagram and Twitter as we go.' Aleksy sounded panicked but just then we heard a commotion and in walked Tommy and Charlie, followed by Franceska and Tomasz.

'I told them I was in charge of filming and then they wanted me to start filming them, which I did because, like the TV talent shows, we can post a video of the queue of people,' Tommy said, almost forgetting to sulk.

'Yeah, it's not as long as those on TV obviously, but we have tricks to make it look longer. Look, guys, we got them to wave and cheer,' Charlie added.

We all crowded round Charlie's screen – it did look as if there were a load of people and noise. There were more people than even I had expected.

'Great job,' Claire said. 'Tommy, Charlie, thank you so much for helping.'

'I am proud of both my boys today,' Franceska said, a little emotionally.

'Hey there's a few kids from school here too, Aleksy, Connie,' Charlie said. He sounded excited, which made us all feel raring to go. 'I thought that they wouldn't want to be in it, but they do!'

'Right, let's begin,' Claire clapped her hands together and as the rest of our family arrived, the auditions began.

It really was nothing like the TV competition, or it was, but mainly the bit when you got those really bad people that made everyone laugh. Claire, Jonathan, Toby, Summer and us cats usually watched those shows on a Saturday night. I didn't always get it, and would often fall asleep, but George loved them and would tell me everything – he really was quite a showbiz cat, thinking about it.

In fairness, our auditions were not all bad. Although, there was a man who tried to juggle – which, as far as I knew, had nothing to do with Christmas, and he wasn't even dressed up as anything – and as he threw the balls around he kept dropping them.

'Thank you,' Claire said as he picked the balls up for what felt like the millionth time. 'Next.'

An old man wearing a suit and top hat walked on the stage with an old woman who seemed to be wearing a long evening dress and carrying a lot of stuff. They not only looked old but walked quite slowly.

'I am Magic Marvin and this is my beautiful assistant, Dolly.' He spoke with a flourish and a wave of his wand.

'Hello,' Claire said. 'Clearly we don't need to ask you what you do.'

What this had to do with Christmas, again, no idea.

'First I will make this rabbit disappear,' Magic Marvin said. Dolly put a table on the stage and out of a big bag she pulled a rabbit, luckily it was a toy one. Marvin placed it on the table, took his top hat off his head and put it over the rabbit.

'I thought they were meant to take rabbits out of hats not put them in,' Aleksy whispered. Connie shushed him.

'Abracadabra,' Marvin said, waving his wand over the hat. He pulled it up with a flourish; the rabbit was still there.

'Dolly, did you set up the trick?' he asked, his face turning red.

'Well, I thought I did,' Dolly sounded confused. 'Do the next one, quickly.'

I tried not to notice Jonathan, Matt, and Tomasz shaking with laughter.

'Right, well, now I shall turn the rabbit into a bunch of flowers.'

We all watched but the rabbit remained a rabbit. He was getting a little red faced and flustered. I really had no idea what was going on and nor did Magic Marvin, by the look of him.

'For my final trick, I shall saw my beautiful assistant Dolly in half.'

We all looked horrified as Dolly handed him a saw.

'No,' Claire screeched. 'I mean, honestly thank you. We probably won't have magic in the show, because it is a Christmas show, but hopefully you can be involved in some way.'

'I could make Santa disappear?' Marvin offered.

I was pretty sure he really couldn't do that.

Aleksy and Connie looked relieved as a group of about five children from their school came on the stage.

'Hey,' Aleksy said.

'Aleksy, Connie, other lady,' one of the lads stepped forward. 'We are going to sing "Drummer Boy", but the Justin Bieber, Busta Rhymes version.' He coughed, and then pressed his phone and music rang out. They all sang and were actually really good. I saw Aleksy and Connie grin at each other and Claire smiled at me.

'This helps make the show modern,' Aleksy whispered to Claire, who nodded. They were followed by a dancing crew who were quite well known locally, apparently; a big group of boys and girls who filled the stage and were really amazing. One even spun on his head, which I thought looked painful but he seemed alright.

'This is getting better and better,' Connie hissed.

Vic and Heather's singing group were up next, mostly people I recognised from Edgar Road, and they sang 'The Twelve Days of Christmas', which was actually really good.

'Thank you so much,' Claire said as they finished.

'Well, you are welcome. We didn't have time to get our costumes together but we will all be dressed the same if we get a part in the show of course, ha, ha.' Actually he and

Heather were wearing the same clothes, but the others looked normal. Not for long, it seemed.

Ralph's choir followed with a very beautiful rendition of 'Silent Night'. They could really sing very well, and the show began to take shape, it seemed.

Everyone cheered when Summer, Toby, Henry, Martha, and Pickles went on stage to do their Rudolph song, which was pretty good. The rap made it even more fun, although Pickles kept wandering off and sniffing things; he didn't fall off the stage, which was something.

'Sylvie, Marcus, and baby Theo,' Connie said, when they'd finished.

'We're not auditioning, love,' Sylvie said, sounding a little panicked. 'We're just here for moral support.'

'But Mum, you have to,' Connie said.

'Well, the thing is, we thought Theo could be the baby Jesus . . . since he's a baby,' Aleksy explained.

'Right, but how can he audition for that?' Marcus asked. 'I mean, he's a baby.'

'He won't be as good as me,' I heard George whisper to Hana.

'He can't, he's got the part. We just need to cast the rest of the Nativity now,' Aleksy said.

'Yeah, we're going to write the script, so it's a bit more modern,' Connie added.

'You can't really mess with the Nativity,' Franceska pointed out.

'No, but we can make it meaningful and fun and with the singing around it, it'll be lovely,' Connie said.

Claire called for anyone who wanted to audition for an

acting part to line up. I was surprised how full the hall was still, even those who had already auditioned were staying to watch. It seemed that already everyone felt the spirit of the show. And as we'd listened to Christmas music, I was really beginning to feel full of festive spirit.

Because the auditions now focused on the Nativity, it was the actors that were taking to the stage. I wasn't sure how many lines were in the Nativity, but everyone had their own ideas. One man even brought a toy sheep with him.

'Hi, I'm Fred and I want to try out for the part of shepherd.'

'Great Fred, so go ahead,' I could see Claire trying not to laugh.

'Good sheep, good sheep,' he kept saying. No one knew quite how to respond to that.

Person after person took to the stage. All the while, Claire, Aleksy, and Connie were making notes. I had no idea what they said, although I was part of the panel — or I liked to think I was. I couldn't read but I could give them a nudge when I thought someone was particularly good. There weren't a lot of nudges going on right now though.

I was surprised as Harold walked onto the stage. He moved slowly as he shuffled to the middle. Harold wasn't one for putting himself forward — we'd had an awful job trying to persuade him to tell Claire about the Sunday Lunch Club. He wasn't full of confidence, that was for sure, but even he wanted to be a part of it all.

'Hello, what's your name and what are you auditioning for?' Aleksy asked.

'You know my name.'

'Well, yes, but there are others here who might not,' Claire pointed out.

'Right, well, I'm Harold, I'm Connie there's step-grand-father in fact, and I'm auditioning for the part of Santa.'

'Oh, we didn't have Santa down on our list, did we?' Connie asked.

'It's a blooming Christmas show. How can you not have Santa?' Harold boomed.

'Good point,' Claire said. 'How about we close the show with Santa? We could do a song at the end like "We Wish You a Merry Christmas", and Santa could give out sweets to the audience, like they do in the panto?'

'I'm not singing,' Harold said.

'OK then, but we could get the children on to sing and you could throw sweets or something into the audience,' Aleksy said. 'The grand finale.'

'Oh I like the idea of being the grand finale.' Harold preened.

'Right, can you say, Ho, Ho, Ho?' Connie asked.

'Ho, Ho, Ho.' Harold boomed as if he had been practising.

'Great, thanks. We'll let you know,' Aleksy said.

'Is that it?' Harold asked.

'Yes, you were great,' Claire said, as Harold looked confused and then shuffled off stage.

I had to admit it was getting a bit tedious as I lay on the table. The auditions seemed to be going on forever, and I knew it was important but honestly, there was only so much 'there's no room at the inn' I could hear. I thought about taking forty winks, but my eyes widened in horror as the woman who threatened George and I walked onto the stage.

'My name is Barbara and I am very experienced in stage work. I was part of my old local amateur dramatics society for years. I also used to be a drama teacher,' she said.

'Right, well great, thank you. Off you go,' Claire said.

'To be or not to be? That is the question . . .'

'What is happening?' Aleksy whispered.

'It's *Hamlet*,' Connie replied.

'I know that but *Hamlet* is a man and has nothing to do with the Nativity,' Aleksy added.

Claire shushed them as Barbara was pacing the stage, saying words that I didn't even begin to understand. Was this a foreign language?

At the end of a very long speech where I really did have trouble keeping my eyes open, she fell down onto the stage and there was silence. Claire, Aleksy, and Connie's mouths were open wide.

'Is she dead?' someone asked from the audience.

'Make way,' Vic Goodman said, Heather on his heels. 'I am trained in first aid.' He ran onto the stage and started poking Barbara.

'Get off me. I'm still acting,' she said, sitting up. I saw Jonathan, Matt, and Tomasz start laughing yet again. Franceska nudged them and told them to stop. Barbara stood up, refusing to let Vic or Heather help her, and then she took a bow.

'Wow,' Claire said. 'That was, well . . . that was something I have never seen before.'

'Thank you,' Barbara said, but I wasn't sure that it had been a compliment.

'Right, well, I think we're done,' Aleksy said. 'It's been great, thank you all for coming and we will make sure everyone has a role in the show because it's for the community and also to raise money for the Helen Street Shelter. So spread the word.' Everyone cheered and clapped. Aleksy was really taking charge as he asked everyone to leave numbers and names so he could get in touch and Claire asked anyone who wanted to help backstage to let them know before they left.

Hang on, this wasn't right. I jumped from the table and went to find Snowball, George, and Hana.

'Um, do you realise that no one has mentioned us?' I said.

'Maybe because you were a judge?' Hana suggested.

'I mean, what if they think we don't want to be in the show?' George said. 'After all, I am probably the most experienced here, so they must want us.'

'I know, maybe we need to show them that we do want to be part of the show,' I said.

'How?' Snowball asked.

'Quick, on stage before everyone leaves,' I said. The four of us made our way onto the stage.

'Meow, meow, come on guys,' I hissed. 'Make as much noise as you can.'

'MEW, MEW, MEW.' We were a bit like a cats' choir. The hall fell silent.

'What is going on?' Barbara shouted.

'Well, it seems that the cats want in on the show,' Jonathan said, and then he, Matt, and Tomasz laughed loudly. I hoped they were laughing with us, not at us.

'Of course they need to be in the show, Aleksy,' Franceska said.

'Oh no, you're right, Mum. We forgot about them,' Aleksy said to Claire.

Yes, you did, how could you?

'Keep going we're filming this,' Tommy said, and nudged Charlie. 'This will be YouTube gold,' he said. Again, as much as he complained about doing this, it seemed that Tommy was forgetting to be obnoxious at times, so this really might work.

We started moving around the stage, mewing and stalking, George did a few jumps and Hana looked a little embarrassed, and stayed very close to Snowball, but I think we got the idea across. We carried on until we were all a little worn out. When we stopped, someone led a huge round of applause.

'The cats are auditioning, that is so funny,' a voice said.

'That is the coolest thing ever,' another person said.

'Who ever heard of actual cats being in a show?' Barbara snapped, but she was soon shot down.

'Of course the cats have to be in the show,' Connie said.

'I can't believe we didn't think of it.' Aleksy was shaking his head.

I couldn't believe it either. George did a sort of jig, Hana swooshed her tail and Snowball rolled around the floor – which I wasn't sure was a good idea as it was a bit mucky from everyone's shoes. I walked to the centre of the stage, sat down and lowered my head in an attempt at a bow. I was soon joined by the others as we sat in a line on the stage, having finished.

'You know, suddenly I think this is going to be the best Christmas show ever,' Tommy said with the biggest smile.

'Meow.' You're welcome, I replied.

Chapter
Fourteen

Post audition, everyone was buoyed up that the show was taking shape. Claire called a meeting at our house the following day, and while the children went upstairs to practise their singing – I had a feeling I would be subjected to a lot of this in the coming weeks – us adults sat around the living room, with Claire, Aleksy, and Connie, who were clearly in charge.

Tommy sat in the corner. He was wearing his sulky face again.

'This looks as if it's going to be bigger than ever,' Claire said. 'We were overwhelmed by the amount of support we received, so I think we owe it to everyone to try to get them into the show.'

'I know there will be some people who will be disappointed though,' Aleksy said. 'But that's show business for you.' Honestly, had he caught it from George?

'Do I still have to be involved if you've got so many people?' Tommy said.

'Yes, you do,' Franceska snapped. 'Now stop that and get involved in something good for once.'

Tomasz put a hand on her arm, in a husbandly way I thought.

'What about the awful magician?' Jonathan asked.

'We are going to give Marvin and Dolly parts in the Nativity, and the juggler,' Connie explained.

'We researched it and there can be a lot of shepherds, so

we thought that we'd have any extra people as shepherds, that way everyone can be involved,' Aleksy said.

'Our thinking is that the running list will be as follows: we open with the dancers who are going to try to dance to something Christmassy, but we'll work on that. They'll be followed by the school singing group, the Edgar Road singers, then Rudolph with the children and Pickles. We thought then we would put the Nativity play on – Aleksy and I are going to write the scripts to make it a bit different, but we won't offend anyone – then, after the first half of the Nativity, Ralph's choir will sing "Silent Night". Then we'll have the second half of Nativity, all with singing as well. We finish with Santa coming on stage with the children and he will maybe throw sweets into the audience, or something – obviously nothing that can hurt anyone – and then everyone will sing "We Wish You a Merry Christmas".' Connie had a list in front of her as she spoke and I had never heard her sound so sure of herself.

'Sounds amazing; you guys have done a great job,' Matt said.

'Can't wait to hear what my part is,' Polly added.

'Meow!' No one mentioned us cats again.

Claire, Aleksy, and Connie exchanged glances.

'We really need you cats to play sheep,' Claire said, carefully.

'Yes, we thought the four of you could be sheep for the Nativity and come on with the shepherds. It's quite an important part of the play,' Aleksy explained.

'Crucial, some would say,' Claire added.

They had to be kidding. A sheep? Really?

Ages ago, George and I were at our holiday home in Devon and we nearly got trampled by a flock of sheep, so I really wasn't keen. Wasn't there anything more appropriate that we could do?

'And, of course, you can do a sort of sheep dance,' Connie suggested.

'What's a sheep dance?' Aleksy asked. I had the same question.

'You know like they did today, a bit of rolling and jigging, it'll be great for the film, then the shepherds can herd them up and it'll look more authentic. Of course you will have to train them to be herded, that might not be easy,' Connie said.

Cheek of it, if we couldn't take direction then no one could. Honestly, how people kept underestimating us I had no idea. The show was my idea, after all.

'And we can make them white fluffy coats to put on, so they'll look like sheep,' Sylvie said.

Oh boy, really? Dressing up wasn't my favourite thing, or George's, but then it looked as if we had no choice. Snowball was the only one of us that even remotely resembled a sheep and that was only because she was white.

'Doris will help with costumes, she's always knitting or making things,' Claire said, making a note.

I was far from convinced, but we would have to accept it for now if we wanted to be in the show. When I spoke to the others – none of whom were here – I'd see what they said. I mean, sheep may not be as cool as cats but we were bound to be able to do something with it. At least we would be doing it for a good cause. I was desperately trying to talk myself into it, but I wasn't sure I was succeeding.

'Anyway, we'll work on the parts and the running list later but we need other things,' Claire explained.

'Like what? I've given you sponsorship,' Jonathan said.

'Yes, which is great because we can now afford to put the show on properly and also make sure we raise money,' Claire replied, giving him a hug.

'We are going to do online tickets, which are easy to set up and also a donation page, which we need to advertise on the posters, and on social media as well,' Aleksy said. 'I've written all the details down.'

'Tommy's doing social media,' Connie said.

'You better not muck it up,' Aleksy warned.

'As if,' Tommy said. But we weren't so sure.

'As lovely as the posters the kids did for the auditions were, we need something a bit more professional for the actual show,' Claire pointed out.

'And my company logo needs to be on there – on everything, if they're sponsoring it – as they do expect to get a bit of recognition,' Jonathan pointed out. Now his company was sponsoring the show he was mentioning it at every turn. No modesty, Jonathan. And it had been my idea in the first place . . .

'No problem,' Matt said. 'I can design the posters. We can have digital copies to put all over social media and physical copies we can put up wherever we can. Now, I did have one suggestion, can we put the show on for people who go to the shelter? So they can enjoy what really is their show, without buying a ticket?'

'Oh Matt, that's a great idea. Why don't you make it the dress rehearsal? Also I volunteer to design the set. It's kind of my job, after all,' Polly added. She was an interior designer. 'I'm thinking we have a sort of Christmas tree forest, with fake snow and stars on the walls, then for the Nativity we need to build some kind of stable, or shed thing, for that, and the final bit with Santa I thought we could do a living room, and have him putting presents round a big tree before the kids come in and find him and it's a great moment before the final song?'

'Isn't three sets a bit ambitious?' Marcus asked.

'Well, I looked at the stage and there's already a curtain, so as long as we have enough people to help shift them around and control the curtains, because it won't be sophisticated like a proper theatre of course, then I don't see why not?' Polly said.

'I think that sounds great,' Sylvie said. 'And we'll help with everything.'

'Ah, well, we wanted to talk about that. We kind of need you two to be Mary and Joseph, Mum, Marcus,' Connie said.

'What?' Marcus looked horrified.

'It's because of Theo.' Theo was sleeping in Harold's arms, oblivious to the fact he was one of the stars of the show.

'Yes, Mum, what if he starts crying in the show? We can't control that, and if some strange man or woman picks him up, that could be a disaster.'

'Imagine if it was the juggler, he'd probably drop him.' Jonathan laughed, but Claire shot him one of her 'looks'.

'But, what if Mum is Mary and someone else is Joseph. I was going to volunteer to help Tomasz with sets.' Marcus sounded panicked.

'You can help me too,' Tomasz said, his lips twitching. 'You can do both.'

Marcus scowled at him.

'Great idea,' Jonathan added. 'You'd make a great Joseph. What about costumes?' Matt, Jonathan, and Tomasz could be so immature at times like this, as they all tried not to laugh.

'We are going to do a modern twist on the costumes to make it more fun, no tea towels on anyone's head . . . Mum's going to be in charge because she knows about fashion,' Connie said.

'Well, I don't know about that, but I'll do my best,' Sylvie said modestly.

'I can sew,' Franceska added. 'So I'd be happy to help.'

'Tomasz and Matt, you will be shepherds because, a bit like with Theo, the cats know you and we're going to have quite a few shepherds in total. Polly, I know you're doing sets but you can also be the innkeeper we thought – you know "there's no room at the inn" – although I think it'll be something more modern than an inn,' Aleksy continued.

'A Travelodge?' Jonathan laughed.

I listened with my eyes widening. There was so much to be done for this show. I thought it would be as simple as a couple of songs and a bit of a play but it was getting very complex. Costumes, sets, running lists, it was all going to take a lot of time and effort, and I was incredibly proud to see how much my families were all banding together to do it. It was warming my little heart. And I was almost happy to be a sheep if it helped. Almost but not quite.

I was woken by George and as I blinked I saw that everyone had gone. I must have dropped off.

'Oh, the meeting's over?' I said with a yawn.

'Did you sleep through it?'

'No, of course not. I listened to the most important parts.' At least I hoped I had. 'It just got very tiring with everyone chipping in ideas. Anyway, I do know what our part is going to be.'

'Tell me, tell me, tell me!' George sounded so young when he was excited.

'Sheep.' I didn't quite know if I could look him in the eyes.

'Sheep?'

'I'm afraid so. In the Nativity there are going to be a few shepherds, and we are going to be their sheep, who go with them when they visit the baby Jesus.'

'I've never understood why there weren't any cats in the Nativity scene,' George said. 'Can't we persuade them to let us be cats?'

'How would that show your acting prowess?' I teased.

'Oh, yes, of course you're right. But it's not me I'm worried about. With my stage experience and natural talent I'll easily be able to be a sheep but you, Snowball, and Hana might not find it quite so. I guess I'll just have to help you all.'

I had no words. But it seemed that George had many as he started lecturing me about characterisation and how to make myself believable. How on earth I was going to be believable as a sheep? I couldn't even make the right noise. And neither could George, to be honest, but I wasn't going to be the one to tell him that. Neither of us had much of a 'bleat'.

We spent the rest of the evening at home because it really

was cold and miserable outside, and also we were both tired. George had to be the stand-in for Pickles (which he did not appreciate) when the children showed Claire and Jonathan how well their Rudolph song was going. Even though he's clearly a brilliant actor – if he does say so himself – George sat there looking annoyed through the whole song.

Claire and Jonathan chatted through logistics – how much money they would spend and how much they hoped to raise, what the ticket price should be, and how they would advertise it beyond social media and putting a few posters up. Claire said she would contact the local paper and see if they would write a piece, Jonathan said he would ask some of the people who worked for him to buy tickets. And they also discussed having a gift donation bank at the show so people could bring a present for the homeless shelter people . . . There were a lot of good ideas going on and I could only feel proud and delighted. Not only because it was for such a good cause and would help so many people, but also because it was all my idea.

Had I mentioned that?

Chapter Fifteen

Chapter
Fifteen

Snowball was laughing, and I didn't think it was funny. I had just told her about the sheep thing, which she thought was hilarious – even the fact we would be dressing up. I thought she would be as affronted as me, but no, she was amused.

'Oh come on, Alfie, where's your sense of adventure?' she said.

'But a sheep? We could have been the wise men, because goodness knows we are wise. Or even angels, because everyone knows angels are good. But sheep? They don't do anything except run around and eat grass.'

'You're an expert on sheep now?'

'I told you about the sheep when we were on holiday in Lynstow—'

'Yes, you did and you don't need to tell me again,' Snowball said, stopping me in my tracks. 'Alfie, where's your Christmas spirit?'

'Goodness, if I had known, I might not have come up with the idea in the first place,' I huffed. I wasn't sure why I was so annoyed, but I think that after all the work we'd done I had expected more of a starring role. I felt that the sheep were just extras really. The more I had time to think about it, the more I wasn't keen.

'You need to get over yourself. I heard Harold talking about how the homeless people will really benefit from this and that's why we're doing it. It raises awareness and money for the problem, and it means that more people at the Helen Street Shelter can have a lovely dinner for Christmas, and hopefully warm clothes and also even gifts. It's more than they normally get, which is sad, and we need to remember how lucky we are.' She gave me one of her stern looks. I was suitably chastised.

'You're right, sometimes I do think about myself too much.' I felt bad.

'Well, I heard Harold on the phone and he said they are all going to the shelter later, not the younger ones because they are too little, so they're staying with Sylvie, but the rest of them are going to help out, meet some of the people who our show is going to help and give everyone an idea as to why we're doing this,' Snowball said.

'We're all going to go to the shelter?' I asked. 'They said us cats would be going?'

'No, Alfie, what have I just said? Sometimes things are more important than us.'

'I do know that,' I huffed again. 'But, surely we'll be going to the shelter.' How could they even think about going without us?

'I'm not sure we're invited,' Snowball said.

'When has that ever stopped us?' I asked.

George didn't take much persuading to come with us to the shelter but Hana said she was tired and would prefer to stay at home.

'Is she alright?' I asked George when we were at our house.

'She's just more exhausted than usual but I think that's

because of the baby. No one gets much sleep in that house at the moment.'

'That makes sense. Hopefully he'll start sleeping more soon and they'll all get better rest,' I said.

'Anyway, I'm excited to go to the shelter and I said I'd tell her all about it. It's good for us to meet the people we're trying to help, so we understand more,' he said.

'You're a good lad,' I said, and gave him a pat with my paw. I was moved. Snowball was right, I had been too busy thinking about myself, and not spent enough time thinking about why we were doing this show. It wasn't for us to be stars, it was to raise money for a very good cause, to show how a community can be when it behaves like a proper community, and also – as an added bonus for us – a chance to spend more time with our loved ones. That was what was important. Not me being a sheep. No, Snowball was right, I needed to get over myself. Not that I would tell her that, of course. She loved being right, and when she was right I never heard the end of it.

Because Sylvie was staying with the children, Marcus offered to help as it was too much for one person. So when Harold arrived at our house with Snowball following him, we were ready to go. Aleksy, Tommy, Franceska, and Tomasz, along with Connie, were meeting us there as it was nearer to their house than ours. Jonathan was going to drive, as was Matt, but no one mentioned us.

'What if they don't think we're going with them?' George asked.

'We go and wait by Jonathan's car and when he opens the door we jump in,' I said.

'Good plan, Alfie.' It seemed that Snowball had forgiven me for my earlier selfishness.

As they got into the cars, we jumped in too.

'Claire, the cats cannot come with us,' Jonathan said.

'Meow.' Why not?

'Look, if they can't go in the shelter, then we'll leave them in the car but if we try to get them out now we'll be late to meet Frankie and the others,' Claire replied, which I knew meant we could go. She indulged us a bit more when it came to outings.

'Why is everything such a drama?' Jonathan said, but as we sat with Harold in the back, he chuckled and stroked us. He was clearly pleased we were going with him. At least someone was.

I had never been in a shelter before. In fact, I hadn't heard of a human shelter before now, only animal ones, but Helen Street Shelter was a massive building, or so it looked from outside. We parked and got out of the car. There was no way they were leaving us out so we practically attached ourselves to one of the humans' legs. I was attached to Jonathan, who didn't look best pleased but what could you do?

'Hey, the cats have joined us?' Franceska looked confused.

'You know what they're like, they come everywhere if they can, but we need to ask the shelter workers if it's OK.'

'Meow.' Of course it will be; they will be delighted to see us.

'Maybe it'll be better if we carry them?' Jonathan conceded, picking me up. Harold picked up Snowball and Claire took hold of George.

'We all have to be brave,' Aleksy said. 'I've been before, and it's hard to see, but remember they are human beings and need to be treated as such.' He sounded so authoritative and grown up. I was proud of him.

'What else would we treat them as?' Jonathan asked.

I hoped the answer wasn't sheep.

I saw Tomasz give Tommy a warning to behave himself, and Tommy actually looked a little contrite as we made our way in. We followed Aleksy — our self-appointed leader of this particular expedition — into a massive room. There were long tables with chairs laid out for people to eat at. Some were already full, others still empty. A feeding station was set up at the front, with people standing organising food and serving. I tried to take it all in but it was vast. There was a part where they advertised clothing, and another one for bedding, a third for toiletries. This shelter was drop in only, Aleksy explained. You couldn't sleep here. They tried to get people beds, of course, and there was an office where people could go to for advice and help round the back.

'Hi, I'm Greg, the manager,' a man said, greeting us. 'And we are all so pleased you're helping us. Really, it means the world.' He was a nice man I decided, with messy blond hair and kind eyes.

Aleksy made all the introductions.

'Meow,' I said, to make myself known.

'Ah, yes you see these are our cats Alfie, George, and Snowball; they like to go everywhere,' Aleksy explained.

'And they are in the show so they really should be here,' Tommy added. I felt relieved, it seemed he was going to do as his dad asked him.

'OK, well not sure if it's a good idea while we serve food but we can make an exception as long as you keep carrying them.'

'Meow,' I reached out and touched Greg's arm with my paw.

'Alfie was homeless when we first met him,' Claire said.

'Mew.' Yes, I was telling him I understood a bit, and although I was now clearly a pampered pet, it hadn't always been this way.

'Well, Alfie, great to have you onboard then. You'll understand how hard it is for some of our guys,' Greg said, sounding ever so slightly bemused.

'Mew.' Of course I understood, but I felt as if I needed to know more.

As we were given the tour, we met some of the people who used the shelter, and those who worked there – all volunteers giving up their time to do good. It was immediately humbling.

I felt choked up as I met some of the homeless people; some were old, and should have been looked after, others too young to be in such a predicament. There was an array of ages, and a mix of females and males. It seemed that homelessness didn't discriminate. But they were all so nice and friendly, some shyer than others. Most wanted to pet us, which of course we didn't mind one bit.

'It's still a bit quiet,' Greg said. 'It'll start getting busier soon as people arrive for an evening meal. And we always need more clothes, toiletries, tents, and sleeping bags, which, if we get extra money, we can buy in, but we still always welcome donations of course.'

'I'm going to get everyone in my office to bring something in for the shelter – I'll call it our Christmas project,' Jonathan said. He was quiet, as if the reality of what went on in the shelter was sinking in, and he kept petting my head, as if for reassurance. I wasn't shocked – I knew from when I was homeless that it can happen to anyone – but I was definitely sad.

Everyone here had a story, you could see it in their faces, their eyes, their tattered clothes. I was so surprised that they were all trying to be cheerful. Despite having so little, they still managed a smile. It was heartbreaking and I realised being a sheep was a tiny, tiny price to pay . . . I was definitely humbled. And I needed to be. We needed to make this the biggest, best show ever, and I knew we would. I could feel it in my fur.

'Oh, I'll get some of the companies I work for to donate as well,' Polly said. Matt agreed that he would get people he worked with involved, and they also asked for ideas for what the shelter could use for Christmas gifts. It was decided that gloves, scarves, and hats would be the most useful, so Claire said if Greg could get her a list of roughly how many women and men he expected for Christmas, she would organise that each got a parcel with that in. She said that they would all be gift wrapped because everyone deserved to get a nice gift wrapped present at Christmas. I felt so emotional as they discussed ways they could help, although I could hear in their voices they all wished they could do more.

'We are so grateful, I can't tell you,' Greg said. 'And of course, we're looking forward to the show.'

'Well, I hope that you can join us for the dress rehearsal,

and we'll put on some food afterwards too,' Claire said. 'We'd love for the cast to meet the people they are doing this for. We can discuss numbers nearer the time, but we'd like to accommodate as many as possible.'

'Thank you,' Greg said, sounding a little stunned. 'You don't know how much this means to us.'

'You're doing a wonderful job,' Polly said. 'This place is amazing.' She had tears in her eyes.

Harold surprised me the most; he was going around carrying Snowball and introducing himself to people, telling them he was being Santa in the show, shaking hands as if he really was Santa. It was funny because he wasn't normally this sociable . . . or this cheerful, for that matter.

'Meow,' I said loudly from my place in Matt's arm, who had taken me from Jonathan. I was thinking of ways to make this even bigger.

'I've got an idea,' Aleksy said. 'How about one evening we get the cast from the show to come here and help out, and we can get the local paper to come to that? Can we do that, Mum?'

'Sure we can.' Franceska put her arm around her son.

'Wonderful idea, Aleksy,' Greg said. 'And, it'll be a real treat for them to see the show, they don't get many invitations.'

'Don't bank on it being that good,' Jonathan said, but he was joking. At least, I hope he was.

'Not funny,' Claire said. She was right; so often his jokes weren't.

'Hi, I'm Lisa,' a young-ish lady said as she came up to us. She was wearing a thick coat, which I was pleased to see looked quite warm, because goodness knew how people were supposed to survive in this weather. 'Can I stroke your cat? I used to have a cat but I lost her and I miss her so much.' Lisa sounded emotional. 'I love cats.'

Matt placed me in her arms and she stroked me. I purred to her to give her reassurance. I was pleased to make a new friend and I nuzzled into her, trying to show her that I cared.

'Hey, you are gorgeous,' she said. 'And the others too. I hope you'll come back again.' She stroked me one last time and gave me back to Matt.

'Meow.' I'd be delighted to.

'Lisa is one of our hopeful cases, we're hoping to get her into some accommodation before Christmas, and then she said she would get a cat as soon as she was able,' Greg explained.

'Yowl.' Lisa was clearly a very clever young woman.

George jumped down and jumped onto one of the empty tables. Before anyone could get him, people lined up to fuss over him. He did a bit of showing off; he jumped a bit, rolled around and then sat looking adorable as they took it in turns to stroke him.

'Honestly,' Jonathan said. 'He's such an attention seeker.' But at least everyone was laughing. The shelter became full of life as George entertained, meeting the people who we were doing the show for. It was wonderful. I had no other words – I felt warm and fuzzy, sad, but hopeful, all at the very same time.

Before we left, I noticed that Jonathan took his wallet out and gave Greg a bundle of notes. I puffed my chest. I was so proud of everyone; we were all working together to do something good. And as we left them enjoying a hot meal and company, chatter filled the hall, and cheers and waves followed us out. I hoped we would get to go again. We couldn't do much but at times doing anything was much better than doing nothing.

My ego was firmly put in its place as we made our way home. I was so lucky and it was time to count my blessings. Even if being a sheep was one of them.

Chapter Sixteen

The shelter visit had made us all see the show as even more important, and so we all upped our game. We knew that if we could raise money, get the gifts and also extra clothes donated, then at least the people there would have a better Christmas than they would otherwise. Everyone was roped in to make it happen. The show was the focus but helping these people was more than just the show, if that makes sense.

Claire had a list of how many male and female people regularly visited the shelter and she was putting together the gifts. As well as hats, gloves, and scarves, she was also going to put a basic toiletry package together, but she said she would hopefully have spares as there could be more people needing them come Christmas. She had managed to get a lot of help for this already. The primary school where Toby, Henry, Martha, and Summer went were asking parents to help, and local shops had also agreed to get involved. Jonathan's company, as well as sponsoring the show – he had put himself in charge of budget and wouldn't let anyone spend a penny unless it was totally necessary – had encouraged its employees to all buy a coat or a sleeping bag, and they had readily agreed. That or they'd been given no choice, I'm not sure which.

Franceska and Tomasz had increased the amount of food they were taking to the shelter every day, now, so more people could be fed. Harold said that his senior centre friends didn't have much money but he would ask if they had any clothes spare, and Marcus, Polly, and Matt were raising funds at their offices to help as well.

In addition to all that, the show was taking up more and more of our time. It had been cast now, and Aleksy and Connie had informed people of their roles and what they needed to do. It was all coming together well as we prepared to start rehearsals. Rehearsals had to be fitted around school and work, so they would be held evenings and weekends and Claire said that they could draw up a schedule to rotate who was rehearsing when to save time. It was actually all very complicated, so I was glad of her organisational skills.

Ralph the vicar had offered to donate mince pies and tea and coffee for the dress rehearsal, when the shelter patrons came to see the show. The Goodwins' singing group were holding a raffle to raise more money on the opening night, and they'd started collecting prizes. As Jonathan pointed out, no one ever said no to the Goodwins. No one dared. Aleksy and Connie said they would get their friends, who weren't in the show, to sell the raffle tickets. It really was wonderful to see how well everyone was working together. It was really a community effort.

I was impressed with how professional Aleksy and Connie were being. They had made a list of the people taking part in the show – and us cats, of course – along with the roles they would be playing. We had six shepherds and only four sheep – or, four cats playing sheep – so Aleksy said they were going to get some toy sheep to make up a flock. There were three wise men, or 'wise people' as Barbara the cat-hating woman was one of them. Jonathan said best not to give her too much of a speaking part in case she launched into Shakespeare again. I was just glad she wasn't a shepherd – imagine her being in charge of us cats? It made my fur shudder. Polly was going to be the angry innkeeper, although she was now an Airbnb owner, whatever that was. Connie said that the innkeeper was always male and it was time for a change because women could be innkeepers too. Sylvie and Marcus were – reluctantly – going to be Mary and Joseph, as they'd agreed in the end. Matt and Tomasz were shepherds along with some of the others who'd auditioned. Sienna, a girl from Tommy's class in school – one everyone seemed to be in love with – was going to be the angel Gabriel and there were going to be four other angels, played by four other women and girls. Jonathan refused a part because he was the sponsor and accountant – he said it wouldn't be appropriate – and Claire was definitely going to be needed backstage to organise the cast and make sure the show ran on time. Aleksy and Connie were both directors and they had also written the script. We all had our roles. We were all systems go.

And Sienna, it seemed, might be the answer to our Tommy problem. He blushed every time her name was mentioned and it was clear he liked her. I hoped that meant he'd be on his best behaviour whenever she was around, and maybe, just maybe, he'd stop being so difficult. Love could really straighten people out after all.

Matt had designed a poster, tickets were going to be available pretty soon, and rehearsals were due to start in a few days. We needed plenty of rehearsal time and, at first, they were doing it in stages, so that not everyone had to be at the hall all the time. It was pretty well organised for an amateur production. That was what Aleksy said anyway. They were taking everything very seriously. And although I was taking it very seriously myself, I was also determined to make sure I enjoyed myself. Have I mentioned that it was my idea?

George was next door teaching Hana how to be a sheep, and also how to have 'stage presence', although he did say that he wasn't sure it could be taught, you might have to be born with it. Honestly, the kitten was becoming a monster. It was quite cute, actually. Annoying – incredibly annoying – but also sweet in a way. Another dichotomy of parenting.

Claire was cooking dinner when the doorbell went. I followed her out to the hallway and waited to see who our latest visitor was. I almost shrank back into the house when I saw it was the Barbara woman, but I was determined to hear why she was here. At the moment, I didn't like her. She had not only chased us with a bin bag and nearly got us run over, but also was rude to us at the show audition. She scowled at us when she thought no one else was looking. The problem was that none of the humans had seen any of this. How dare she come to our house?

'Hello,' Claire said. 'It's Barbara, isn't it?'

'Yes, it is.' Standing on the doorstep, she spotted me and her eyes narrowed.

'Would you like to come in?' Claire was so polite but she didn't know how awful this woman was. I hissed. 'Alfie, don't hiss,' Claire chastised. No idea at all. But I really didn't want the cat hater in my house. So I stepped closer to the door-step. She wouldn't dare attack me in front of Claire, I was pretty sure, but I hoped it would put her off coming in.

'No, no, I don't need to come in.' She glared at me again.

'Right, well what can I do for you?' Claire asked. Yes, I wanted to know that too.

'It's about the show.'

'The show?'

'Yes, you've put me down as a wise man.'

'Yes, it's a pivotal role – you're going to have a few lines, sing, and give the baby Jesus a gift. We really thought we needed someone with your experience to pull it off.' Claire smiled. Barbara did not smile back.

'But as I explained, I used to be a drama teacher and I've always acted; I was the star of our old amateur dramatic group before I moved here. I'm wasted being a wise man, I should be Mary or the angel Gabriel – a main role.' I took a step back. Was she mad? Mary was so much younger than her and the angel was supposed to be this ethereal being (I heard Claire say that), and although I wasn't one hundred per cent sure what ethereal meant, I was pretty sure Barbara wasn't it. I would never get the picture of her swinging a black bag at me and George out of my head.

'The thing is, we cast the actual mother of Theo, who is going to be the baby Jesus, in case he cries, and we chose a teenager for the angel Gabriel because we wanted to get the youngsters involved, you see. We thought your audition was brilliant but it's just a Nativity, so there's not a huge scope for speaking parts.' I could hear Claire trying to be diplomatic, but Barbara did not look happy.

'I am not happy about it. Not at all. It's wasting my talent.' See, I was right.

'I'm sorry but Aleksy and Connie are doing this to help

the homeless shelter and they're doing a great job, so we need to all work together. I really hope you still want to be a part of it. The wise men will probably have the best costumes anyway.' Poor Claire was really trying. 'And, I know you're new to Edgar Road, so it might be a really good opportunity to meet others in the community. Do you live alone?'

'I do, but what's that got to do with it?'

'Well, we have a Sunday Lunch Club whereby people on their own can join another family for lunch a few Sundays a month.'

'I'm quite capable of making my own lunch,' she snapped.

I was relieved. I really didn't want her joining us. By the look on her face, Claire was no longer keen, either.

'Of course, I was just thinking that if you wanted to meet people . . .' Claire shook her head. She didn't know how to deal with this woman.

'I shall probably still take part but I hope you have noted my displeasure at not being given a bigger role.'

'Duly noted.' Claire glanced down at me, her eyes wide.

Without another word, Barbara turned and walked away. I looked up at Claire, she shook her head. See, this woman was not normal. Not normal at all.

'I don't know, Alfie,' she said, picking me up and shutting the front door. 'I hope she'll just be happy to be part of it, but she didn't seem very happy did she?'

'Yowl.' She certainly did not.

The rest of the week passed quickly and largely uneventfully. George insisted on getting Snowball, me, and Hana together to practise being sheep, which involved a lot of standing and pretending to eat grass. I wasn't sure how much rehearsal we needed if that was all we had to do. I was slightly disappointed not to have a bigger role, still, but then I would remember Barbara's reaction and think of the shelter and all the people there who were so happy to see us. Sometimes, you had to put your ego aside, and this was one of those times. I just hoped that Barbara would too. I knew it wasn't always easy but it was definitely the right thing to do.

'Dad, you are still not standing right,' George chastised as I realised I'd been thinking and therefore not concentrating.

'Sorry,' I said.

'Honestly people, you need to take this seriously. We are doing a show, we are raising money for charity and we are also going to be all over social media, so I would suggest we all pull our socks up, and work harder.'

'I don't wear socks,' Snowball said. She was getting impatient with George, but she was amused at the same time.

'You know what I mean. Right, let's take it from the top. Annnnd stand. Now look up. Now look down. Now pretend to eat grass. Oh my goodness, how hard can it be? I knew working with amateurs wasn't going to be easy but still . . . it's a disaster.'

Hana, Snowball, and I watched as George flounced off, and then we all laughed. I felt bad but he was really too funny.

'He's really trying,' Hana said, she was the softest out of all of us.

'A bit too trying,' Snowball said.

'I said it earlier, we've created a monster.'

'A monster in sheep's clothing,' Snowball finished and we all grinned.

Chapter
Seventeen

We were wrapped in Christmas suddenly, although not literally. Because of the show, our Christmas started even earlier than normal. At home, we played Christmas songs all the time, and at the hall we played Christmas songs all the time. By the time we were ready to hold the first rehearsal, I was fully in Christmas mode.

As they were opening the show, the first rehearsal involved the dancers and the singers. They had decided to do a routine to 'Santa Claus is Coming to Town', and they'd found a version which was fast and more modern. The crew – that was what they called themselves – were made up of boys and girls from the same dance class. Their teacher, a relatively young man called Nicky who wore very low-cut baggy trousers, coached them and they were actually pretty good from what I could tell. Aleksy, Connie, Claire, and myself were watching and George had insisted on tagging along. Polly was thankfully able to look after the children and Pickles. Tommy couldn't make it as he actually had to do some urgent homework, so Aleksy was filming bits so he could upload to social media later. We were getting quite an online following, apparently, and us cats had naturally caused quite a stir after the auditions. They hadn't actually thanked us yet, but they were very busy at the moment so I was going to let it go. For now.

After they ran through the routine, with only a couple of mistakes which I didn't actually notice, they sat on the stage to talk to us.

'We've got the parents all buying tickets as soon as they're available,' Nicky said.

'You know, we might need to do more than one show, I mean more than one paying show. We're doing the dress rehearsal for the people from the shelter to come and see,' Claire said. 'But if we have enough ticket sales we could maybe do two nights?'

'We'll definitely sell enough tickets for two nights,' Aleksy said, confidently. 'What if we do Friday and Saturday night?'

'We could do a third on the Saturday afternoon, I mean it will be a bit tiring but that's what they do in the theatre,' Franceska, who was helping with stage management, suggested.

'Yes, and younger children would maybe come to the earlier show, that's a good idea,' Connie said.

'So now we have to sell out three shows?' Nicky said.

'Yup, and we will somehow do it,' Connie said. She sounded full of determination. We had quickly gone from a one-off show to three shows. Could we do it? Of course we could.

'And what a great opening to the show this is going to be,' Claire said. 'You guys are amazing so, if you're happy to do three shows?'

'It's really good experience for us,' Nicky said. 'We might go on a TV talent show next year.'

'Well you are definitely good enough,' Claire said kindly.

'You see,' George hissed. 'If we tried harder – and by we, I mean you, Snowball, and Hana – we could maybe be on a TV talent show. Although, thinking about it, maybe I would be better as a solo act.'

I raised my whiskers but kept quiet.

'Before you leave, we want the people in the show to visit the shelter at some point, so we all understand what we are raising money for. I know most of you are quite young and it's quite hard to see, but would you be willing to?'

'Hey, how about the crew take a shift helping serve food one weekend? We could then document it on our social media as well as the show's,' Nicky said. The dancers all chorused their agreement.

'Brilliant, we'll get a date in,' Claire said, making another note in the big notebook that she carried around for all things show related.

After rehearsal, Claire went home and switched with Polly, while Tomasz, Franceska, and Matt discussed the sets. Franceska had said she would rather not be in the show but she was doing lots of different things and she was also sort of job sharing with Claire when she couldn't be there. It was doing her good, because she was so worried about Tommy that this seemed to be making her a little more relaxed, which made me happy, because I did hate to see anyone – but especially Franceska, who was the kindest person ever – upset.

There was an awful lot to do. They were making a forest of decorated Christmas trees, which the dancers would emerge from in the first song, that would stay there until the Nativity scene. Then there would be a big shed-like shelter, which had to be made out of light wood so it could be easily transported on stage. For the Santa scene at the end, there would be a living room with a fully decorated six-foot tree, presents around it, and an armchair. It all sounded ambitious to me but as they all chatted through it, they seemed to think they would be able to do it. Polly and Franceska wrote down estimated costs as they had to run them by Jonathan, who continued to rule the budgets with an iron fist.

'The idea is to make money for the shelter, not spend it,' was Jonathan's new favourite catch phrase.

Claire tried to point out that spending money on the show would mean we made more money, but Jonathan wasn't too keen on that logic.

Most of the materials – the trees etc. – had been donated, so the costs were pretty low. It was all going so well, and I was feeling very optimistic. Excited, too. I really couldn't wait for this show. Even being a sheep was something I looked forward to now. Because being in the hall, seeing the first act rehearse and also everyone discussing sets, it felt real. More and more real by the minute.

But although it felt as if we were obsessed by the show, normal life still went on – we still had lots to do outside of it. It was Sunday and time for our Sunday Lunch Club. Jonathan went to pick Doris and Clive up while Claire cooked a really lovely roast dinner. The children, although only Summer and Toby, were planning on doing their Rudolph song for them, and George was annoyed because again he had been roped in to play Rudolph in place of Pickles. I thought I had escaped and could just spend a quiet day watching and resting, but no, because Doris had kept her promise and brought me my 'cat bonnet'. It was bright green – to match my eyes, she said.

'Doesn't she look gorgeous?' Doris said.

'Meow?' She?

'Alfie's a boy, Doris,' Claire said quickly before Jonathan could make an inappropriate joke.

'Oh, I know, but he's so pretty, I shall call him a she.'

I raised my tail. Not only was I wearing a bonnet but I was now a girl? George almost fell off the arm of the sofa he was trying so hard to contain himself; and then he did fall off.

'Yowl,' he said, as he rolled himself upright again.

'Yowl,' I replied. Serves you right.

The talk over lunch was all about the show and also about Christmas.

'Maybe you could do a performance for us,' Clive said. 'I, for one, would like to see it but of course it might be hard to get us all there, all the Sunday Lunch Club.'

'Oh goodness,' Jonathan said. 'We've got enough members to fill the hall, and of course then we'll need to be able to transport you all, seeing as most of the families you go to are in the show . . .' He scratched his head.

'There must be a way,' Claire said. She lapsed into thought. 'Leave it with us.'

I had a brainwave. On Christmas Day, we were all going to be hosting our Sunday Lunch Club for all members who would be alone. And most of the people involved in the show, as Jonathan rightly said, were involved in the club, so Christmas Day would be perfect for us to do a show for them. It might have to be in the evening and maybe not everyone could make it, but surely we could put on an edited version? It would be better than nothing, and like the people in the shelter, the Sunday Lunch Club didn't get to go out very often so it would be special for them.

I jumped onto Claire's lap, and mewed at her, trying to convey my idea. But of course she didn't understand. How could I tell her what I meant?

'We'll sort something out,' Claire said again, looking at me with a puzzled expression. I would have to keep trying, because clearly she wasn't quite as advanced in ideas as me and this was a tricky one to convey. I thought maybe I would try again at the next family day, because if everyone was there, someone might understand me. Or maybe George and Snowball could help me explain it to Harold. That might work. In the meantime, I would just enjoy some nice lunch treats that Jonathan had put down for George and me. Although I was still wearing this awful bonnet, and there wasn't a damn thing I could do about it.

Later, with everyone at home and the bonnet gone, I went to see Snowball to see what she thought about my latest idea.

'I agree it's a very good idea but how to tell the humans? Maybe they'll come to the same conclusion themselves?' she said, hopefully.

'I agree they might . . . After lunch and games we all have a bit of time before we have to arrange for everyone to go home, so maybe if we did the show then – like a kind of finale – that would be a great end to Christmas Day.'

'Ah, Alfie, it's lovely, it would be perfect and mean that everyone we care about gets to see the show. It'll be like a family showing. Otherwise our Sunday Lunch Club family might miss out.'

'You know what, Claire said she's drawing up a list of who from the Sunday Lunch Club is going where for Christmas

Day, because some families go away, so we double up, don't we? If we can see the list and maybe jump around on it or something she might get the idea.'

'It's worth a try, but,' Snowball yawned, 'I still think that if Claire tells the others that Clive said he wanted to see the show, they will come up with the idea themselves.'

Snowball had a lot more faith in the humans than I did.

'Or we could do our sheep bit when it's next family day, so that might give them the idea.'

'We could, or we could wait for them to get the idea themselves,' Snowball reiterated.

'Or we could wait until they put the Christmas tree up and all climb it – OK, actually just George – so they get the idea.'

'Or we could wait . . .' Snowball licked her paw. 'Alfie, you don't need an elaborate plan for everything, you know. Do as you said, see if they come up with the idea at the next family day and if they don't then we'll think of something. But, whatever you do, don't tell George about the idea of climbing the tree, you've only just got him to stop doing that.'

'Fair point.'

We strolled around Harold's small garden and though it was cold and dark, my mind was whirring. Could I really trust the humans to come up with my brilliant idea on their own? Without my help? I really didn't think I could.

Chapter Eighteen

'Alfie, I feel as if I haven't seen you in ages,' Nellie said. 'I'm sorry.' I was. I knew I had neglected my friends yet again. Rocky, Elvis, and Oliver were all at the recreation ground and I felt even more guilt as they seemed so pleased to see me.

'So, fill us in? We're dying to hear about the show. We saw Snowball briefly, although she was in a hurry because Harold needed her at home, but she said it had been busy.'

'Understatement of the year. There's so much to do. Who knew when I came up with the idea—'

'Dad, will you stop saying that? We all know it was your idea, we've heard it a thousand million times,' George interrupted. I hadn't seen him approach.

'As I was saying, there is so much to do. It's hectic, and of course we feel as if we ought to keep an eye on everything.'

'Not least because, of course, I have so much stage experience,' George added. Clearly, it was OK for *him* to boast, then.

We took turns to tell them about the show, and we also filled them in about Barbara.

'Oh my, I met her,' Nellie said. 'I was walking past where she lives, just minding my own business and she shouted at me to get away, but I was on the pavement, not even in her garden. I did run a bit though.'

'Remember, we nearly got killed by her bin bag,' George

said dramatically. He then did a mini re-enactment by running, spinning and then falling over. Although they had heard about it, they indulged him.

'Definitely not a cat fan then,' Rocky added.

'She was also mean to us at the auditions,' I explained. 'Even suggested we shouldn't be in the show.'

'We ought to give her a bit of a wide berth, if we pass her flat we should cross the road, you don't want to provoke people like that,' Elvis said. 'Never know what might end up happening to you.'

'Or we could find out why she's like that.' I studied my paw and waited for the reactions.

'No, Alfie,' Nellie, Rocky, Elvis and Oliver shouted at the same time.

'We can't avoid her though, she's in the show,' George pointed out.

'Perhaps we just win her round, we've done it before,' I suggested.

'No,' they all chorused.

'Oh goodness, please be careful around her and if you need our help then you can always come to us,' Rocky said, which moved me. My friends had my back, and although we had so much to do, I needed to make sure I made time for them too. Although, because they were such wonderful cats they did understand that it was tricky at the moment.

We hung out for a while longer and I promised to visit at least once every two days to check in. I still couldn't persuade them to come to the hall – it was out of their comfort zone to venture past the recreation ground, actually

– but they said they would still love to hear all about it. When George and I went home I thought about the fact that I must go and see Dustbin soon. I didn't want to neglect him – and Ally – either.

'I've tried to tell him that he needs to be more reindeer but you know Pickles, he's a bit limited isn't he?' George said. We sat on a table by the stage watching the children and Pickles' first rehearsal. They had fixed a soft red nose to Pickles but he kept trying to eat it. They hadn't yet put the antlers on but I doubted that they would fare much better. The door banged open just as Toby and Henry started their rap. The hall went quiet and turned to look. It was the awful Barbara.

'Hi,' Claire said. 'We didn't expect to see you.'

'I was just passing so I thought I'd see if I could help you at all.' Barbara smiled, but I didn't like the smile. Of course, I also just didn't like her.

'What's she doing here?' George hissed. I raised my whiskers; I had no idea. I wondered if she had decided to put her meanness aside and try to join in finally. I know that Salmon said she was missing her husband, and I understood grief better than most cats, but still, my grief didn't make me mean. Hopefully she had come round and was ready to be a part of the community. People did change after all. I had seen that happen time and time again. My theory was that people who were horrible were sometimes just unhappy, and I had to keep remembering that.

'Oh,' Claire said. 'Well, we are doing early rehearsals, just finishing today's actually, but if you want to help with sets we are asking for volunteers to paint, decorate trees, help out with costumes, that sort of thing.'

I narrowed my eyes at Barbara, but she smiled again. Still a bit scary, but perhaps that was just her face. I tried to give her the benefit of the doubt, while remaining cautious.

'I would be delighted. By the way, you haven't changed your mind about the parts? I mean, I would be happy to understudy anyone.'

'We hadn't thought about understudies,' Aleksy said, eyes darting towards Connie. George glared at me. He still felt that Summer and Toby were treating him as Pickles' understudy, although I hadn't even known what that was until he explained it.

'Well, it doesn't hurt to be prepared, in case anything happens to the cast,' Barbara said. I felt a bit of a shiver in my fur. What on earth could happen to anyone? 'You know, if they got ill or something. It is the time of year for colds and flu. But never mind, I'm happy to do whatever it takes to make this show a success, as it is for such a good cause.'

'Thank you so much,' Connie said. 'Come with me and I'll take you backstage, show you what we're doing.'

As they went behind the stage, George leant in close.

'I don't trust her, Dad,' he said.

'Me either, son, not totally anyway. We'll have to keep an eye on it.' I didn't like the way she made me feel one little bit, but then again, maybe, just maybe, she had changed and we had all just got off on the wrong paw.

We watched from a safe distance as she ingratiated herself with everyone. She was smiling, jolly, nothing like the woman we had seen the past few times we met her. I raised my whiskers. 'Everyone deserves a second chance, son,' I said, and although he didn't seem convinced, he reluctantly agreed.

'Let's go and see how she reacts to us, see if she's different with us now,' I suggested.

'Isn't it a bit risky?'

'No, George, because there's lots of people around. She wouldn't dare do anything to us.' I hoped she wouldn't, anyway.

'OK.'

I took off backstage, George dragging his paws behind me. We found Barbara near some of the trees, admiring them with Connie.

'We're going to spray the tops with snow, so it looks a bit like a Christmas card,' Connie explained.

'That's a lovely idea.' Barbara spotted us. She narrowed her eyes but turned back to Connie. 'Well, dear, as I said, I am happy to help with everything.'

'Thank you, I better get back to rehearsals but just ask if you need anything.'

George and I exchanged glances as we sat by the tree, not too far from Barbara. Were we going to see if she had changed towards us? I tentatively put my paw towards her foot but she saw and pushed a tree.

'Run, Dad,' George shouted, as the tree was about to fall on me. I sprinted away, just escaping before it fell to the ground.

'Yowl!' I shouted, narrowly having missed being squashed by a fake Christmas tree.

'Oh dear,' Barbara shouted. 'One of the trees fell, I think the cats knocked it.'

'Be more careful, guys. Maybe you shouldn't be back here,' Matt said as he and Tomasz came to see what was happening. George and I lay down, trying to catch our breath.

'Never mind, it looks fine, as do the cats,' Tomasz said, and picked the tree up again.

'Thank goodness it didn't get them,' Barbara said innocently.

George and I raised our whiskers. This was worse than we thought. She hadn't changed, she was just pretending she had. All my deliberations about her being unhappy not horrible, that she deserved a second chance, were a waste of my precious time. I was done with her. She was nothing but a cat hater; it was no longer up for debate.

'Keep well out of her way from now on,' I said to George.

'It isn't me you need to tell, it's yourself,' he hissed. He wasn't wrong.

Claire took us home shortly after, leaving some of the others still working in the hall. We were glad to go, still shaken up from our ordeal. I wasn't going to let that woman ruin the show for us. Her involvement wasn't something I could control, but I wouldn't let her get the better of me a third time. Mark my whiskers.

With just over a month until the first show it was all hands on deck. The show was consuming us, but we had been consumed by much worse. I just hoped that Christmas still carried on as normal, and I also hoped that the humans would find a way to let the Sunday Lunch Club enjoy the show as well.

Despite my weariness, I remembered my friendship resolution. It was too late to see Dustbin that night, but I resolved to go first thing in the morning, no matter how foul the weather was. It was time to remember to be a good friend, even if it did feel as if I was spreading myself a little thin at the moment. But then, I did have a lot of fish to fry. Um, I really could do with some fish right now, actually.

Claire was telling Jonathan about Barbara before we all went to bed.

'She was really nice, not at all like the way she was with me when she came round here.'

'Did she recite a long Shakespeare monologue?' Jonathan joked.

Claire rolled her eyes. 'No, she did not. She was quite pleasant. Anyway, Heather and Vic told me that her husband died and she was forced out of her home due to money issues, so she was pretty miserable about moving into the flat. Maybe that's why she was acting up a bit.'

'Ha ha, good pun,' Jonathan said.

I had no idea what he meant.

'I didn't mean to say that.' Claire laughed and gave him a playful tap on his arm. 'What I mean is that maybe she was angry about everything – you know, how unfair life can be and missing her husband – but now she's turned over a new leaf. Maybe she's so lonely that she realised the only way to feel less so is to use the show to make friends.'

'Maybe. Anyway, we don't need to collect any more people do we, Claire?'

'Meow.' Of course we did, we could never collect too many people. But not Barbara, we did not need to collect her. He was right about that.

'Jonathan, being kind doesn't have a number limit,' Claire said.

As I slept that night, I decided that Claire was right. I knew I shouldn't give Barbara a third chance – I wasn't stupid – but kindness was inherent in both Claire and I, and we couldn't just switch it off. We wouldn't want to anyway, so I decided that no matter what anyone said I would be kind to Barbara and show her that friendship was much better than being angry with people. I would just have to do it from a safe distance, that was all.

Chapter Nineteen

I was surprised when George came in via the cat flap just as I was about to leave for my visit to Dustbin.

'I thought you were with Hana,' I said.

'She kept falling asleep, so I said I'd let her rest. Theo's still keeping them awake most of the night but Sylvie's taken him out this morning so Hana can catch up on some much-needed sleep. Connie now has ear plugs so she doesn't hear him. It's the only way she can make it through the school day, and of course she's got the show to work on so she can't afford to be so tired. Who knew something so small could be so troublesome?'

I thought of George as a kitten. I knew, but I wasn't going to tell him that.

'Apart from Pickles, of course,' he added.

I decided not to argue.

'Do you want to visit Dustbin with me?' I asked.

'Might as well,' he said. 'Nothing better to do.'

Sometimes George could sound a little like a teenager still. We set off and it was quite windy. There were also more hazards on the street, probably because the weather was so awful and people couldn't see where they were going. At one point I was pushed right to the end of the kerb, nearly falling into the road.

'George,' I hissed. 'Let's jump on garden walls, it might be safer.' We chose the harder, less direct, but definitely safer route. By the time we reached the restaurant we were tired

– our fur both cold and warm, if that's possible – and also a little relieved. Sometimes cat travel can be dangerous; I can't count the number of times my tail's been stepped on, or my paws for that matter. But, of course we love our freedom, so it's a small price to pay.

Dustbin greeted us, and then Ally emerged from behind one of the big bins.

'We haven't seen you for a while, the show's been keeping us busy, and I didn't want you to think I'd forgotten about you,' I said.

'We've seen all the comings and goings, so I know it's been hectic, but we've missed you,' Ally replied.

'The show definitely seems to be one of your better ideas, everyone seems so happy about it,' Dustbin added. I preened.

'Please don't start him off,' George said with a groan. We all laughed a bit.

'Tommy seems to be slightly better,' I said, deciding not to be accused of boasting this time.

'Yeah, he and Charlie have been working hard on ideas, from what we can see,' Dustbin said. I loved that he was my eyes and ears on the family here. It made me feel as if I wasn't missing out, even though I didn't see them every day. Although I was seeing much more of them at the moment, with the show. 'But, I think that Charlie needs to take credit for keeping him on track. He's a different kid when Charlie's around. When he's just with the family he turns all surly and rude again.'

'And . . .' Ally stopped to laugh. 'Tommy has a crush on the girl who is playing the main angel or something. He talks about her a lot to Charlie, but only out here. When Aleksy asked him about it he went all huffy again.'

'Ah, teenage love, I remember it well,' George said. I glanced at him in confusion. Since when was he such a grown-up?

'Yeah, well, the main thing is that he's starting to do better,' Dustbin explained.

'It's music to my ears,' I said. 'So, anything new with you?'

'Just really busy here,' Dustbin said. 'The restaurant is always full, which is great, but of course it means we have more pests to keep at bay.'

As we chatted and caught up, I was surprised to see Aleksy walking towards us. Shouldn't he be at school?

'Meow,' I said, rubbing his legs.

'Don't worry, Alfie, I'm not skipping school, I've got to go to the dentist. I'm just going to meet Dad at the restaurant as he's taking me.'

Ah, I didn't know much about dentists, but I was glad he wasn't doing anything he shouldn't be. I didn't need any more troublesome teens in my life.

'I'm going to take one of the new posters to the dentist to see if they'll put it up. And don't forget we have a meeting at the hall tonight after school, to look at where we are with sets, so if you want to come along?'

'Meow.' Try keeping me away.

As he walked off, fussing us all before he went, Dustbin grinned.

'They all treat you as if you're a human.'

'I know, and sometimes I feel as if I am, although of course us cats are cleverer than humans. Listen to my latest idea,' I said, and I filled him in on the idea of getting the Sunday Lunch Club to the show on Christmas Day. The more I thought and talked about it the better it sounded.

'Most people are tired on Christmas evening though,' Ally pointed out. 'All that food and drink, and the cooking and clearing up.'

'I know and I had thought of that,' I replied. 'But if we did it early, like after lunch, it would be such a lovely way to end the show and Christmas Day too. It also means that the Sunday Lunch Club will already be with those who are in the show so transport won't be a problem. Most of them could walk, it's not that far.'

'Yeah, I can see that,' Dustbin said. 'Hey, Ally, if they do it what about us sneaking in to watch?' He raised his whiskers.

'Really?' George said. 'I would love you to see us being sheep. I'm pretty good but the others need work. I have high hopes that they'll be OK by opening night though.'

My fur bristled but I kept quiet.

'I'd love to see you be sheep too,' Dustbin said.

'I have no idea what sheep are, but I'm pretty sure we should be there to see it,' Ally added.

I was even more excited. To get them out of the yard took a lot, but it seemed that our friendship was enough. It moved me and I resolved to work hard to be a good sheep, whatever that meant.

'So,' Aleksy said later, as we met him at our house, ready to go to the hall. 'I've given the Nativity script to the others, but obviously as you're cats you are not able to read.'

Me, George, Snowball, and Hana sat facing him, all of us listening intently to our pep talk.

'Mew,' I said.

'But, what happens is this. You will be in the field with the shepherds, which will be in the middle of the stage, just after Mary and Joseph are told they are having a baby and they set off to go on their journey to take part in the census. We tried to get a donkey for Mary to ride on but apparently it's not safe, so we need to think about that. Connie thinks that as we're doing a different version we could have them go on a bike, which might be fun, but we need to ask Sylvie and Marcus what they think about that. Anyway, where was I?' He scratched his head.

'Meow,' George said impatiently.

'Oh yes, so, you and the shepherds will be in the middle of the stage and you'll be frolicking like sheep – jumping around, and playing, you can improvise – and then it goes dark and we have the song "While Shepherds Watched Their Flocks by Night". After the song the angel comes, and you listen while she says a baby has been born and you have to visit. Then the shepherds herd you together and you all set off on your journey. That's the first scene. We then break for Ralph's choir to sing and come back for the second scene where you meet the baby Jesus.'

I realised that I'd stopped listening because I was thinking about the song and whether I'd heard it before, which I thought I had but couldn't be sure . . .

'Meow, meow, mew.' George was telling him he understood. Thankfully, it seemed he'd been paying attention. Hopefully Hana and Snowball had been too.

Claire appeared and said it was time to go and get Connie. I was the only one going with them as Snowball and George were going to Snowball's house, because George felt as if he had neglected Harold, and Hana was going home to rest as she was still really, really tired.

Before we parted, George said we would have to start rehearsals properly the following day as we all had a lot of work to do. It seemed that although Aleksy and Connie were directors of the show, George was the self-appointed director of us. We all agreed before I jumped into Aleksy's arms. I had done quite a lot of walking today so I fancied being carried. One of the perks of the cat job.

After picking up Connie, she, Claire, and Aleksy chattered away about the rehearsals, and I enjoyed listening to them as we made our way to the hall. It was cold, so I snuggled into Aleksy as he carried me. We reached the hall and Claire unlocked the door using the keys Ralph the vicar had given us. She flicked on the lights as we walked in and then gasped.

'What is it?' Aleksy asked.

We all stared as Claire pointed at the stage. There were large, bright yellow footprints all across the stage.

'How on earth?' Claire said.

'It looks like a man's footprints,' Connie said. 'And we had yellow paint to make the big star that the wise men are going to follow.' The star was huge and was to be attached to a person, though I wasn't entirely sure who or how. Aleksy had said that maybe we could suspend the star in the air, as if it was in the sky, but apparently not on this amateur production's budget. Jonathan said it would cost a fortune, not to mention something called health and safety. I loved how Aleksy had big ideas, but most of them did have to be reined in.

'Who would do this?' Aleksy asked. I was shocked. The stage was a mass of bright yellow footprints, as though someone had danced across it. Would this ruin the show?

I put a paw in the paint and found it was dry. 'Meow,' I said to draw their attention. Claire bent down and put her finger in.

'It's dry, so it was done a while ago,' she said. 'OK, the sets were being done last night, so it must have happened then? Aleksy, I'll call your dad and ask if he saw anything.'

Claire walked up to the stage and pulled out her mobile.

'It's going to ruin things,' Connie said, turning to Aleksy.

'No, it won't. We just have to get it sorted.' However, he looked confused and upset as he hugged Connie. I took a closer look. They were large footprints, with the tread of a boot or shoe. It was a lot of paint, but who would have done this? What a mystery.

'Your dad is coming down here,' Claire said as she hung up the phone. 'He was here last night and locked the door himself, and he said that they definitely weren't there then.'

'That's so weird,' Connie said. 'Do you think someone stood in the paint by mistake and didn't realise?'

'I think they'd have noticed, don't you? It's bright yellow so even if it was dark . . .' Claire ran her fingers through her hair. 'And it's all over the stage; it's a total wreck.' Her voice was full of emotion. I understood. We had worked so hard on the show so far, and it meant so much to everyone. We didn't need this.

'It makes no sense,' Aleksy said.

I agreed with him. I tried to see if I could find any clues, but there were none. All we knew was that there were footprints, which were from large feet – bigger than Claire, Aleksy or Connie's – which suggested a man. The footprints weren't here when Tomasz left last night so it must have been done after. It had to have been, because otherwise the paint would still be wet. Curiouser and curiouser. I looked forward to chatting it over with George to see what he thought.

Tomasz arrived and he was as baffled as the rest of us.

'There were about five of us here, and we all left at the same time, around nine o'clock last night. They definitely weren't there then and when we left the hall was empty.'

'And no one else has keys?' Aleksy asked.

'No, just me, Claire, and the vicar,' Tomasz said.

'What if the vicar did it by accident?' Connie asked.

'I'm pretty sure it's not Ralph,' Claire said. 'But I'll call him.' She went off to do so.

'It doesn't make any sense,' Tomasz said and we were back to square one.

'Dad, the stage is ruined, what are we going to do?' Aleksy said, trying to focus on the only issue we could solve at this point.

'Don't worry son, I'll get it sorted.' Tomasz put his arm around his son, and I nuzzled his leg. I knew Tomasz would fix this, he was that kind of man.

'Ralph hasn't been here, he had no idea,' Claire said, coming off the phone. 'Can we get some white spirit and clean it off?' she asked.

We were all examining it closely.

'Honestly, it's pretty thick. I think we're better off sanding it down and then re-varnishing the stage. The paint won't come off easily and it will still probably leave a stain. We have someone who sands all the restaurant floors for us so I'll give him a call. I'm sure he'll do it for a good cause.'

'But it'll put the stage out of action for a while,' Connie pointed out.

'What about rehearsals?'

I ran to the back of the room. They could clear a space and do it here.

'MEOW,' I shouted.

'Ah, yes, we can use the back of the room, just for now,' Aleksy said. 'Good idea, Alfie.'

'And we'll get the floor done really quickly.' Tomasz was already on his phone.

'But still, how on earth did it happen?' Claire asked again. We kept coming back to that.

I thought about it. Someone must have got in last night when no one else was here. I knew it wasn't Tomasz or Claire and it was ridiculous to think that the vicar would ruin his own hall, especially as he was a big supporter of the shelter and the show. I tried to come up with the answer, but my brain was getting tired. Then I saw Tomasz walking behind the stage to the back of the hall. I vaguely remembered seeing another door there, didn't I? I followed him out back, brushed past him as he talked on the phone and . . . yes, there *was* another door, although it was off on the side, so not obvious. In fact, I wasn't sure it led to the outside but it was worth a try and, from what I could see, it had a bolt on the inside, which didn't seem to be across. I nudged the door with my head, it moved a bit. It was open! Ah-ha! I had my answer.

'Yowl,' I said at the top of my lungs. 'Yowl, yowl, yowl.' Finally Tomasz came to see what the noise was and I nudged the door again.

'Come, quick,' he shouted to the others, and they all joined us. 'Look, Alfie found another door and it's unlocked,' he said, pushing it.

'Oh no, it looks as if it needs to be locked from inside, I didn't even realise it was there,' Claire said.

'Me either,' Aleksy agreed.

'At least we know how whoever it was got in,' Connie added. Tomasz slipped the bolt across and pushed the door, which didn't budge.

'So that mystery's solved,' Claire said. 'And now we can make sure it's always locked.'

'I didn't know, otherwise I would have checked, sorry,' Tomasz said.

'Hey, it's not your fault, we didn't know the door was even here,' Claire reassured.

'Well done, Alfie,' Aleksy said, rubbing my head. 'But it doesn't solve who did it,' he pointed out.

Goodness, I wish I knew, but I couldn't perform miracles. I had figured out how they got in, but it would take me longer to figure out who. But we were looking for someone with very big feet and so at least I had my first clue. So, if I looked at everyone's feet when they came to work on the show, I might be able to crack it. I was hopeful.

'Let's hope it was an accident and a one off,' Tomasz said as we checked that there was no other way into the hall.

'Yes, probably was,' Claire agreed as we shut the lights off and locked the hall, checking it more than once. Aleksy and Tomasz went off to their house, and Claire carried me as she and Connie went back to Edgar Road with a new mystery to solve.

Chapter Twenty

It was time for our first proper rehearsal of the Nativity. The stage wasn't yet ready so, in the meantime, a space had been set up at the back of the hall for rehearsals, as per my suggestion. George had been working us quite hard, leaving very little time for trying to solve the paint mystery, seeing my friends, or anything not sheep related. I had managed to steal a bit of alone time with Snowball, and also a few short visits with Elvis, Nellie, and Rocky – and sometimes Oliver and Salmon – but really, our time was taken up with learning how to be sheep.

When we first got given the part I was indignant because I was pretty sure that it was too easy – not to add beneath me – but actually, according to director George, doing it properly was a lot harder than I ever thought it would be. He was a strict taskmaster.

'Try to be more convincing,' he kept shouting at us. 'Call yourself a sheep?' was another of his favourite phrases. Even Hana, who was the sweetest cat ever, lost her temper a couple of times. When faced with rebellion, George would just say: 'It's show business, deal with it.' Half the time I didn't know whether to laugh or cry.

Aleksy put all the shepherds together first and then got us to stand in front.

'Can I just make a suggestion?' Peter – the man who had been a terrible juggler but was now a shepherd along with Magic Marvin and Dolly – said. I looked at his feet, they were big, possibly about the right size for the yellow paint intruder. I made a mental note.

'Sure, what is it?' Claire asked. Franceska was with us today too.

'How about I juggle the sheep?'

'Yowl!' I shouted, no way. George, Hana, and Snowball backed away.

'Not the cat sheep, but stuffed ones.'

Franceska looked at Claire, who looked at Aleksy, who looked at Connie.

'If we get some toy sheep we can try it, maybe,' Connie said, with her face scrunched up. That seemed to be good enough for Peter.

'Right, action,' Aleksy shouted.

As the shepherds watched us fondly, we began to frolic. George was going for it, bounding around like an overactive lamb, and we all jumped a bit, shuffled and Snowball and I did a good impression of eating grass.

'Brilliant, cats,' Connie said, as she gave the cue for the song. As the music started and the shepherds started singing it wasn't terrible. Tomasz and Matt, who were shepherds, looked a little embarrassed as they seemed to mumble rather than sing, but thankfully the other four shepherds were pretty good, so it didn't matter.

Sienna the angel couldn't make it today because she had a dance class, so, in the meantime, Claire read her part. Before we knew it, we were finished. The next scene was the wise men, and so we went to rest while they did their bit. Barbara, who seemed to think she was leading the wise men, spoke very loudly, and when they sang their song 'We

Three Kings', she drowned out the other voices. And not in a good way.

'It hurts my ears,' George said.

'That was great,' Claire said, as they finished. 'Um, we couldn't hear Steve and Cath very well. Perhaps you guys could sing a bit louder,' she suggested. I could tell she didn't dare tell Barbara to sing more quietly.

'Or, maybe this is a better idea, you each have a verse of your own and sing the chorus together,' Aleksy said. The kid was a genius. It was a very fair idea.

'But, perhaps you need my expertise to carry the song,' Barbara said. Cath shot her a dirty look.

'I think it's much nicer for everyone to have a part and then join together in the chorus, as Aleksy said,' Claire said diplomatically. Barbara first looked as if she was going to argue, but she then seemed to change her mind.

'Of course. I'll do the first verse,' she said, quickly. I saw Cath and Steve – two people from our road – smile at each other. Barbara was one of those difficult people, she seemed to think she was an expert on all things to do with the show. She had a lot in common with George, in that respect.

The rehearsals finally came to an end. We didn't have the Mary and Joseph scene today, as Aleksy had said we would rehearse each part before putting it all together, so the weekend would be the first full run through of the Nativity. It really felt as if it was all coming together. Now I could see the reality of the show and I felt as if I would burst with excitement. I just hoped the stage would be finished so we could rehearse properly soon.

'Great work everyone,' Aleksy said, sounding happy.

'It's really going very well,' Connie said. 'And you are all doing such amazing jobs.'

'Right, see you all at the weekend,' Claire said with a massive smile on her face.

Most of the cast left then, Matt rushing off to relieve Polly, who was coming here to work on sets, and I stayed with Aleksy and Connie because I wanted to be involved with everything. I also wanted to find the paint culprit which meant I had to be here as much as possible. The others all went home with Claire – not even Snowball could be persuaded to stay, as she said Harold would be expecting her home for dinner.

We all said our goodbyes, and I went to the backstage area to look at feet. Tomasz was supervising a team of people, some painting, others building things, and it was really quite noisy as they chatted, hammered, and assembled bits and pieces. They were building a shed-like structure, which would be the place where Mary and Joseph had the baby Jesus, and where we sheep and the shepherds would go and visit. When she arrived, Polly would be assembling props to go in it. They'd decided on hay bales for seats and Tomasz was building a manger with a couple of helpers. It was going to be quite minimal, to show that they didn't have a luxury place for the birth, staying true to the original story. Also, I gathered they needed something that could easily be placed on the stage; we weren't an elaborate production after all. Not with Jonathan in charge of budgets, in any case.

As they worked, I checked out as many feet as I could. There were only a few suspects, feet-wise, I mean. I ruled out all women – their feet were far too small – and only a few men had the right size feet and kind of shoes. None had yellow paint on, but then they would have got rid of them, wouldn't they? One of the men had yellow paint streaks on his overalls, but then he had been painting the star before the stage sabotage happened, so I needed to keep that in mind.

Of course, it had also crossed my mind that the culprit might not be here at the moment. We had so many volunteers and they didn't all come at once, because of the roster. In order to find out who did it I would have to be here all the time and even I couldn't do that. I just had to hope that whoever it was hadn't meant to tread paint over the stage but was too embarrassed to own up, and therefore wouldn't be a problem again. I crossed my paws.

The evening passed nicely, actually. Even Barbara was friendly and nice to people, although she ignored me. I gave her as much space as I could and I was glad when Polly said it was time to finish up and she picked me up to take me home. I was tired and hungry. Food and bed, that was all I wanted.

But then Barbara offered to walk home with Polly and I. I was glad to be safely in Polly's arms, I can tell you.

'The cats seem to come everywhere with you,' she said.

'Yes, they are important members of our family,' Polly said. 'And of course they have to be involved in the show. Aleksy said it was Alfie's idea.'

'Meow.' Finally, some recognition.

'Really?' Barbara sounded full of disbelief. 'I'm pretty sure cats can't have ideas.'

'It's a long story, but Alfie is quite remarkable. In fact, we are all friends because of Alfie.'

'I never much liked cats,' Barbara said.

Who'd have guessed? I narrowed my eyes at her but she didn't look at me.

'My late husband, he loved dogs, and we had one for years but when she died we were both so heartbroken we couldn't think about getting another one. And now he's gone too and I have nothing left.' She began to sob.

'Oh Barbara, I'm so sorry. It must be awful, losing him and then moving to a new place. Do you have family nearby?'

'No, my daughter and her husband live up north. She encouraged me to join the play actually, said it would be good for me. She thinks I'm depressed.'

'How long since your husband died?' Polly jiggled me so she was holding me with one arm and touched Barbara's arm with the other.

'Six months. I had very little money left and had to sell our house in Richmond and move somewhere smaller. I hated leaving it. It felt as if he died all over again.'

She was properly crying now and Polly put her arm around her. I somehow found myself squashed between them but I didn't object. I felt sorry for Barbara; she was obviously heartbroken. And she was crying, so she couldn't hurt me, right?

'Hey, listen, on Sunday we have a couple of friends coming round for lunch, would you like to join us?' Polly asked as she stepped out of the hug.

'That's kind, but, no, no thank you. I'm happy to do the show but not quite ready to be in that sort of situation.'

'Of course, you have to do whatever's right for you, you're the one who matters,' she said, and I nuzzled into Polly, because she was right.

'Yes, yes, whatever's right for me,' Barbara said.

We'd reached my house and Polly said goodbye to Barbara before taking me to the front door and ringing the doorbell.

I couldn't help but think that Barbara's actions towards me and George were a result of her depression. Perhaps I could learn to forgive her . . . I was pretty sure I could. It was confusing but I was trying to be compassionate. I knew how much grief could mess with anyone. On the other hand, this woman had tried, more than once, to hurt me and my kitten. I was really feeling mixed up about it. Did I do what I normally would do – try to win her round, and make her feel better at the same time? Or did I take the more sensible option of keeping well away from her? I just didn't know.

'So, you had to walk home with the cat hater,' George said when we were alone together that evening.

'Yes, well, Polly held on to me so I was quite safe. But remember, she has had an awful time of it, losing her husband, moving house and she doesn't even have family nearby.'

'Oh Dad, I said I'd give her another chance, but this would be her third or fourth chance. And I still don't see how we can trust anyone who doesn't like cats.'

'She did say she liked dogs rather than cats, so you're not wrong there, son. Anyway, I'm declaring tomorrow a show-free day. I am going to see my friends, spend time with Snowball, and just do normal things, because I need a day off.'

'Yeah I understand, but we will have to fit in one of our rehearsals. I'm sorry but you guys really need to practise more, otherwise the show will be a disaster,' George said.

'A disaster?' Really, George was melodramatic.

'Yes, if we can't be good sheep then the whole thing falls apart,' he said.

I decided not to argue with him. I didn't think he was right, but I knew that there was no point. So, it seemed that there was no such thing as a show-free day for me after all.

Chapter
Twenty-One

The next day, I visited Snowball and we set out to see our friends. We had a nice stroll, we both napped, and really, it was all the things that cats like best. If I had been given pilchards it would have been perfect. But there were no pilchards. Never mind, it was still a pretty good, relaxing day until after school, when Aleksy and Connie came to our house, visibly upset.

'The dance crew wanted to go to the hall so they could use the stage to practise, and we said great, we would let them in. I was going to use Dad's key – he said he had his in his jacket pocket – but we looked and it's gone.'

'Oh, Jonathan loses his keys all the time,' Claire said. 'Your dad has probably put them somewhere else and thinks it was in his pocket. Take these for now and I'm sure they'll turn up,' Claire said. 'I can't come with you, unfortunately. Polly and Matt are working late and I've got all the kids.' It seemed Claire might like a show-free day too, although the kids were upstairs practising their songs at the top of their voices, so it seemed that there was no such thing as a show-free day for her either.

Aleksy and Connie trotted off, and we settled down in our basket for a pre-dinner rest. Pickles was supposed to be up practising with the children but he joined us instead – clearly he had also had enough of the singing.

'Apparently I am the best reindeer ever,' he told us.

'I doubt that,' George said, but thankfully Pickles didn't hear him.

'I'm sure you are, Pickles,' I said, giving George a 'look'.

'Guess, what though, I can even make a reindeer sound,' he said.

'What's a reindeer sound?' George asked.

'Woof, woof, woof.'

'Really good,' I said, silencing George again.

I closed my eyes as George and Pickles bickered like siblings, and took another short cat nap. My nap count today had been impressive to say the least.

I was woken by a commotion as Polly arrived with Aleksy and Connie.

'Calm down,' Polly was saying. 'You're both talking at the same time, and I can't understand – oh there you are Claire, thank goodness; maybe you can get some sense out of these two.'

'What is going on?' Claire asked. I sat up, yawned, and blinked. What *was* going on?

'The hall, we went there and the dancers got on stage to practise, so we went backstage to see how the props looked and it was a total mess. The star was all ruined, the stable had been broken, and there was mess everywhere. Nicky said that we should call the police, but then we thought we would ask you first,' Aleksy gushed.

'And there was no sign of a break-in?' Claire asked.

'No, and then I thought about how we couldn't find Dad's keys, so that means maybe . . .'

Surely they weren't accusing Tomasz. Yes, he did have very big feet and he had keys but he wasn't the sort to do—

'Of course I'm not suggesting it was Dad, of course,' Aleksy said. Ah, OK, I thought so. 'But after the paint, we think maybe someone took his keys and did it.'

'Yes, someone must have taken his keys last night, stolen them,' Connie said, as if we were in any doubt as to what Aleksy meant.

'Really?' Polly scrunched her face up in disbelief. 'Isn't that a bit, well, extreme?'

'I think we need to take it seriously,' Connie said. 'Weighing up all the evidence it looks as if someone is out to sabotage our show.' Connie wants to be a lawyer and she's very sensible, so I had to agree with her.

'Oh my goodness, why would they do that? It's for charity, it's for the community and there are children involved.' Claire's voice was pitched a bit high; she was clearly upset.

'Right, we need to find out who did this. Come on, I'll get Matt to come pick up the kids and we'll go to the hall and survey the damage. Can your dad make it?' Polly asked.

'No, he's working tonight, covering for one of the chefs, so we'll have to tell him later. Besides he'll blame himself because of the keys,' Aleksy said, sounding so upset. I nuzzled him but I feared that was little comfort at the moment.

'It's not his fault,' Claire said. 'But if we find out who it was, they better watch out.'

I was with Claire on this one. We would find out who it was, and when we did they would be sorry they messed with us and our show. Although, I was still worried about those big feet. Someone could do some serious damage to a cat like me with feet that size.

★   ★   ★

All the children and George were tucked up and I was with Claire and Jonathan, in our living room, as Claire explained the situation to him.

'If it ruins my budget, they will be sorry,' he said.

'Always thinking about the money. Thankfully, Polly said that although it was pretty bad it's nothing we can't fix. More worrying is why would someone want to hurt the show.'

'So, it looks as if the paint on the stage wasn't an accident?' Jonathan suggested.

'No, and the keys, well, they were definitely Tomasz's keys. He feels awful, but clearly someone took them without him knowing,' Claire added.

'You don't think Tommy would do it, do you? He's been in so much trouble lately . . . I hate to think badly of him – because he's a great kid normally – but maybe he's in a worse way than we thought? Maybe he did do this?' Jonathan looked pensive. I knew what he was saying but I couldn't believe it was our Tommy. No, no there was no way he would do this.

'You mean for attention? I guess his acting up could have been a cry for attention, it often is with teenagers,' Claire said.

Thinking about it, Tommy's behaviour had been erratic – good one minute, terrible the next. But no, it couldn't have been Tommy. I was pretty sure of that. He might be a bit of a wild one but he was working really hard for the show, and he'd been to the shelter with us; he'd met the people that the show was going to help. No, no way it was him, I'd bet my fur on it.

'No, I'm pretty sure it's not him; he wouldn't. He's turned

over a new leaf and at heart he's a good kid. Plus, he loves his role in the show,' Claire said.

'Yeah you're right, it was just a thought because of the keys. But if Tomasz had them in his jacket, I guess anyone could have taken them. It'll be tricky to find out who did it.'

'We need to find out soon, before they do anything even worse,' Claire added.

'Agreed, I'll start paying more attention when I'm there, look out for anyone suspicious,' Jonathan said. I didn't have high hopes for him as he wasn't the most observant person ever. 'And, we have family day this Saturday. We'll get everyone onboard trying to discover who did this,' Jonathan said.

'No one can ruin our show, it's so important,' Claire said.

'No one will. I promise, my love,' Jonathan replied.

No, no one would because now I was on the case. Or I would be after a good night's sleep and a decent breakfast. And first port of call would be to speak to the others – George, Snowball, Hana, and our other cat friends, because they would help us get to the bottom of it. As much as I knew the adults meant well, I also knew it would come down to me and my cat gang in the end. It always did.

'You mean they did more damage?' George asked when I filled him in the next morning. I waited until after breakfast when the house was empty, but we did have Pickles with us.

'What does that mean?' Pickles asked.

'You wouldn't understand, you're a dog,' George said, and I put a paw on him. He really had to remember to be kinder to Pickles. He was a dog, yes, but he was still a baby. George really needed to have more patience.

'Actually I am Rudolph the red-nosed reindeer,' Pickles retorted and ran around in a circle.

'Anyway,' I said, bringing the conversation back to the matter at hand. 'The point is that we need to foil whoever it is who is doing this and so far we have very little evidence.'

'What is evidence and can I eat it?' Pickles asked.

'See what I mean?' George raised his whiskers. Yes, my defence of Pickles was wearing a little thin.

'So far, we know the person has big feet, the size of Tomasz, Matt or Jonathan's.'

'But none of them would have done this,' George said.

'No, of course not. I'm just using their feet as an example. The person also managed to access Tomasz's keys, but as Claire said, he had it in his jacket pocket so it could have been anyone with access to the jacket while he wasn't wearing it.'

'Right, so this evidence is really not very good. We are looking for someone with big feet,' George summed up.

'You're right, it's not a lot to go on.' I scratched my head; it was a perplexing situation.

'We'll have to go to the hall when they're making sets or rehearsing and see if we can see anything suspicious. Search for clues, watch people,' George suggested.

'There's a rehearsal tonight, and Polly said they would be setting up the trees as well.'

'Great, well at least we have a starting point,' George said.

'Can I come?' Pickles asked.

'I guess you'll have to, seeing as you're a reindeer,' George replied.

'I'm not a reindeer, I am Rudolph – the best reindeer ever.'

'You are,' I said quickly before my son could say anything scathing to the poor pug.

'So, I can help you catch the baddie,' Pickles said.

George shook his tail. I knew he thought that Pickles would be more hindrance than help, but then, you never knew. Maybe he would be able to help us. Or, then again, maybe he wouldn't.

I needed to go and rally my troops. It was going to be a long day, I could feel it in my fur, but I would make sure that I was prepared.

'George, I have to go and see Snowball. You can go and fill in Hana, I guess?'

'Sure thing, Dad.'

'What about me?' Pickles asked.

'What I really need for now is for you to stay here and keep guard. Note anything suspicious and tell us when we get back. Think of yourself as being in charge of ground control.' I knew I wasn't technically supposed to leave Pickles but Claire would be back any minute – or so I hoped – and this was an emergency. It was a case of neighbourhood security after all.

'Oh, now that does sound important. Am I important?' he pushed.

'Very,' George said, staring at his paw. 'Right, I'm off. Let operation foil the saboteur begin.'

'What's that mean?' Pickles asked.

'I'll explain later,' I said. 'For now, we really have to go and you need to stay here and be in charge.' I followed George out of the cat flap and the house before Pickles could ask any more questions.

★   ★   ★

It wasn't even midday and we were already weary. My first stop had been Snowball, but Harold was clutching her, so we'd had to wait, because he really didn't let her go for a minute. Thankfully Sylvie called round with Theo, and Snowball was at once discarded and replaced by baby Theo. That baby was proving very useful, it seemed. We quickly ran outside and finally had a chance to chat.

'We'll get it sorted,' Snowball said reassuringly when I finished telling her.

'Yes, but we don't have much time and we need a plan,' I said.

'You and your plans! But yes, this time I agree, it's import-ant.' Snowball sounded serious, she wasn't even taking the opportunity to tease me . . . much, anyway.

'It's vital. And we cats will probably end up having to solve it as usual,' I pointed out.

'You're probably right. Alfie, what if the person is really bad? The show is for charity so to try to ruin it is awful; we don't want to put ourselves in danger.' Her fur shook.

'No, Snowball, I promise I'll make sure that we aren't in danger.' Thankfully she didn't notice that I had my paws crossed. I couldn't promise any such thing, but I could hope, and I certainly hoped we wouldn't get into too much danger. But then, sometimes danger did seem to be my middle name.

Our second stop was the recreation ground, where I filled in our other cat friends. They all sat to attention like an army as they listened to me.

'Right, so we need to see if we can find out who is doing

this?' Oliver said. He was quite a smart cat so I had high hopes for him being able to help.

'Yes, and as a lot of the people involved in the show live on this street, you guys can be our eyes and ears here on Edgar Road,' I explained.

'Got it, I'll see if there's anything suspicious going on,' Rocky said.

'We can do a bit of a patrol of the street between us,' Nellie said.

'Rest assured, Alfie, we are on your team,' Elvis finished.

'I know I can always count on you,' I said.

'Now we need to find Salmon. If anyone knows anything, it'll be him,' Snowball said. So off we trotted.

Salmon was sat just outside his front door, under a shelter. He looked as if he was guarding his house and I was glad for his, and his humans', busybody behaviour for once.

'I heard about this,' Salmon said when we finished telling him what had been happening. 'Claire phoned us and Vic and Heather are already on the case. They are talking about organising a neighbourhood watch meeting to help sort this out.'

'Good,' I said. For once I was keen for a neighbourhood watch meeting. Normally I wasn't, because they went on for ages and ages and were incredibly tiresome. Jonathan had fallen asleep in quite a few, which annoyed Claire, but I honestly couldn't blame him.

'Don't worry, Alfie,' Salmon said kindly. 'We'll catch the culprit and save your show.'

I was suitably reassured as we left Salmon to go to our last port of call for today, which was Dustbin. Although Snowball agreed with me that it couldn't be Tommy doing all of this, we both felt that it would be a good idea to go and check that he was alright. I was worried that others might be pointing the finger at him, the way Claire and Jonathan had.

'It's been a long day, already,' Snowball said as we made our way to the restaurant yard in the freezing cold. It was as though she could read my mind.

'God, it has, and if we don't get this sorted, every day might be long from now on.' I wanted to time our visit for after school so I could get a sense of whether it possibly could have been Tommy.

'At least we'll get some food when we get there,' she said, suddenly cheering. Oh yes, we had definitely earned some treats, as we'd been working so very hard.

'Ah, I thought we might see you,' Dustbin said as we greeted him. 'And I think you are just in time.' He gestured to the yard behind Tomasz and Franceska's house, where Aleksy and Tommy were stood, staring at each other.

'You did it,' Aleksy was shouting, his face red. Uh oh, it wasn't just Jonathan that thought Tommy could be our culprit.

'No, I did not.'

'You said you're helping with the show but you still call it stupid and now look what's happened.'

'It is stupid but that doesn't mean I did it.' Tommy and Aleksy were standing quite close together. I ran to get in the middle.

'Meow,' I said loudly.

'Alfie, Tommy is the one ruining our show,' Aleksy said.

'Yowl.' I really don't think he is.

'I'm not,' Tommy shouted back. Thankfully, Franceska appeared.

'What is all the shouting about?'

'Tommy won't admit that he's the one messing up the show.'

'Aleksy, your brother wouldn't do that; right, Tommy?'

'I didn't, Mum. Look, I may not have been as supportive as I should have been but I am trying, and I wouldn't do anything to ruin it for the shelter. I'm not a monster.'

'You are a monster,' Aleksy shot back.

'Aleksy, stop it. Listen to me, if Tommy says he didn't do it then that's good enough. And last night he was definitely here all evening, so it couldn't have been him.'

'See,' Tommy said.

'Yes, but Tommy you have to see that your behaviour has been so bad lately that people might suspect you, and for that you only have yourself to blame,' she added.

'Right.' Tommy looked at the ground.

'Can we try to stop this? Christmas is coming soon and the show needs you and Charlie for the social media. He has been doing a good job so far, hasn't he, Aleksy?' I was glad that Franceska was able to remain so calm.

'He has,' Aleksy said grudgingly.

'So can we agree that Tommy, you'll make more effort, and Aleksy, you give your brother another chance.'

'I am sorry, Aleksy, but I really didn't do it and I wouldn't hurt the show.' Tommy sounded sincere.

'OK, I'm sorry I accused you, but maybe you could stop taking the mickey out of me now and just get on with it?'

'Deal.'

The boys shook hands and I felt we had made a real breakthrough. But then, if it wasn't Tommy, we still didn't know who was the show wrecker in our midst.

That night at rehearsals, it all seemed normal as I patrolled the backstage area. I was so tired from the day's adventures but as George kept saying 'the show must go on'. No one seemed hostile, no one was acting suspiciously. Tomasz still hadn't found his keys and he asked if anyone had seen them – they had not. But then, if someone had taken them they wouldn't say, would they? Polly was ranting about the damage, and how it was taking money from people who already had less than nothing – how you could have less than nothing I wasn't sure – but again, I looked for reactions, but no one looked guilty. The only conclusion was that either the person wasn't here tonight, or they were very good at acting. Oh boy, that gave me an idea. I went to find George.

'George,' I hissed.

'What?' I ushered him into the corner. I would have rounded up Hana and Snowball as well but Harold was holding them both, one in each arm, so I couldn't tell them yet.

'You know I've been looking for clues and I discovered that no one showed any guilt backstage, which means that the culprit either isn't here or is a very good actor.'

'And what does that mean?'

'It means that we are looking for someone with big feet who is also a good actor.'

'But apart from me we don't have anyone that good in the show,' George pointed out.

'Well, yes, OK, but we need to look closely at the people in the Nativity. Not Matt and Tomasz of course, but the men we don't know. So, our first step, pardon the pun, is to look at everyone's feet and pick out those who have the biggest.'

'What do you mean, about the pun?' George eyed me as if I was a little mad.

'Never mind, just keep your eyes open for a big-footed actor.' How hard could he be to find? It wasn't as if we had a cast of thousands.

Thankfully my musings were interrupted as the children climbed onto the stage. They looked cute, although they weren't yet wearing their costumes – neither was Pickles, because he kept trying to eat the red nose – as they had said they'd save it for the night.

'Rudolph the red-nosed reindeer . . .' they trilled as they tried to get Pickles to do the dance they had taught him. Henry held a dog treat and Pickles went on his hind legs and danced in a circle on them. It was very cute but definitely more dog than reindeer, or so I thought, anyway.

'He looks sweet,' George said, showing a rare moment of fondness for Pickles.

'He does. As do our children.'

Everyone clapped as the song came to an end and Pickles licked the stage.

'Woof, woof, woof,' he said, standing in the centre and looking pleased with himself.

'Bravo,' Claire shouted.

'Great job, everyone,' Aleksy said, taking his director role seriously.

'And now, we have the Edgar Road singers,' Connie said. As Vic and Heather led their group onto the stage, I sat down. This was too important to everyone, I just *had* to find the culprit, there was absolutely no choice.

Chapter
Twenty-Two

The neighbourhood watch meeting was, luckily, being held at our house, which meant I could attend. It was Monday evening and a rare evening away from the show. We were no closer to finding out who had done the damage so far, but it was early days and thankfully nothing else had happened. Because some of the sets had been ruined, Tomasz and his crew were working late to re-do them all, so maybe the bad person just hadn't had the opportunity to ruin anything else. Or maybe they had stopped. I could only hope that they'd stopped.

'Right let's get started,' Vic said, clapping his hands. Claire and Jonathan were rushing around making drinks for everyone, and the living room was full, standing room only. The doorbell rang and Vic tutted loudly. He hated anyone being even one minute late.

Polly opened it and came back with Barbara.

'So sorry I'm late,' she said, with a big smile. 'I'm here to help.'

I was unsure whether I believed her or not, but she sounded genuine. She didn't even glare at me, so I thought perhaps she was actually becoming nice. Or nicer, at least.

I settled down in a good listening place, on Matt's lap. He stroked me as he listened to Vic.

'We will not let anyone ruin all our hard work,' he was saying.

'No, and also Edgar Road does not tolerate crime of any description,' Heather added.

'We will catch whoever it is and they will be sorry they messed with us,' Vic shouted, making Matt jump.

I concentrated as they tried to come up with an action plan. Some of the ideas were immediately discounted. The first was to install cameras, but Jonathan vetoed that on the basis of the cost being too high, especially as they only needed it for a short time. Then Vic said they could arrange security to be at the hall at all times, but again this wasn't practical.

'I don't see how it would work. We've got a fair few weeks until the show and everyone's busy enough as it is,' Jonathan replied.

'I agree, it's not feasible to have someone stationed at the hall at all times,' Vic concluded.

Although it did give me an idea. If it came to it, maybe we cats could keep watch. Yes, that wasn't a bad idea at all. Honestly, the cat neighbourhood watch could foil this before the human one did. But then, we usually did.

The meeting conclusion was a pretty woolly plan where everyone would keep their eyes and ears open and report anything suspicious . . . which was pretty much my, and my cat friends', plan too. But it was still gratifying to see everyone firmly behind making the show a success and trying to stop anyone from doing it harm. Surely with us all working together, the show would be safe now.

'Right, so we know what we're all doing?' Vic said, after a lot of waffle. I would have been surprised if anyone knew what they were doing.

'Pretty much nothing,' Jonathan muttered and Claire swatted him.

There was a bit more chatter before Jonathan finally

managed to get everyone out. Matt and Polly stayed behind for a last drink and a debrief.

'Do you think the person who did it was here?' Polly asked, sipping her wine.

'Probably. I would be, if it was me, to see what we knew,' Matt replied.

'I just don't understand why anyone would try to sabotage the show,' Polly said.

'Me either,' Claire agreed.

'No one seems to know anything though; that's the problem,' Jonathan said.

'True, and no one was acting in a suspicious manner,' Claire said, which I agreed with, because I had been watching and I had very good intuition.

'So maybe they weren't here. What if they have nothing to do with the show but they just don't want it to go ahead?' Polly mused.

'But why?' Matt was as confused as I was.

'Well, I'm pretty sure it can't be about the charity. No one could object to supporting the homeless shelter, surely?' Claire said.

'People can be strange and have weird motives for doing things. By the way, Tomasz called me. They couldn't be here tonight because of work, but apparently Aleksy accused Tommy of doing it,' Matt said.

'Unfortunately, that possibility did cross my mind too,' Jonathan said.

'But he didn't, and he had an alibi in any case,' Matt explained.

'Just shows how mud sticks,' Polly said. 'Tommy was just

being a teenager and now he's trying to join in with us, become part of it, and I really think he's turned a corner.'

'I agree, and he wants the work experience with Jon, so he really is trying,' Claire said.

'Anyway, I feel bad for doubting him, because it definitely wasn't him, and we can be sure about that. Tommy has turned over a new leaf,' Jonathan added.

'Which brings us back to square one. No idea who has been messing with the show,' Polly sighed.

'No idea at all,' Matt sighed.

They were wrong, I thought, as I settled into my bed, I wasn't at square one. We knew it wasn't anyone we were close to, because they all cared too much. The more I thought about it the more I thought I would have to sneak into the hall overnight and act as a watchcat, but I didn't fancy doing it alone and I had to have a long hard think about who would be happy to do it with me. Snowball would be my obvious choice, but I was pretty sure that there was no way she could sneak out without Harold noticing, and if she disappeared overnight he would probably panic, which could hurt him. George would probably love the adventure but what if the person did turn up and we were in danger? I couldn't put him in danger, he was my kitten. Hana wasn't even on the list as she would be terrified and I wouldn't put her through that. None of the cats from the recreation ground would be that happy to spend the night away from Edgar Road, and although I knew if I asked them they would, I didn't want to put them in that position. And, of course, Dustbin and Ally would join me if it was an emergency, but night time was the busiest time in the yard and they needed to keep the rodents at bay – that was their job after all. So, really that left me with only one option – an option that I wasn't overly keen on – but I could see no other way.

I went to see Salmon the next morning and told him of my plan. He stared at me with narrowed eyes.

'We stake out the hall?' he said.

'Well, yes, but only if there's any more problems, of course, which they decided last night there might not be. But if we're going to catch the culprit . . .'

'I agree. I would be happy to step into the breach with you; my owners would want me to help out. And although it might be dangerous, I accept the mission.'

'Right, uh . . . that's great.' Salmon was more dramatic than me sometimes.

'What next?'

'We have a rehearsal tonight, and I'm hoping we'll find everything intact, but if not then we shall have to spend at least one night there, maybe more, until we find out who is doing this.'

'Alfie, as much as I don't relish spending a night in a cold, dark hall with you, I agree it might be the only answer. I'll come to rehearsal tonight so I can see the lay of the land for myself.'

'Great. OK, well, I guess I'll see you there later.'

We said a nice, friendly goodbye and I went home. Goodness, I could only hope that we caught the person on the first night out there, because more than one night alone with Salmon might be more than this cat could cope with. I was beginning to regret my plan but I told myself that it was for a good cause, and it would be worth it if we were able to save the show.

When I told Snowball and the others at the recreation ground, they all had a good laugh at me. Only Elvis was missing, and Nellie said she couldn't wait for him to hear about this.

'Listen, I am making the sacrifice for the greater good,' I said, my fur bristling.

'But, Salmon? I mean, it wasn't long ago that he tried to fight you all the time,' Rocky said.

'That was years ago, and Tiger used to see him off,' I said with fondness.

'No one would mess with Tiger,' Snowball said. We often shared memories of her, because she had been an important part of all our lives. Although Snowball had been my girlfriend first, when she came back after Tiger died and heard about our relationship she was happy for us, rather than jealous. But then, they were friends themselves back in the day. It was nice to be able to talk freely about Tiger with Snowball. I couldn't help but think she would have done the overnight in the hall and she was far feistier than me, so if there was any danger lurking, it would probably be her that would have faced it. I shook my head. Those thoughts weren't going to help us now, so instead I would use my memories of Tiger for strength, as I often did.

'Anyway, Salmon and I are almost friends,' I said. 'So, let's not worry about that right now.'

'We can worry about the fact that if the person comes to the hall when you're there and sees you, you could be in danger,' Nellie said.

'Oh gosh, I hadn't thought about that,' Snowball said. 'Alfie, you have to promise to be careful.'

I brushed their concerns away.

'Listen, we don't even know yet if we'll have to do it, but if we do, Salmon and I will stay hidden, I promise.' I shuddered. I had been in enough danger in my life, I certainly didn't need more.

That night, Salmon and I made our way out of the hall after rehearsals. We decided the best thing to do was to wait outside, hidden in the shadows, to see if anyone came. I was hoping someone would, but also scared because what would we do if they did?

'So what do we do, if we have to confront someone?' Salmon asked.

'I was thinking the same. Perhaps if we just make enough noise to scare them off?' I suggested.

'OK, but if they look dangerous, then we definitely leave them alone.' Salmon sounded nervous but I was too, so I understood.

We crouched behind a wall in front of the hall, as it was the only way someone could get inside. I shivered – it really was bitterly cold – and hoped we wouldn't be here too long.

'So, what's your favourite thing about Christmas?' Salmon asked me, to pass the time.

'Only one thing.'

'One thing.'

'Family and friends being together,' I said. I would have said the food but that was shallow and I am not a shallow cat.

'I agree, it's a wonderful time if you have a nice family,' Salmon said.

'Gosh, that's deep.'

'I'm thinking of the shelter, the people who probably don't have family, because if they did, they wouldn't be homeless, would they?'

'No,' I agreed. 'There would be someone to take care of them. When my first owner, Margaret, died, I had no one to take care of me, but I was lucky enough to find a new family.'

'And your Toby, he found a new family.'

'Yes he did, but it might not be so easy for grown-ups as it is for cats and children,' I mused.

'Sad, that.'

We both lapsed into our thoughts before being shaken by the sound of footsteps.

'Quick, look,' I said, standing up. Salmon did the same. It was dark but we saw a shadowy figure approach. I checked the feet, they were big. Whoever it was, was big, and also not Tommy, I was relieved to see.

'Ready, let's pounce,' I said as the footsteps came closer.

'God help us,' Salmon said and we jumped out.

'Yowl,' I said at the top of my voice.

'Meow!' Salmon shouted.

'Oh my God, you nearly gave me heart failure.'

We both became silent as we stared at Tomasz. Not the saboteur then. Or was he? No.

'What the hell are you doing? I left my phone here – Franceska says I lose everything – and I was coming back for it.'

Ah, that explained it.

'Were you waiting to see if the sabotage person came back?'

'Meow,' I admitted.

'What clever cats you are, but you need to be careful. Whoever it was had quite big feet, Alfie.'

I shuddered. Tomasz was right and I'd already thought about the damage those feet could do.

Chapter Twenty-Three

I was distracted from the show for a moment because it was Christmas tree day. Finally. It seemed that since we had started the show we had been waiting to be able to get Christmas properly started and now we were. It might be a little early but Claire said they were working so hard on the show that if we didn't get the tree now, we might not have the time to all do it together. I think secretly she liked the idea of putting it up a bit earlier than usual. And as the show was so Christmassy, it seemed only fitting that we enveloped ourselves in all things Christmas.

Like everything in our families' lives, Christmas tree day was crazy. Tomasz came with us because he had a van and that could fit ours, Polly and Matt's, and their tree in. We had offered for Sylvie and Marcus to come but they said with Theo being so tiny they were going to put up an artificial tree, and Harold said he had one that he'd had since Marcus was a boy and it was good enough; he wasn't going to waste money on a tree that only got used for a month. Jonathan agreed with him but he was outvoted by the rest of us.

The only downside to Christmas tree shopping was that us cats were banned. As was Pickles.

George, Pickles, and I could only sit at home and wait for the tree to arrive.

'I am so excited,' Pickles said.

'Remember no trying to climb it this year.' Last year had

been the first year when George hadn't climbed the Christmas tree, but he'd encouraged Pickles to do so. This year I was hoping for no tree issues for the first time in a long time.

'No, I won't. Can I eat it?' he asked.

'No, it's prickly and could hurt you,' George cautioned. I gave him a stare of approval.

'No eating the decorations, or the tinsel either,' I said.

'So many rules.' Pickles didn't like to be told not to do something. None of us did, really, and Pickles generally did the opposite of what he was told, which never turned out well.

It felt like hours but finally they returned with the tree.

'Did we have to get one this big,' Jonathan moaned as he, Tomasz, and Matt carried it in, straining under the weight.

'Yes,' Claire said simply.

'It's the best tree ever,' Summer said.

'Why isn't ours as big?' Henry asked.

'Our living room is a bit smaller so we have two – one for the living room and one for you guys to decorate exactly how you want,' Polly explained.

'Why haven't we got a tree to decorate exactly how we want?' Toby asked.

'Because you got the world's most expensive tree,' Jonathan said. He was still a little red faced from the exertion. It was a very big tree.

'Why isn't ours the world's most expensive?' Martha asked.

The adults all shook their heads.

'We'll go and drop yours off next,' Tomasz said to Polly, Matt, Martha, and Henry. 'Then I better get mine back to the house, as Franceska is insisting the boys help to decorate it. I thought Tommy would say he was far too old but he agreed. Although as Connie's coming over, he's allowed to have Charlie too.'

I was pleased by this news. Although Tommy wasn't quite his old self, it sounded like he was getting there.

We had a lovely afternoon. Claire put on her favourite Christmas music, someone called Michael Bublé, who apparently was a very handsome Christmas singer. Even Jonathan began to stop moaning about the cost of the tree as they started getting the decorations out.

We had got all the decorations down from the loft earlier and Claire was sorting them out, with Toby helping.

'All I want for Christmas is you,' the singer sang.

'All I want for Christmas is you,' Claire joined in, laughing, and gave Toby a hug, then Summer and Jonathan. As the family danced around the living room – including Jonathan, who had Summer dancing on his feet – George and I joined in. We danced until our paws hurt.

'I know, let's make hot chocolate and have marshmallows while we decorate the tree,' Claire suggested.

'Yay!' Toby and Summer said.

'Put a shot of whisky in mine,' Jonathan said.

'I might, if you promise not to be grumpy,' she replied.

'Mew,' George said to me. He was a bit partial to marshmallows, which weren't exactly cat friendly and which I didn't like because they were sticky, but each to their own.

It might have taken us hours but the tree did look impressive when it was finished.

'Wow, it's beautiful,' Claire said quite emotionally as

Jonathan climbed up the stepladder and placed the angel on top.

'That's the angel both you kids made last year,' Jonathan added. 'Right, who is going to do the big light switch on?'

'Me, me, me,' Summer said.

'Meeee,' Toby said.

'I'd say it's a draw, so as we have two sets of lights, you can plug one in each on my count.'

I could barely contain my excitement as the children took the plugs and got ready to put them in the socket.

'Ten, nine, eight, seven, six, five, four, three, two, one, go,' Jonathan said.

'Wow,' Claire said as the lights all sparkled and the tree lit up.

'Mew,' I said. It was beautiful.

'Yowl,' George said. 'It's going to be hard to resist climbing that one.'

'Please try.' I flicked my tail.

'Silent Night' started playing and we all huddled round the tree, admiring it.

'Plenty of room for Santa to put presents,' Summer said.

'But remember, it's not just about presents,' Toby said. He was pretty mature for a kid.

'No, it's about family, love, and caring about those who aren't as lucky as us,' Claire said.

'Like the homeless people,' Summer said.

'Meow.' Maybe Summer was maturing too.

'Family photo time!' Claire said.

Jonathan got his phone as Summer put tinsel round George and we all stood by the tree – Jonathan and Claire at the back, Summer holding George, and Toby holding me at the front. Jonathan took it as a selfie.

'That will be our Christmas card this year,' Claire declared as she looked at it. I managed to jump onto the chair arm and see it; we did look like a perfect family. But then, we pretty much were.

We'd gone back to admiring the tree when the doorbell went. I ran after Jonathan to see who it was. Tommy stood on the doorstep, looking sheepish.

'I thought you were decorating your tree?' Jonathan said.

'We did it. Apparently our tree is normal and yours is a monster.'

'It is,' Jonathan agreed.

'Aleksy walked Connie home, so I thought I'd come and see you.'

'Come on in.'

'Actually, can we talk here? It's just that I don't want the kids to see me and think I'm mean for not playing with them again.'

'OK, sure.' I stood outside with Jonathan even though it was bitterly cold.

'I came to say sorry.'

'What for?' Jonathan asked.

'I know you said that if I behaved myself and got good grades I might be able to do work experience and I was grateful but for some reason I just managed to get into more trouble. I feel like I upset everyone in my family and now I've realised that I don't want to be that person anymore.'

'Right, well that's a good start. But what's made you realise this?'

'I was angry all the time, and I didn't want to have to join in with the show, I thought it was dumb and that's not nice. But I realised how much I've been missing out on by being so bad, and I want to go back to how I was. I still get a bit angry at times but Mum explained it's hormones. And I think the shelter is such a good cause and I love doing the social media; I even told Aleksy that. I pretended to hate it at first but it wasn't true. My friend Charlie has helped me see how awful I was being, and now I want to do better.'

'Well, that's great. I have to admit, I heard Aleksy thought you were the one who sabotaged the show, and it had crossed my mind as well.'

'I know. Once you're a trouble maker then you're branded. But, I understand and that was my wake-up call. I realised that if people thought I would really do something that bad then I must have been really horrible. But I want a second chance to prove myself.'

'That's great. You do it and that offer of work experience might still be on the table.' Jonathan ruffled his hair and I nuzzled his leg.

'That would be awesome, thank you. I won't let you down.'

It was an early Christmas miracle.

Chapter
Twenty-Four

We saw Elvis bound down the street towards us as I was recounting the events of the previous few days to my friends at the rec ground. It was frosty most mornings now, but we cats were brave when we needed to be.

'Alfie, wait until you hear this,' he said breathlessly as he skidded to a halt.

'What?' Snowball asked.

'So, I was walking here, and went past the flat – the one where the cat hater lives.'

'You mean Barbara?' I was still a little confused by her. She had tried to hurt us, but she had also offered her help with catching the person sabotaging the show, and was being friendly with everyone on the street, so it was hard to figure her out.

'Yes, that one, well,' he interrupted my thoughts then had to stop he was panting so much. He almost sounded like Pickles when he ran too fast. 'Sorry, I was trying to get here too fast.'

'Elvis, get to the point,' Nellie said.

'Sorry. Yes. So I was about to walk past her flat, but I remembered what you said, so when the front door opened, I crouched down by the gate of the next door flat, hidden, as she approached the bin. I saw her look both ways before she lifted the lid and what do you think she put in there?' He paused and sat down, looking at us expectantly.

'Rubbish?' Snowball volunteered.

'Nope. Not exactly.'

'What was it, Elvis?' I said, impatiently. He was making a real meal out of this, which reminded me that I was a bit peckish and my stomach rumbled.

'A pair of shoes with yellow bottoms.'

'Right and?' Rocky said. 'Oh, you mean?'

'Yes, they were big shoes and the bottoms were covered in yellow paint, and she threw them in the bin.'

'Are you sure?' I was shocked from my whiskers to my paws. I had almost decided to give her another chance after she had seemed so sad when Polly and she walked home the other night.

'Yup.'

'But, she's got little feet,' I added.

'Go and see for yourself. I saw her leave after she threw them away. She had a shopping bag with her so if we go now, I can show you and she won't see us.'

We all set off together. We reached her flat, and the bin outside, but the lid was, of course, closed.

'How do we look inside?' I asked.

Snowball jumped up on the wall. She gently eased her paw under the lid and lifted it a bit.

'Quick, jump up and see if you can see anything,' she said. I did as she asked and, balancing precariously on the rim of the bin, I peered in.

'They are in there and it's the same colour as— Ahhh,' I lost my balance and fell onto the path, landing on my tail. The others tried not to laugh; they failed. Snowball let the lid fall, and jumped down to join me.

'Alfie, are you OK?'

'My tail is a bit sore,' I said, embarrassed. It was easy to lose your footing on the narrow bin rim, but falling in such an undignified manner in front of Snowball and my friends wasn't great for my ego.

'But you saw the shoes?' Elvis said excitedly.

'Yes, and you are right, they are definitely the footprints we found, which means that she must know the person who did it. She must know a person with big feet.'

'Oh Alfie, it was probably her. She wore shoes that were too big for her to throw us off the scent,' Nellie said, slightly patronisingly.

'Oh, yes, of course.' I hadn't thought of that. But then, I was still nursing a bit of an injury so my brain wasn't working as well as normal.

'Remember how the kids used to put on the adults' shoes sometimes and flap around the house?' Snowball asked. I nodded.

'Of course, she put the shoes on just to make the footprints.' That made more sense.

'So, she made the footprints, which means it was probably her who managed to damage the sets and stole Tomasz's keys. But what do we do now we know?' Snowball asked. It was all falling into place in my mind as Snowball spoke. She was at the meeting to hear of any plans to foil her. Was she doing this because she was annoyed that she didn't get a bigger role in the show? Would a grown-up really do that? Or had her grief at losing her husband and having to move house made her slightly mad? It could happen. I knew from my own experience how grief could change you into a totally different person. However, regardless of her motives, one thing was certain: we had to stop her and I didn't have long to come up with a plan. I needed to put my thinking cap on – and no, that wasn't the one knitted by Doris.

'So, here's how it's going to work,' I said a bit later to my troops, who were lined up listening to me. I had gathered every cat I could get my paws on. Nellie, Elvis, Rocky, Oliver, Salmon as well as Snowball and George. 'We will go to the perpetrator's front garden. We will wait until one of our adults walks by – it'll be either Claire or Sylvie, by my reckoning. When we see them, George, you will be our lookout and will give us the signal. The rest of us, from behind the bin, will push it with everything we've got so it tips over and reveals the shoes to our human.' A brilliant, brilliant plan, if I did say so myself.

'What's the signal?' Salmon asked.

'Yowl as loudly as you can,' I said.

'Or I could be more creative, I could do my sheep impression?' George said.

'No, we won't be able to see you, so just yowl and we will know it's time,' I said. I wanted to keep it as simple as possible.

'What if Barbara sees us?' Snowball asked.

'Then we'll have to abort our mission so hopefully she won't. We'll tuck behind the bin and if she comes out of the house George will give us a signal,' I said.

'What's the signal?' Salmon asked again.

'Meow as loudly as you can.'

'Right, let me get this straight,' Rocky said. 'He meows and we tip the bin, he yowls and we hide?'

'No, the other way round.' I went through the whole thing one more time. We had to get it right.

It was cold and had started to rain by the time we made it to Barbara's flat. We took up our position behind the bin, with George out front, and waited.

'Ow, I think someone stood on my tail,' Nellie said.

'Careful,' I cautioned, although I think it may have been me.

'Keep quiet, or we could blow this whole thing,' Salmon said.

'Imagine if Barbara finds us here, she'll go mad.'

'She won't find us.'

Just as we were all getting on each other's fur – we were soaking wet and also uncomfortable being crammed in together – we heard George.

'YOWL.'

'Is that push or Barbara?' Rocky asked. I rolled my whiskers.

'Push,' I commanded. We all shoved the bin with all our strength and with the help of the wind it fell over with a crash.

'Whatever is that?' Sylvie said. Us cats made our way round to the front but tried to stay hidden in a bush. George and Sylvie stood by the bin. 'How did this happen?' she asked. She went to pick the bin up, putting the break on Theo's pram first, and as she did I felt like mewing in despair. The bin was empty, which was probably why it had been pretty easy to push over. Sylvie picked it up and put it back in place, still looking perplexed, then she walked on. We all emerged from the bush.

'Didn't think about the fact it might have been emptied, did we?' Salmon said.

'No. Oh, how disappointing,' I said, feeling dejected.

'Oh Alfie, it was a very good plan, and it's not your fault that the bin men must have just been.'

'How could I be so stupid? I heard Claire reminding Jonathan to put the bins out earlier. I didn't think.'

'Never mind, there's always another plan, Alfie,' Nellie said.

She was right, there was.

'I think that Salmon and I will have to try to catch her red-handed, as per the original plan. And now we know it's her, we need to act quickly.'

'But she tried to hurt you before, what if she does something now?' Snowball asked.

'OK, well, maybe we won't confront her, but we have to stop her from ruining the show somehow. But just in case, George, if I am not at home when you wake up, come and find these guys – if you can make sure you come here in the morning everyone, and Snowball, if you can't get away, someone will come to your house. Is that OK with everyone? Are we all clear?' I was surprised to find that I was beginning to feel nervous.

'Hold on, if she doesn't come to the hall tonight, you might get locked in, anyway,' Elvis pointed out.

'Yes, which is why I need George to find someone to come get us out if that's the case,' I said. I thought I had explained my plan clearly, but still they had questions.

'I should be coming with you,' George said sulkily.

'But son, I need you at home, in case you need to raise the alarm,' I repeated.

'Humph.'

'OK, Alfie, but do you still need to do it now we know it's her?' Nellie asked.

'We have to stop her, and this is the only way I can think of.' I stood my ground.

'Then you need to be doubly careful,' Snowball said, sounding worried.

'She's definitely sneaky but hopefully by tomorrow her plan will be foiled.' I tried to sound more confident than I felt as we did need to catch her in the act, and I would have Salmon with me. I just had to be brave. 'And, in the meantime, we better scarper. We definitely don't want her to find us here.'

Chapter Twenty-Five

Salmon was surprisingly chipper about staking out the hall a second time, although this time we were going inside. George, however, wasn't quite as happy. He was still very upset at not being invited. He had let the first one go because we were just hanging out outside, but now he seemed to think that he should be involved. I told him it might put him in danger. He didn't accept that and said that, as his dad, I shouldn't put myself in danger either. I couldn't argue, but I reiterated that I needed him here, because if Salmon and I got into trouble he would be able to raise the alarm if we weren't back by morning. Still, he refused to be pacified, insisting that the plan would work much better if he was directly involved. I had to get quite firm with him, which I don't like to do but, as he said, I was his father. He might be grown up, or think he was, but he still had to do what I told him. Especially as this was for his own good.

I was quivering with anticipation and cold as I met Salmon that night, and we got to the hall while people were still working. Polly and Franceska were spraying the trees on the stage with fake snow and it was beginning to look like a proper winter wonderland. Tomasz and some others were putting the finishing touches to the stable where baby Jesus would be born, and the star was now re-made and hanging up. An old armchair had been cleaned up, ready for the Santa scene, and someone was making a fake fireplace where stockings would be hung. It was all looking amazing.

'We better hide,' I said to Salmon. We didn't want anyone finding us and making us go home.

'Right, Pol, let's go, we've got a dinner reservation,' Matt said.

'Just coming, love,' Polly replied. The children and Pickles were spending the night at our house – another thing that had annoyed George. He felt as if he was getting left behind with Pickles, and that he was being treated as a baby. I hadn't had time to argue though and I did think that with the house full it would be less likely that anyone noticed I wasn't there for a bit. If everything went to plan, that was.

We could hear everyone leaving – saying goodbyes, footsteps heavy – from where we were hiding.

'Can you hear that?' Salmon said.

'What?'

'I just heard a lady saying "I'll lock up, I just want to finish tidying up," and I think it's Barbara. Surely she wouldn't be so obvious as to do anything when she was the last person in the hall?'

'Yes, if she does anything then they'll suspect her, surely,' I said.

'Maybe she has a plan. You might not be the only one with plans, you know,' Salmon grinned.

'I have a lot of plans,' I admitted.

'And I'm glad to be participating in one of your plans, I like working with you Alfie, and this is right up my street.' We both raised our whiskers. It seemed we made a good team. We snuck towards the backstage to find somewhere to hide.

'Look, here's a good place.' He pointed his paw towards

one of the backdrops that was leaning against the wall at an angle, leaving just enough space for a couple of cats. We went to slide behind it, but I bumped into something. Something soft and a bit smaller than me.

'George,' I hissed. Salmon had managed to get close to me but there was not much room.

'Oh hi, Dad. I couldn't let you do this alone; I was worried,' George gushed, looking guilty.

Something licked me.

'Oh my God, Pickles, is that you?'

'Woof.'

'George, what on earth are you and Pickles doing here? Salmon, what are we going to do?'

'I'm not sure.' Salmon wasn't sure about Pickles, which was understandable because he didn't know him. It was dark, but we cats have very good eyesight in the dark, so we could see them both. Standing there, as if pilchards wouldn't melt . . . 'But, I don't think it's a good idea that they're here,' he added.

'Dad, I decided to come here before they all left because I was worried about you and Salmon. And, well, Pickles followed me. It wasn't my fault.'

'How did he get out?' I snapped. I was pretty annoyed. Salmon and I had it all figured out and now George – and, more to the point, Pickles – threatened to ruin everything.

'The cat, or dog flap,' George said, innocently.

'But how did he get out of the garden?' They always made sure our gates were closed since Pickles had a habit of following us, something which had led to all sorts of trouble in the past. Actually, now was a case in point.

'Ah, a courier came earlier with a package and no one thought to check the back gate like they normally do,' George admitted.

'Guys, this explanation is all well and good but now they're here, what are we going to do?' Salmon asked.

'We'll have to leave; our plan is ruined.' I stamped my paw. I was incredibly frustrated. They would notice Pickles missing before they even thought we might be as well, and all sorts of chaos would ensue if we didn't get him home.

'Now you know what it was like when I was visiting Harold at the hospital,' George said defiantly. I had to admit that I had no answer to that, because I had followed George to the hospital and Pickles had followed me . . . It hadn't ended well, but that was not the point.

'Are you going to go on about that forever?' I snapped.

'Woof.' Pickles said.

'Quiet,' I hissed.

'Now you know how it feels,' George said again.

'This arguing is all well and good, but don't you think we should decide what to do?' Salmon said reasonably.

'Let's catch the baddie,' Pickles said. 'And I can lick and lick them until they surrender.'

'George, what on earth have you been telling him?'

George started to examine his paw, trying and failing to look innocent.

'What the hell is all that noise,' a voice – Barbara's voice – boomed. We all tried to shrink into the wall as she moved the backdrop and we found ourselves staring at her. 'What are you all doing here?' she snapped. Her eyes did not look kind. Her voice didn't sound kind either.

'Yowl,' George said, aggressively.

'Woof,' Pickles added. Salmon and I exchanged glances.

'Right, you come with me,' she said as she picked George and Pickles up. I tried to scratch her but she shook me off. 'Get off me you horrible cats. And dog.' As Salmon and I watched helplessly, she took Pickles and George into the dark props room and then she came back, scooped both Salmon and I up and did the same. 'You have no right to be here,' she said. 'No right at all.'

'Meow,' I said loudly and tried to scratch her again. I am not a fan of violence – I don't condone it – but this woman was hurting those I loved. She sidestepped me and kicked out with her foot; I managed to dodge her and decided it was safer to keep my distance. We were supposed to find out who was sabotaging the show, which we had, but now, now what on earth was going to happen?

'I am going to lock you in, it serves you right for what-ever it is you think you're doing.' I barely had time to turn around before the door slammed close.

The four of us stared at each other for a few moments, blinking to adjust to the pitch black room.

'How are we going to get out?' George asked. I looked around. Only one door and no windows.

'I have no idea.' The door handle was high up and there was no way we could reach it. And it wasn't the sort of door you can push open. The prop cupboard was dark, dusty, and cold – not somewhere I fancied spending the night.

'At least she won't be able to damage anything,' Salmon said, sitting down.

'But we could be here all night, locked in this room and

imagine how much they'll panic when they find Pickles missing.' I was so angry, our carefully thought out plan had gone completely wrong.

'I'm hungry,' George complained.

'Is there anything to eat?' Pickles asked as he tried to lick a cobweb.

I had a feeling it was going to be a very long night.

'Right,' Salmon said after a while. 'I've been thinking. This isn't a total disaster.'

'Salmon, with all due respect, we're locked in a cupboard. How is it not a total disaster?' I asked.

'We have caught Barbara being here when she shouldn't be. So, she might not have done any damage tonight but I am pretty sure she was planning it. My thought is that she might have made it so she could come back on a night when she wasn't the one locking up.'

'Yes, that makes sense,' I said.

'Woof, I can see myself,' Pickles said, looking in a mirror. I shook my tail.

'Carry on, Salmon,' George said. He was still unwilling to admit he had ruined our plan because he was stubborn, but at least now he was trying to be helpful.

'And I know she only found us because you two snuck in here, but in a way at least, because of Pickles, we have a better chance of being found because everyone will be looking for him.'

'True, but why would they look here?'

'When they realise the three of you are missing, I am guessing they'll try the hall as you've all been here so much.'

'Humans aren't always that bright,' I said. 'But, being optimistic, it's possible.'

'Right, and even if they take longer, someone will find us, as they are here all the time. When we hear footsteps we just make a lot of noise.'

'Right Salmon, that makes sense,' I said.

'And we can do as many stake outs as necessary to foil her,' Salmon said.

'But shouldn't we be worried about what she might do to us?'

'No. She swings at us, and locked us in here, but she's not going to hurt us, I could tell. I think she's all bluster and meanness but not violent,' he said, as if he was totally confident in that conclusion.

I looked at Salmon, and I never thought I would say this, but I was so glad he was here and so sensible. Because he was right. One night locked in a dusty props cupboard would not put us off.

'Right, so we just make sure we're here every night until we can get the humans to catch her,' I suggested.

'Yes, and also, if we're here, we can probably try to stop her ruining things, somehow,' George said.

'But she's not nice, I mean, she didn't hurt us but she shut us in here so we have to be careful,' I said. My mind was ticking over. 'Salmon, you are so right. We ensure she knows we are on to her and as soon as we can we get the humans to find out too.' I had no idea exactly how we were going to do that, but somehow we would figure it out.

'And me too. I can be here all the time,' Pickles said. I glared at George.

'Hospital,' he said, and stalked off to a corner to resume sulking.

I really was getting very hungry, and so was Pickles, who was trying and failing to find anything to eat. He wasn't so keen on cobwebs it seemed, but he gave them a good go. George had even tired of sulking and was trying to show Salmon his sheep acting, in order to keep us from thinking too much about how long we were actually going to be here. I lay down, but it was cold and dark, and it smelt funny. Pickles started whining.

'I need to eat,' he said.

'Pickles, just hold on, someone will come and get us shortly.' I looked at Salmon. Would they? It felt as if we were going to be here all night. We might even freeze to death.

'Right, let's try to make a comfortable area, so we can try to get some rest,' I suggested.

There was a blanket, which had paint on it, but would at least provide some warmth.

'We should all huddle together to keep our body heat up as much as possible,' Salmon suggested.

'How do you know that'll work?' I asked.

'Because my humans are survival experts,' he replied. That did not surprise me, although why they needed to be when Vic and Heather rarely seemed to go beyond Edgar Road, I had no idea.

We huddled together on the blanket.

'What if we never get rescued?' George asked. I wanted to tell him that that was why I didn't want him here but knew that wouldn't be helpful.

'As much as I'm angry you brought Pickles – and don't say hospital again – at least with him here they'll look for us more quickly.'

However, as more and more time passed, hope began to fade.

We stayed huddled together for what felt like forever, then Pickles moved and I had to as well, as my paw had gone to sleep.

'This is silly, I'm going to rehearse,' George said. 'I'm bored.'

'I'm bored and hungry,' Pickles added.

I raised my whiskers at Salmon, as if to say: 'See what I have to put up with?' He gave me a sympathetic smile.

What if they didn't think to come here until the next rehearsal? We had hours to go until daytime and hours more until evening when the rehearsals were held. Thankfully someone rehearsed almost every evening and, if they didn't, people came to work backstage. Still, we would have so long to wait. And Pickles, who was already complaining about being hungry, would be unbearable. What would we do? I felt panic rising. George was prancing around being a sheep now, but how long before he got scared? I lay down again. This had not gone according to plan at all and Barbara needed to be stopped. But more than that, we needed to be rescued.

'Shush,' I said, as George was mid sheep.

'Don't shush me,' he said.

'No, I can hear something,' I said.

'Me too, voices,' Salmon said.

'Wait, and when they get closer we all make as much noise as we can. And that includes you, Pickles,' I said. We waited and when we could clearly hear Claire and Jonathan we all started crying out.

'Yowl.'

'Meow.'

'Mew, mew, mew.'

'Woof, woof, woof, woof.'

The door swung open and I blinked as Jonathan put the light on.

'What the hell?' he started.

'How did you all end up in here?' Claire asked.

'Is that the Goodwins' cat?' Jonathan was scratching his head as usual.

'I am so sorry,' Barbara said.

'Hiss.'

'Alfie, stop it,' Claire chastised. 'Barbara, it's not your fault, you couldn't know they were here. And thanks for coming down with us; you didn't need to, I've got keys.'

'Oh, well, I wanted to check they were alright. If I had known they were here I would never have shut the door, they must have been hiding.'

I looked at Salmon.

'YOWL,' he said at the top of his voice.

'MEOW,' I shouted.

'WOOFWOOFWOOF,' Pickles added.

'HISS,' George said.

'Oh goodness they must be so distressed from being shut in,' Claire said, missing our point entirely.

'Right, let's get them home,' Jonathan said, putting the lead on Pickles and scooping George up.

'What on earth?' Claire was asking. I glanced at Salmon.

We would have to do much more because they weren't even remotely suspicious of Barbara.

'How did you know they were here?' Barbara asked.

'We checked everywhere else, so we thought we would give it a try. They have been coming to rehearsals, and hanging around here, so I thought it was worth a shot before we had to call the police. It was Pickles that was the real worry. He's not allowed out without one of us,' Claire explained.

'They somehow always manage to go to places they're not supposed to be,' Jonathan added.

'But we are so glad we've found them safe and sound,' Claire said. 'Thanks again, Barbara.'

'Of course. Oh and Claire? You can have the keys that Polly lent me; you'll see her before me no doubt.' She smiled innocently. Oh she was good. She was very, very good. But even so, she was no match for this cat.

Chapter
Twenty-Six

We were in the dog house. Not literally, unless you counted Pickles. Claire and Jonathan were furious that we had stowed away, as they called it, in the hall and got ourselves locked in. As if it was our fault. We were doing it for them, but did they appreciate that? No, no matter how much noise we made, they simply wouldn't listen to us. We slunk home and the only saving grace from the evening was that Salmon had been very sensible, and that we knew, without a whisker of a doubt, that Barbara was the culprit. And she was, despite Jonathan's thoughts, a very good actor. Because the way she was with Claire and Jonathan when they found us, and the way she spoke kindly to us as we walked home, was so convincing. I almost forgot she was a crazy woman trying to ruin our show. But not quite, because I knew that we would have to stake out the hall again the following night. Now, though, Barbara didn't have keys so how would she get in? Part of me hoped she wouldn't, but part of me knew she would. She was clever and there was no way she didn't have a plan.

I was so tired and hungry when we got home that I ate my supper under a cloud as Claire kept on about how we had to be more careful, especially with Pickles. As if it was my fault he had come with us. Even George felt bad enough to apologise, but I was too tired to chastise him, so I ate, cleaned up and went to bed. My sleep was restless though, full of nightmares about what Barbara might do next.

And that dark, dusty prop room wasn't much fun, I can tell you.

The following day, George slunk out early to see Hana, and probably to get away from me. Claire took the children to school, with Pickles, and although she was still a bit cross with me – Claire could certainly hold a grudge – I was too tired to be upset. Jonathan was at home, which was unusual, but he explained that he was working from home today, in order to get something called admin done. He rarely worked from home so it was a treat to have him here. I sat next to him in the kitchen as he finished his coffee. Thankfully, he stroked me and relaxed into it.

'Why exactly were you at the hall last night?' he asked. Ah, good, someone was thinking about it in the right way.

'Meow!'

'I know, I talked to Claire about it and I said I was sure you were trying to tell us something, but what?'

'Yowl.' If only I could talk, and tell him everything. It would save me a lot of effort, that was for sure!

Jonathan sighed. 'If only I could talk cat.' He stood up and went upstairs and I was pretty sure there was no way I could get him to understand right now.

I had to see everyone, obviously, and Snowball was my first stop. Luckily it was Harold's senior centre day so she was free.

'I am so tired,' I said as I explained what had happened last night. She listened, horrified at first, then amused.

'So, it went wrong?' she said.

'Well, you could look at it like that. Or you could say that we have successfully fulfilled phase one, which we would have done a little more successfully without George and Pickles, but still . . .'

'Right, but Alfie we already knew who it was, and now you have to get her caught,' Snowball pointed out.

'Yes and I am working on it. Salmon and I are going to watch the hall every night until we do catch her.' I bristled. I was trying to stay positive but Snowball wasn't helping.

'But how are you going to do that?' she pushed.

'I am going to discuss that with Salmon,' I replied, a little snappily. I was still tired.

'OK, so you and your new best friend,' she teased, and I relented and grinned.

'Sorry, I am still tired and grumpy. We were in that dusty room for ages before Claire and Jonathan found us.'

'It must have been awful. Let's go and find the others and start working on the next part of the plan,' she said.

We made our way to the recreation ground, happy to find Nellie, Elvis, Rocky, and Salmon there.

'Has Salmon filled you in?' I asked.

'He has, and Alfie we told you it could be dangerous.'

'I have had another idea, Alfie, really based on what you said,' Salmon said.

'What is it?' I was happy for someone else to contribute to my plan. More than happy, in fact.

'Well, you said we'd go back tonight, and every night as necessary, right?'

'Right, we cannot let anyone ruin our show,' I agreed.

'Well, I thought, how about we mobilise a bit more of an

army, you know, like how Vic and Heather do with the neighbourhood watch when they need to patrol the area?'

'Yes, I think I see'. I began to feel a fizz in my fur. 'I think I get it. So we get all these guys involved too?'

'If we all patrol the hall then if Barbara does come in tonight we can charge at her, or scatter, or something, so she can't get us all. Even if we can't get the humans there, we should be able to put her off,' Salmon explained. 'Strength in numbers, and all that.'

'I think it's a good idea. Who's in?' I asked.

'We all are, Alfie,' Nellie said.

'Even me,' Snowball agreed. 'Harold should be OK without me for one night.'

'Do you think we should try to get Dustbin involved?' I asked.

'Let's try with just us for now, and George of course,' Snowball said. 'There's no way he'll be left out.'

'OK, we'll give it a go. But, the thing is, Barbara made a show of giving Polly's keys back yesterday, so she won't be able to get in,' I said, thinking.

'Hang on. Did Tomasz ever find his keys?' Salmon asked.

'No, no, she must still have them. But they have a new padlock on the door,' I pointed out. Jonathan had refused to pay for cameras or security so instead he put a big padlock on the front door which only Claire, Ralph, and Tomasz (who promised to wear it round his neck so he couldn't lose it) had a key to.

'She must have some plan on how to get in, I just don't know what,' I said. It was so frustrating.

'God, it sounds as if she's clever,' Rocky said.

'Not as clever as us.' I sat up straight. 'We are going to get her.' We all put our paws in together, to show we were a team, united in our goal.

'Salmon, you are a genius,' I said. Credit where credit is due, I say.

'But, Alfie, if you hadn't come up with the plan in the first place I'd never have thought of it,' he replied, magnanimously.

'OK, OK, we get it, you're both clever. Now we need to make sure we all know what we're doing, because we need to get this done before any more trouble ensues,' Snowball finished.

It seemed we were wrong about one thing. Last night, we were sure that Barbara wouldn't have done anything, but it turned out that when Claire went to the hall, the curtains – the ones for coming across the stage – had been slashed. I heard about this when we were at home, after I'd filled George in on the latest part of our plan. Claire was telling Sylvie.

'Is it bad?' Sylvie asked.

'I don't know, but it looks bad. Tomasz and Frankie met us there, and Tomasz said that if we took the curtains down they could maybe be sewn up.'

'Where have they been cut?'

'Quite near the bottom.'

'I have to see them, but I'm thinking I could use a different piece of material and sew it across, so it looks as if it is supposed to have a panel,' Sylvie suggested.

'That might work. Do you fancy a walk down there later?' Claire asked. 'I'll get Frankie to meet us there too.'

'Yes, let me feed my little one and we can take him in the pram. I just don't know who would do this?' Sylvie sounded confounded. I wished I could just tell them.

'Me either. Jonathan and I locked up last night when we found the animals there, and it was fine then. Barbara gave us Polly's keys back and came home with us, and the padlock was definitely on.'

'Did you check the back door?' Sylvie asked.

'Oh God, no, because it's always locked. I'll check with Barbara if she did. Oh goodness, I hate to think how much damage is being done. If someone is intent on ruining the show it'll devastate us and the shelter. Think about Aleksy and Connie and all they've put into this. Not to mention everyone else.'

'Meow,' I said. I wouldn't let it happen.

I was beginning to think that Barbara was a sort of criminal mastermind. She used big shoes to throw everyone off the scent, then she made a show of locking up and showing she was trustworthy, but she must have made sure the back door was unlocked. Then she went back last night, despite us all trying and failing to scare her off. I had no idea if tonight would be the end of it, but I sincerely hoped so. I wasn't sure how many more late nights I would be able to cope with.

The rehearsal went on later than usual. All the acts were now running through the show so it took quite a long time, especially as there were a fair few mistakes. Pickles was over excited and he snorted loudly the whole way through the song, which annoyed the children, but Polly explained that he couldn't help it. It seemed Pickles wasn't in any trouble after last night, by the way. He caused all the trouble and didn't get any of the consequences. The story of my life.

Also, Sylvie was right about the back door, as it was unbolted when they went down to look at the curtains. Still, it didn't occur to them to blame Barbara. To me it was obvious, but maybe that was because I knew.

Tomasz waited until after the rehearsal had finished to get some of the guys to help take the curtains down. Franceska and Sylvie were going to get some similar material and make a panel to go across the width of them and it would look fine. But, still, it was piling more work onto people who had enough. Sylvie had Theo and Franceska had the restaurants and her boys. We needed to stop the saboteur, enough was more than enough now.

Barbara was, again, hovering around, being overly helpful. She threw herself into her wise man role with gusto. And even though she only had a few lines she definitely milked them. She was so charming and helpful to everyone, definitely not acting as if she was remotely guilty.

We did our sheep part pretty well tonight, according to George. It wasn't long until the dress rehearsal and I knew that if we didn't do our best, George would never forgive us. So we all threw ourselves into being sheep. Hana was particularly good, she even looked a bit like a sheep having put a bit of weight on. Apparently she was so tired she was eating all the time. It actually suited her, but then she probably would need to start exercising more if she kept going that way. Not that I would tell her. I had learned from Claire that to comment on a woman's weight was definitely not a good idea.

When the rehearsals ended, everyone moved to leave the hall. Pickles was on his lead, so there was no way he was staying behind. Hana bid us goodbye and went with Connie, and Snowball managed to get away from Harold, who had performed a great Santa finale and was so pleased with himself that he didn't seem to notice she was still here.

The plan was that we would go and check if the back door was locked and if it was open we would know that Barbara was going to come back later. If that was the case, then we had to move quickly. George, Snowball and I would hide, Salmon would go and get the others, who would be waiting outside by the back door. Snowball, George, and I would all push the door as hard as we could and let them in and then we would be ready for Barbara. It was a very good plan.

However, as we went to the back door, I saw it was locked. I'd heard Claire asking someone to check it, and they obviously had done. Then Barbara left with the Goodwins. We ran out and sat on the front step of the hall as Claire locked up and bolted the padlock. I went to tell Salmon and the gang that our mission was aborted for now and we all went home heavy hearted. Although I was tired, I knew that we still hadn't sorted this awful situation. Barbara might not be going in tonight but that didn't mean she'd stopped and we had to do this every night until we caught her. I felt tired from the tips of my claws to the tips of my ears just thinking about it.

Chapter
Twenty-Seven

It was another day of agitation, waiting for the evening to come around again. I knew you shouldn't wish time away but when you had a bad person to catch it was different. There was no rehearsal tonight, but a lot of work going on with the sets and the costumes, so I wasn't exactly sure if Barbara would be there, but we assumed she would be. We were sure that she was going to strike again, yet somehow it felt as if she was toying with us.

To pass the time I sat in the window and watched the weather. It was cold and people on the streets were wrapped up in warm coats, scarves, and gloves. I also played with some of the baubles on the lower part of the tree. There was no way I was going to harm them, but I liked to see them spin a bit and then watch my reflection in them. I was still waiting until the advent calendars arrived, because then I knew we had only a few weeks to Christmas. The anticipation was killing me; because we put the tree up early I was ready for Christmas now. But not ready for the show just yet. We needed to get Barbara out of the picture before we were ready for that.

I couldn't sit still, so I went to see Dustbin, to update him. I knew there was no news from him because he or Ally would have come to find us. I went alone as George was with Hana, who was trying to rest as much as she could. The show and the baby were really taking their toll on her. But then, she was quite a delicate cat. Snowball was spending the day with Harold, to alleviate her guilt about having to leave him at night, depending on whether we could figure out if Barbara was going to strike again, of course. Although my instinct was that we had to risk it.

I let thoughts run around my head as I made my way to the yard. We were pretty sure we could catch Barbara but how could we make sure a human discovered what she was doing? I had no idea yet. We could all foil her but would that be enough? I kind of felt that if justice was to be done she needed to be found out by the humans.

I was still mulling it over when I went into the yard and found Ally and Dustbin.

'Hey guys,' I said, trying to sound upbeat.

'Alfie, how are you?' Dustbin said. I filled them both in on our situation.

'Wow, so you are all going to stay in the hall, and make a big fuss and stop her from doing any more damage to you and the play?' Ally asked.

'Well yes,' I said.

'But you really need the humans to find out it's her?' Dustbin said.

'Yes, but we don't know how. She obviously damages things at night when no one is around and how on earth would we get someone to the hall in the middle of the night?'

'It would be impossible. So, maybe you're right. Maybe you have to just keep interrupting her plans until the show opens?' Ally suggested.

'That's what I thought, although it seems to be a bit of a job and of course we can't all be there all the time, which is a worry. Also, we're all tired, so I can't expect everyone to come out night after night. What we want to do is figure out how the humans can catch her red handed but that is eluding me so far.'

'Right, well, if there's anything we can do to help, just let me know.' Dustbin was trying to help but none of us really knew how to get Barbara caught.

'We might get locked in again and I don't think Claire or Jonathan will look for us unless we don't turn up for breakfast,' I said. 'But they would check the hall, so I think that we'll be OK', I replied. Without Pickles there wouldn't be the same panic. After the other night though, at least they would know to look for us there. We just had to hope that we could foil Barbara and get out in plenty of time for breakfast. I really did like my food first thing in the morning.

'We'll just carry on being your eyes and ears here, and if we do hear anything, we'll come and find you,' Dustbin said.

'Perfect, so we all know what we're doing. I hope we can stop the woman. We've had to fix the stage, re-build the shed, and re-do the stars. Sylvie also had to fix up the curtains and she's got enough to do what with Theo and being Mary in the Nativity. I am so fed up with Barbara ruining our wonderful show.'

'You'll get her to stop, I just know it,' Dustbin said reassuringly.

'I hope tonight's the night. My nerves won't take much more of this,' I pointed out.

Franceska came out just as I was about to leave so I fussed her. She looked tired as well.

'Hey Alfie, I heard about you getting locked in. What are you up to?'

'Meow,' saving the show.

'I have to go and do some sewing now. I am so worried that if someone ruins the show, not only will it be terrible for the shelter but it will devastate Aleksy and even Tommy now.'

'Mew.' I knew, which was why I was doing something about it.

George and I went to the hall when I knew the doors would be open and the work in full force. As well as making the sets, it had been decided to try to decorate the hall so it looked more Christmassy. At the moment, it was still just a hall, although I was pleased to see that Aleksy and Connie had a number of youngsters from school helping them, along with a new and improved Tommy.

'Look at all the decorations we got for free,' Tommy said proudly. Charlie was filming it all for social media. I still wasn't quite sure exactly what social media was, but I was obviously going to be involved, as was my George. They had giant paper chains to hang around the top of the walls, and the grown-ups had to help with that, because of the ladders and something called health and safety. I tentatively put a paw on a rung of the ladder but I was too scared to venture up too far, not only because of my fear of heights, but also because it didn't look safe. Sienna and one of her friends were spraying the windows with what looked like snow and making patterns. Tinsel was being hung around the light fittings, and all sorts of Christmas decorations were being placed around the room. It looked a little disorganised – Polly's words – but it was beginning to look a lot like Christmas.

Especially when Tommy found two small Santa hats, and put them on George and I. We were then filmed. George couldn't see out of his, which was a bit big, and he bumped into me, sending me flying into Tomasz, who was about to go up the ladder. No damage was done but all the kids found it funny as George yowled, and then ran around in circles until someone took pity on him and sorted his hat out.

In the background, Christmas carols were being played, and it was so lovely and cosy. I really was glad we had decided to do this show, for so many reasons. The main one was the shelter; I wanted those people to have a happy – or happier – Christmas. I wished it for the whole world, but then I'm only one cat and there's only so much I can do. But looking around, it really had brought everyone together in a wonderful way. Everyone, that is, apart from our saboteur, Barbara.

Connie had managed to hang some Christmas lights around all the windows, so they decided to put them on and turn the main lights off. Wow. As the room lit up with dancing lights, it was really beautiful.

'You guys have done an amazing job,' Polly said, putting her arm around Connie.

'I am so proud of you,' Franceska added, grabbing both Tommy and Aleksy.

'Get off, Mum,' Tommy said, blushing and sneaking glances at Sienna, but she was smiling at him, so he didn't need to be embarrassed.

As soon as we got a chance we snuck away to check the back door. The bolt was open but we needed to see if anyone closed it. They had all said they would make sure they checked it after the other night but I also knew how forgetful humans

– especially Polly and Tomasz – could be. George was stationed by it, slightly hidden, so he could see if anyone locked it. I went to the front door, dodging legs, and found Salmon, Nellie, Elvis, Rocky, Snowball, and Oliver waiting for me.

'She will have no chance against all of us,' I said as confidently as I could muster.

'No, not unless she throws something at us,' Snowball replied.

'Oh my, she won't do that, will she?' Nellie asked.

'Of course not.' I crossed my paws, I really wouldn't put it past her.

I hid them away at the back of the hall and as I noticed people packing up, I went to find George.

'No one checked the lock. You'd think after last time . . . but no. Tomasz and Polly are the worst when it comes to security,' he said. He was right. Polly and Tomasz were busy laughing and joking rather than checking the doors. If only Franceska hadn't left early to go and do some work, she would have made sure we were secure.

After a while the hall was in darkness and we cats were there alone. I felt adrenaline pumping through my body. Tonight was going to be it, I could feel it in my fur.

'This is a bit spooky,' Oliver said.

'Ah, reminds me of the good old days,' Elvis said.

'What on earth do you mean?' Nellie asked.

'You know, when people went to the theatre regularly.' That made absolutely no sense, but Elvis did sometimes come out with random things, so we just ignored it.

'Right, so now we just wait, employ stealth, and be quiet,' Salmon said.

'What does that even mean?' Rocky asked.

'It means when we hear the door open, and I am pretty sure we will, we stay quiet. We have to catch her in the act,' I commanded.

'No repeat of the other night, lad,' Salmon said to George.

'Of course not, Pickles isn't with us and I do know how to behave,' George grumbled.

'He isn't, is he?' I asked, paranoid.

'No Alfie,' Snowball reassured me.

'Phew, I think my nerves are getting the best of me.'

'Right, well, I think we all know what we need to do,' Salmon said, trying to sound in control.

'You mean nothing,' Nellie said.

'Well, nothing for now,' he replied. Honestly what kind of army were we?

We all did our own thing. I fretted and Snowball tried to reassure me. Elvis explored and George showed him around, giving him a guided tour. Salmon sat upright and alert, as if ready for anything. Nellie and Oliver were climbing on some chairs and Rocky had closed his eyes. I repeat, what kind of army were we?

'Um,' I cleared my voice. 'This is not a holiday camp, it's serious business.' They all looked at me and carried on with what they were doing.

It felt like we had been there for hours. I was about to ask Salmon if we should give up and leave out of the unlocked back door – we could push it with all of us and get out easily – but then we heard a noise.

'Listen,' I said, and everyone crowded round. We could

hear footsteps and I saw a light from a torch appear. There was a dark figure, and though I couldn't see clearly who it was, I assumed it was Barbara. She made her way towards the stage. As she got closer I saw that it was definitely her. She was wearing all black, carrying a torch in one hand and something else in the other, I couldn't make out what.

'Right, prepare for action,' Salmon said. I had told him he could give the commands. We watched as she got onto the stage and muttered some words I couldn't make out. Then she knocked over one of the Christmas trees. As it made a loud crash, I looked at Salmon and blinked. 'We are a go, I repeat, we are a go,' he said.

The new few minutes were pandemonium. George and I ran for the stage from the centre, Salmon, Snowball, and Oliver went left, and Rocky, Nellie, and Elvis right. It was a good strategy; though she tried to chase us, we were all running in different directions, which confused her. She then pulled out a can, and before I knew what she was doing she had pointed it at George.

'George, watch out,' I hissed, but it was too late as his tail and backside were sprayed bright red. She was obviously planning on doing the same to the trees. She was spraying at us but the paint was hitting the stage, making even more mess. Nellie tried to scratch at Barbara's leg, but she managed to throw her off, however, she did drop the can. Thankfully, Nellie was quicker than her as she ran around in a circle, confusing Barbara, whose arms were flailing around. She spun around and around, making herself dizzy and increasingly unsteady as she tried, and failed, to chase us.

'You awful cats, I will get you and you'll be sorry,' she

shouted, but she wobbled as she tried to grab Snowball and missed, almost falling over her own feet.

We ran around some more with Barbara chasing us, but finally Salmon and Snowball launched themselves under her feet. I watched in horror in case my beloved was in trouble, but Barbara lost her footing, wobbling backwards, arms swinging to try to steady herself as she fell into the trees. It was as if it was all in slow motion as she went backwards, landing on the stage with a number of the trees falling on top of her.

'Ahhhhh,' she screamed, and then as she lay still all went quiet.

'Oh my goodness, do you think she's dead?' Nellie asked as we all crowded around, pretty much unable to see her.

'Of course she's not,' Salmon said. Although how he knew, I wasn't sure. The trees were quite light, I reasoned, so it wasn't likely that she was.

'I've got a bright red tail,' George lamented, spinning around as he tried to see it. 'How am I meant to be a sheep with a bright red tail?' he asked.

'Shush, what are we going to do about her?' I asked.

'We'll have to get a human,' Snowball said.

'She might be badly hurt,' Elvis said. 'I've seen it on TV, my owners like hospital drama so I'm something of an expert.'

'Who would be the best grown-up to alert?' Salmon asked.

'It depends on how late it is. Quick, let's go to our road and see who is still up.'

We all left, pushing the back door with all our might and squeezing out one at a time until Rocky, the last of us, made it out. I had been slightly worried about that part of the plan. As we made our way home, hearts still hammering, I was pretty exhausted but pleased that we had a) made it out in one piece, b) would now have Barbara banged to rights, and c) our only casualty was George's red tail. I was so proud of all my friends and how brilliant they had all been. I felt a little bit proud of myself, too.

'You were all so brave tonight,' I said.

'But I hope she isn't really hurt,' Nellie said.

'My tail,' George repeated.

'We don't want her to be hurt,' Snowball said. 'Just stopped.' I knew it wasn't our fault, she fell into the trees, but I agreed, we didn't want her to be hurt. But we did want to stop her, and it looked as if we may have succeeded in that.

Chapter
Twenty-Eight

I led the gang back to ours, to see if we could find a human to help us.

'Hey I can see a light on our front step,' I said. There were a lot of Christmas lights outside our house though, so I wasn't sure that anyone was there until we got closer. Thankfully, we struck gold. 'Right, we go as a gang, and they'll have to take notice of us.' I led my army up to our front door, where Jonathan was stood, talking to Matt.

'What on earth?' Matt said as he saw us. On cue we all started making an almighty noise, prancing around and making a general fuss.

'Oh God, not this again . . . Is George's tail red?' Jonathan asked. We made our way to the front gate.

'What are they trying to tell us this time?' Matt asked. We all started making noise again.

'OK, I'll get my shoes.' Jonathan went into the house, leaving Matt staring at us, confusion in his eyes. As Jonathan came out and shut the front door, we saw the Goodwins' door open.

'What is going on?' Vic asked as he strode across to us, Heather trotting behind him trying to catch up. 'Salmon, what are you doing?'

'Meow,' Salmon said.

'No idea,' Jonathan said. 'They are all here screeching away, so I think we need to follow them.'

'This is most bizarre,' Heather said, looking at Salmon, who raised his whiskers.

The other cats went home but Salmon, George and I led them back to the community hall and to the back door. I was excited, this was one of our more elaborate – and dare I say it, dangerous – plans and we seemed to have pulled it off. Matt opened the door and turned on the lights, which made me blink as my eyes adjusted to the dark. We led them all to the stage where they looked at the mess, and we tried to draw attention to where Barbara—

'She's gone,' George hissed.

'Oh no, what a nightmare,' Salmon said. I was bitterly, bitterly disappointed as I glanced at the humans.

'Who the hell did this?' Jonathan asked. 'My budget won't stretch to new trees, not if we're going to make money for the shelter.'

'Do you think it was the cats?' Vic asked.

'Meow.' Of course not.

'No, the cats won't have done this and look there's a can of spray paint. Even I know that cats can't use spray paint,' Matt said with a laugh, then stopped when he saw how downcast Jonathan looked. 'Hey, the trees will be alright mate, but we'll need to clean this red paint pretty quickly. Not just on George's tail and bum it seems.' Matt put a reassuring hand on Jonathan's shoulder.

'Yowl.' George really wasn't happy.

'We'll bath him at home, but let's get the stage cleaned up right now,' Jonathan said. Heather and Vic went to the kitchen then came back with a bowl of water and started scrubbing the stage.

'But what were the cats doing here?' Heather asked, glancing quizzically at us. Matt and Jonathan started picking the trees up and it was soon apparent that it actually looked much worse than it was. But where had Barbara gone and how on earth were we going to catch her now? The red paint was coming off the stage with a bit of elbow grease, hopefully George could be restored as easily.

'Of course,' Vic said, standing still, tree in one hand.

'Of course what, Vic?' Matt asked.

'Heather, why didn't we think of it? We got Salmon a camera collar, it records everything. No sound, mind, it's not that sophisticated, but we can watch the footage.'

'You mean to tell me you have a camera on your cat?' Jonathan looked incredulous. As did I. If I'd known that it would have made my plan so much easier. I glared at Salmon.

'I didn't know what it was for,' he hissed at me. 'They only put it on me yesterday.'

'We bought it after he got shut in the prop room the other night. I said to Heather, if he goes missing and we've got a camera on him we'll always be able to find him. Didn't occur to me that we'd be able to use it to fight crime, but what a bonus.' Vic sounded very pleased with himself and for once I was pleased with him too. Busybodies who liked to know everything that was going on came in handy on a number of occasions.

'You put a camera collar on your cat?' Jonathan repeated, scratching his head.

'I spoke to some of our friends in the security and cat-loving community we're part of and they suggested it. Said it was very good for making sure our cats were safe and it's also interesting to see what they got up to.'

Goodness, would Jonathan get me one? It would make

my life so much easier if I could communicate to my humans that way. Although of course there were times when I valued my privacy and didn't want them to know what I was up to . . . Um, thinking about it, I wasn't sure. No, in fact, no, I definitely didn't want a camera on me.

'So how do we see what it recorded?'

'It's linked to my phone. Oh, how exciting, this is the first time we get to use it and we might have solved the great mystery. I told you it was a good idea, Heather,' Vic said.

'You did, Vic, and you were right,' Heather replied.

'So, we can see what happened here tonight?' Matt asked, clearly trying not to sound impatient.

'We certainly can. Come and look.' As Vic did something to his phone, they all crowded round the screen and I was pretty sure we had managed to do exactly what we set out to do, although not exactly how we set out to do it. And as Barbara wasn't even hurt, she would hopefully be caught this time. As they started to watch the footage I felt nervous. Would it be clear it was her? Would they only see us and the trees? If this didn't work then I didn't know what we'd do.

'It's very dark and fuzzy,' Matt said.

'Well, it is a cat cam,' Heather said defensively.

'I can make out the cats running riot on the stage,' Jonathan said. 'Blimey, you guys were crazy.'

I tried not to take offence – we were saving the show *and* Jonathan's budgets at the time.

'How on earth did all the neighbourhood cats get involved?' Matt asked, sounding confused. 'Oh look, there's a pair of human feet, not big feet either,' Matt pointed out.

'So, by the look of this, the cats were trying to stop whoever it was from doing any damage,' Jonathan said, scratching his head.

'Ah, Salmon, chip off the old block, he is the cat neighbourhood watch,' Vic said proudly. I decided to let that one go. I mean, I didn't do all this for praise, but they could have acknowledged me.

We finally struck lucky. Just as I thought they wouldn't identify her from her feet and ankles, Jonathan shouted.

'Look, there, the cats sort of trip the person up and oh, she, it's a she, fell under all those trees,' he exclaimed.

'My goodness, is that Barbara?' Heather asked. She was identified by her springy grey hair, I assumed.

'It looks like her,' Vic said, a bit uncertainly.

'Meow,' I shouted. Yes it was.

'She fell under a lot of trees,' Matt said.

'You know, ever since she did that awful audition I knew there was something dodgy about her,' Jonathan added. Actually, in fairness, he did. It was Claire who said she was fine. He never trusted her.

'Well, it looks as if we have our culprit,' Vic said.

'But why would she do it?' Matt asked.

'I guess we'll find out when we confront her with our evidence,' Vic said. 'Good work Salmon and friends.'

So, OK, it probably should have been Alfie and friends but again, I was going to let that go because she was there on film, so finally our work here was done. Lucky, as I was beyond tired. Being a crime-fighting cat is not for the faint-hearted.

Chapter
Twenty-Nine

Chapter
Twenty-Nine

'So I didn't even need to install cameras, I could have just put the cat in there the whole time,' Jonathan said as he explained to Claire what had happened.

'So you're telling me the cats foiled the plan and it was . . . Barbara? Have you called the police?' Claire asked.

'No, we talked about what to do, and we agreed to confront her, or rather for Vic and Heather to, I'm going to be at work. We don't know if having her arrested would be good for the show – it's pretty low to try to ruin a charity show and Vic said that maybe we should find out why she did it first.'

'I wouldn't have expected him to be so reasonable. I'm furious. I was nice to her and the other night she came with us to find the cats, but she must have been the one to shut them in there.'

'I know, it's a shame Salmon hadn't got his camera collar on then. But the main thing is, it's over. Vic and Heather said they will confront Barbara tomorrow morning and will call you so you can go along too. We'll need to tell Aleksy and Connie, but let's see what she has to say first.'

'You're being reasonable.' Claire sounded surprised, which made sense given that Jonathan wasn't known for being reasonable.

'Matt said her husband died and she cried with Polly the other day so maybe we shouldn't judge too harshly, but you know what a softie Matt is. Regardless, we won't let her anywhere near the show, that is not in dispute.'

'Oh Jonathan, I'm just so happy the show is saved.'

'And my budget,' Jonathan replied. 'No more damage to worry about once we confront her. We should really thank Alfie, George, and their cat gang; it was them that sorted it. Again. And the cat collar camera thing was mad, but actually really useful,' he added.

'I'll buy them pilchards tomorrow, after we've confronted Barbara,' Claire said, and my tummy rumbled with anticipation. 'But first, George, we need to bath you and try to get the red paint off.'

'Meow.' George was a little strange as he didn't mind water and baths. Not very cat-like, if you ask me, but then I often said that it takes all sorts.

I rested in my basket as George got bathed, thankful it wasn't me. I really disliked baths and when I had taken them in my past I had found them really quite unpleasant. But poor George needed it as he did look funny with a red tail and backside. I didn't know whether to laugh or cry.

I was so tired but also feeling victorious when George emerged from the bath. He was pretty much his usual colour, although there was a bit of a pink tinge still on his tail.

'It wasn't easy to wash my tail,' he explained. 'Claire tried to be gentle but it wasn't the most fun bath ever.'

'Sorry, son, but thankfully a bit of red paint was the only casualty of the evening.'

'What about Salmon's camera collar though; whoever heard of such a thing?'

'I hadn't, but in this case it was lucky we had it. I thought

Barbara would still be under those trees when we went back with the humans.'

'Me too, I don't know how she got out.' George looked pensive. 'I hope that they don't get ideas and give us cameras, I like my privacy.'

'I was thinking the same. But Salmon will probably like it. It'll give him even more power on the street,' I said.

'How come?' George asked.

'Well, if he comes to see us and he's wearing it, we'll all have to be on our best behaviour,' I pointed out.

'Not to mention looking our best,' George finished. I hadn't even thought of that, but then I pride myself in looking my best at all times.

'Anyway, I am going to go with Claire, and Vic and Heather, when they confront Barbara, are you coming?'

'I'd love to, Dad, but I have to go and see Hana first thing – I promised I would – so I might not be back in time. To be honest, I'm just glad we exposed her and didn't get hurt. Apart from my tail, of course.'

'That was just a bit of paint, George.'

'Yes, but I was the only one affected, so I think that makes me the hero of the night.'

I decided not to mention the fact that I had masterminded most of the plan, rallied the troops and it was actually Salmon and Snowball who got Barbara to trip over. I also didn't mention that Salmon's camera was possibly the actual hero of the night . . .

'George, you are always my hero,' I said instead, and nuzzled my boy.

★   ★   ★

I was so excited to go to confront Barbara, and waited patiently the following morning until Claire grabbed her coat and said it was time to go. We had Pickles so he went with her, and if Claire was surprised when I followed her out she didn't show it.

It was quiet as we left our house, and I could see that another frost had settled in overnight. We went to collect Vic and Heather, and of course Salmon. After our eventful night I expected all the other cats would be having a bit of a lie-in this morning. They deserved it.

Salmon and I raised whiskers at each other and hung back from the humans.

'Sorry, I didn't know about the camera. They just said it was a new collar,' he said.

'Hey, no, don't apologise. As much as I'd like to take the credit, it was actually Vic and Heather who basically won the day with that collar,' I grinned.

'Yes, but now they can watch my every move. I'm glad I had it on the one paw, but on the other, I think that when I do anything – just going about my normal business – I'm going to be so self-conscious.'

'I know, I was thinking the same about having one. Maybe we can find a way to get rid of it?'

'Another one of your plans coming up, Alfie?'

'You know it.' I grinned again. I felt as if we had cemented our friendship over the last few days and I was proud of us both. How to get his collar off though . . . That would take a whole lot of new thinking. For now, we had to run to catch up with Claire, Vic, and Heather, because we had reached Barbara's flat.

Some of the houses in Edgar Road had started hanging their Christmas decorations, which we were able to admire as we walked, but Barbara's flat didn't have any sparkly lights or bright tinsel hanging in the windows. Maybe she tried to ruin the show because she didn't like Christmas?

They rang the doorbell and waited until Barbara answered. She wasn't looking her best. She had a bruise on her cheek, and I could see some streaks of red paint in her hair.

'Hello,' she said with a smile, and I resisted the temptation to go and stamp on her foot. I know that wasn't nice but she had shouted at us and chased us last night. Not to mention poor George's tail.

'Barbara, we have come to you with a very grave and serious matter,' Vic said.

'Very grave, indeed,' Heather repeated.

'What? What's wrong?' She ran her hand through her hair and . . . yes, definitely red paint.

'It has come to our attention that for some reason you have been the person sabotaging the show,' Vic said.

'No, you must be mistaken, it certainly wasn't me.' She really was a good actress. There was no flicker of guilt in her eyes, no awkward gestures that people sometimes make when they're lying.

'I'm afraid we know it was you,' Claire said. 'We have no doubt at all, so it's probably best that you admit it now.'

'Why on earth do you think it was me?' she asked, but her mask was beginning to slip.

'The cats,' Heather told her.

'What do you mean the cats? You mean the cats told you

315

it was me?' She seemed to notice Salmon and I for the first time, and she didn't look pleased to see us.

'No, of course not. Cats can't talk,' Vic said. 'But cat collar cameras can,' he added.

'I really have no idea what you're talking about.'

'Barbara,' Claire sounded annoyed now. 'You're a grown woman. We saw the footage of you chasing the cats on the stage and then falling over the trees. Also, the spray paint. My George's tail and bum were bright red. We have proof it was you.'

'You mean there's a camera on the cat?' Her voice squeaked.

'On Salmon, our cat, yes,' Heather explained.

'And we have no alternative but to make a citizen's arrest. I hereby arrest you in the name of the—'

'Please, don't arrest me. I did damage some things but honestly, you can't go to the police.'

'And why on earth can't we?' Heather said. I was pretty sure she had some handcuffs in her handbag, ready and waiting.

'Oh goodness, I am sorry. Really.' Barbara had turned very pale but then I remembered she was an actress, so I wasn't sure if she was putting on yet another act. 'I mean it. I should explain. I've been in a rage since I moved here – and I didn't know why I was angry all the time – and my daughter said to try to get involved with the locals and then I saw the poster for your show. I thought with my acting experience I could get involved, but I felt side-lined, pushed to a small part, and no one even asked for my help and advice, even after I told you all about my experience with amateur dramatics. So I felt my rage building and I wanted to ruin the show. I have no excuse, apart from perhaps feeling mad with grief, having lost my home and my friends because I had to move away. Plus I hardly ever see my daughter.' She was babbling, talking so fast I could barely follow her words.

I saw Vic, Heather, and Claire exchange glances. Were they softening? Was I? I still wasn't sure she was genuine.

'While that is all very sad, you behaved in a totally unacceptable way,' Vic said.

'It's for charity. Not only that, but Aleksy and Connie are kids, and they are doing something so, so great. For a grownup to try to ruin that for them and for the homeless shelter is just unimaginable.'

I was tempted to add my two tails' worth but I kept quiet.

'I know, I know. I wasn't thinking straight. I think it became an outlet for my anger. I'm going to see my doctor, tell him how I haven't been sleeping, or feeling like myself at all. Look, I can't tell you how embarrassed I am. I behaved in a totally unacceptable way and I don't expect you to forgive me but if you could just understand that I actually do need help.' Tears rolled down her cheeks.

Claire, Vic, and Heather moved away from the doorstep and gathered in a huddle. Salmon and I joined them.

'I think we should let her go on the understanding that she gets help and stays away from the show,' Claire said. 'I don't think arresting her would be the right thing. It's nearly Christmas, after all.'

'You're right. As much as we never condone breaking the law and we always like to see justice done, you can tell she's really not in a good way,' Vic agreed, which surprised me. He normally loved having people arrested.

'It's agreed then,' Heather said. 'We will give her the chance to get help but not let her near the show. We can't risk that.'

'No and I don't think Aleksy and Connie would be able to forgive her so easily. Right, let's tell her,' Claire added.

We returned to the doorstep.

'We're not calling the police this time,' Vic said.

'Oh thank you. I am sorry.' She sounded sorry, she looked sorry, but I still didn't trust her.

'But you have to stay away from the show and I think it would be good if you wrote a letter of apology to Aleksy and Connie,' Claire added.

'Yes, yes I'll do that. And I'll keep away from the show. I think the idea of Christmas without my husband also hit me very hard.' I saw tears streak down her face, but again, she could have been acting.

'We are sorry about that,' Heather said. 'But for now, I think you need to figure out how you are going to live on this street with people like us and not want to do anything to hurt us.' I didn't often say it but I did agree with Heather.

'You have my word that I am genuinely sorry. And I know if you hadn't caught me I might have done something again, which is such a horrible thought but I really am not myself, I think I might have been temporarily insane or something.'

'I hope the doctor can help,' Claire said sadly, and we all turned to leave.

* ⋆ *

Salmon and I stopped by the recreation ground where Nellie, Elvis, Rocky and Oliver sat. We told them all about the confrontation that had just taken place.

'And what do you think?' Nellie asked.

'I'm confused,' I admitted. 'She sounded sorry, and she seemed to have realised how deranged she was being but then she is an actress, as she keeps telling us.'

'I think she was sorry though,' Salmon said. 'I think she meant it.'

'Only time will tell,' Rocky said. 'Last night, when she was chasing us all over the stage, I really thought she would try to kill us.'

'Well maybe not kill us,' Elvis said. 'But she definitely wasn't playing tag.'

'People are funny,' I mused. 'Anyway, I must go and see Snowball, she'll want to hear the latest.'

'See you later, Alfie. And you're right, people can be funny. If only they were more like cats,' Oliver said.

Chapter
Thirty

I was so ready to welcome family day at the end of one of the most stressful weeks of the year. It felt as if it might be the last one before Christmas Day, what with the show and everything. The house was looking amazing, fully decorated with tinsel, lights, and of course our wonderful tree. Claire had put candles around, which had Christmas trees on them, but she wasn't going to light them – she had done that once and poor George caught his tail on fire, so they were now purely for decoration.

I was still a little tired, having had barely any time to catch up on sleep between seeing Snowball and then my friends, rehearsing for the show, and looking after George and Pickles, although George wouldn't take kindly to me saying that. And I wasn't without worry, even though we'd saved the show.

George said that Hana was still very tired and lethargic, barely able to muster up enthusiasm for the show. I knew she was having a tough time sleeping – she was a light sleeper and woke whenever she heard Theo – but it had been going on a while now. George was unable to get her to come out on their usual walks, and he said when he visited the last few days she just fell asleep. I told him he needed to be understanding, which he agreed with, but I could see he missed the fact they used to have more fun together. I knew that it was hard for them both. I just hoped it didn't ruin their relationship. Marcus and Sylvie had had a few more rows than usual when Theo arrived, because they were both tired, but they had worked it out and I hoped George and Hana would do the same.

In light of everything, family day – which was again at our house – was a welcome day without any show rehearsal, and with the people we loved the most. Our house was a fair size but with us all there it seemed small, and I loved that. Harold and Snowball, Sylvie, Marcus, Connie, Theo, Polly, Matt, Henry, Martha, Franceska, Tomasz, Aleksy, and Tommy – oh and Pickles, of course – all crowded in our kitchen for lunch. Hana didn't come because, as George said, having a quiet house was important for her to catch up on her rest, and he did seem to support her in that, which made me proud and also a little relieved. We put all the Christmas lights on, and the children chose Christmas music to play, which they insisted on singing along to. It was a very, very noisy house today so Hana certainly had the right idea.

After lunch, the children went upstairs and the adults, and the older children, went into the living room. Pickles and George went upstairs to play, but Snowball and I stayed downstairs.

'So, now the younger ones are upstairs, can we talk about Barbara?' Polly asked.

'I was so mad at her, but she sent us a letter saying sorry and, well, I don't know why but it made me sad,' Aleksy said. He was a sensitive boy. He really did have a big heart.

'I would have called the police,' Tommy started. 'Locked her up, thrown away the key.'

'Tommy, you more than anyone know about giving people second chances,' Franceska admonished.

'Yeah, but I didn't do . . . OK, fair enough, but what if she is just pretending to be sorry?' Tommy did make a good point.

'She wasn't that good of an actress, not if that audition we all had to watch was anything to go by,' Jonathan said.

'The letter said that she was going to get help – some counselling for her grief – and also the doctor had given her something to help with her depression, so she was taking steps to feel better and behave better,' Connie explained.

'But she's not in the show, right?' Tommy asked.

'No, I can't cope with re-making anything else,' Tomasz said, but with a laugh.

'You've all worked so hard and we're not doing anything to jeopardise that. We are pretty sure she won't do anything else, but just in case we have three checks a day at the hall and this time we're making sure the back door is locked,' Claire said.

'Oh goodness, I think that was my fault; I didn't check it,' Polly said. 'I feel awful.'

'Me too,' Tomasz added.

'I should have known. You are terrible at locking up, always losing your keys,' Franceska said to her husband.

'No need to blame anyone; it's over now,' Sylvie said. 'And, thankfully, nothing that we couldn't fix happened. I'm just glad the cats are alright.'

That was a matter for debate, George's tail was still a bit pink and no one moaned about that more than him. Especially as he said it hindered him being a realistic sheep.

'But, that does leave us with a problem,' Marcus said.

'What?'

'Who's going to be the wise man now she can't do it?' Marcus asked.

'Jon will have to do it,' Claire said. Jonathan choked on his drink.

'No, no way. I'm in charge of—'

'Budgeting, yes we know but that is all really done now, isn't it?' Claire said.

'What do you mean?' Jonathan said.

'Well, we've spent all the money we need and now we just have to watch the money coming in,' Aleksy said.

'So, I need to be in charge of that,' Jonathan replied. 'I absolutely need to be in charge of making sure that the money is all counted and correct.'

'But it's all online, mate, so we don't need to make a song and dance about it,' Matt said.

'Good pun, Matt.' Tomasz laughed.

'I am not going to sing.' Jonathan looked panicked.

'OK, how about you do the speaking but not the singing,' Connie suggested. 'We can't get anyone else at this short notice, the dress rehearsal is only a week away.'

'Which reminds me, it's nearly time for the advent calendars and I also want to get started on Christmas shopping,' Claire said. 'Who's in?'

As they discussed Christmas shopping – and to my delight, Christmas lunch – I was reminded of my old plan about the Sunday Lunch Club getting to see the show.

I gestured for Snowball to come with me.

'What is it, Alfie? You look as if you have something on your mind,' she said.

'I was hoping we could get them to realise that the perfect

time to have the Sunday Lunch Club to see the show would be on Christmas Day. It would also be such a lovely way to end Christmas.'

'Right, I remember you saying, but how do we tell them that?'

'That's what I can't figure out,' I said. 'I know they have to think of it and I am guessing maybe Harold or Aleksy would be our best bet for coming up with that idea,' I suggested.

'Well, I could work on Harold and you work on Aleksy but I'm still not sure . . .' Snowball trailed off. She was right, this was a difficult idea to convey. But we had to try.

We returned to find Tommy showing the group some of his latest videos that he'd done for the show.

'They are so good and they've really helped to promote the show. The first show is almost sold out already, and there are really strong sales for the other two,' Aleksy said.

'And there's already been quite a lot of donations, so the shelter will be getting a good amount of money this Christmas,' Jonathan added.

'Can we get a cat camera for Alfie?' Tommy asked.

'Yowl!' No, I replied.

'Why?' Jonathan asked.

'We could put the footage on social media, make a story about the show from a cat's point of view. It'd be so cool,' Tommy pushed. I did not like where this was going.

'But the footage was pretty bad – grainy and it wasn't that easy to see – so unless you've got loads of cash—' Matt said.

'Which we absolutely do not,' Jonathan interjected.

'So that's a no then,' Franceska smiled. She was definitely

happy to have her lovely son back rather than the terror he was becoming when this all started.

'No,' Jonathan said. I felt relieved.

'Sunday Lunch Club tomorrow,' Polly said. 'We've got our two coming. I feel bad because they keep asking about the show and I don't know how to get them to see it.'

'Yes, Clive and Doris are the same,' Claire said. 'But, as we're all in it, there's no way to get them there, take care of them and get them home again.'

I looked at Snowball.

'Mew, mew, mew,' she said, sweetly, nuzzling Harold.

'What is it?' Harold asked, shaking his head.

'Meow,' I said.

'Oh God, here we go, trying to tell us there's another baddie in our midst?' Jonathan said. I despaired of him at times.

'Yowl.' I did a running leap and jumped onto Aleksy's lap. He looked at me, and I tilted my head slightly, trying to convey my idea to him.

'I've got it. How about we do a show for them on Christmas Day, after lunch? We'll all be together then anyways,' Aleksy said.

'Meow.' Yes, thank you, that was my brilliant idea.

'But we've got so much to do on Christmas Day, what with the kids and lunch and then, well, normally we chill out,' Matt said. 'It's sort of like adding more work for us all.'

'Imagine, how magical it will be if we could do one final show for them though. And if any of the cast want to bring people, we won't charge, it'll be like a friends and family show,' Tommy said. I glanced at him in surprise, he really had turned a very big corner.

'Not everyone will be able to make it though, as people already may have commitments. It is Christmas Day,' Sylvie pointed out.

'But how perfect for those who we have adopted as friends, as family, to do it on Christmas Day afternoon. We'll still have the evening to chill out. Please say we can do it,' Aleksy begged. I purred loudly in agreement.

'It would be a great way to end the show's run and imagine how the Sunday Lunch Club will enjoy themselves. We can't get them together any other way, really. While those who need to change into costumes and get ready to perform, those who aren't in the show can chat to them and keep them entertained. I think it'll be brilliant,' Connie added.

'I would also love to be Santa for them,' Harold added. 'In fact, I could wear my costume all day, save me having to change.'

I wasn't sure that was a good idea. Harold as Santa might end up with most of his lunch in his beard, as it was a very big beard.

'And if I do a film, I'll be able to do some social media about the Sunday Lunch Club, which we've never really done. Harold, I could interview you about how you came up with the idea in the first place!' Tommy added, sounding excited now.

'Well, yes, but you'll also have to interview George, Snowball, and Alfie, as they all helped me.'

'Fine by me.' Tommy grinned.

'We have to transport the Sunday Lunch Club anyway,

which means we can easily get them from the restaurant to the hall, I guess,' Jonathan said. 'And the others who are with families on Edgar Road could possibly get them there pretty easily. I mean, most could do the short walk, couldn't they?' I thought if anyone would object to the idea it would be him, but he seemed quite happy.

'Oh it would be a brilliant way to bring everyone together on Christmas Day, and these people, who always have to go back to empty homes after being with us, deserve it,' Harold pushed.

'How can anyone argue with that, Dad?' Marcus hugged him.

'Right, well, I'll speak to Vic and Heather, and Ralph, and Aleksy, Connie, you speak to the dance group, your school singers and Sienna.'

'I can ask Sienna,' Tommy said, and I noticed a blush creep up his cheek.

'Great, so we'll have lunch and then don our costumes one last time,' Claire said.

'You don't actually have a costume,' Jonathan pointed out, as if he'd just remembered he had been roped in to play a wise man.

'Which reminds me, Jon, Barbara's costume won't fit you, so I'll need to get you sorted this week,' Sylvie said. Jonathan scowled. And I purred contentedly. This had gone even better than I ever could have hoped for.

Chapter
Thirty-One

Snowball and I had spent a very lovely time at the recreation ground. Cold, frosty mornings were normal now, and the cars on the street wore white blankets most mornings. It wasn't snowing, but it often felt as if it might. Christmas was evident all around us, the houses decorated – some lit up inside and out – and the way that that made us all smile a bit more was evident on Edgar Road. It was a truly magical time. I loved pausing by the windows to admire the twinkling lights and the decorations that hung in each one. It made me feel so warm inside. Christmas was coming and this cat was getting more and more excited by the day.

Now the show was saved, I had a little more time on my paws. I was still busy with rehearsals and keeping my humans in check, but with the dress rehearsal looming we were all very pumped. The Christmas tree now even had a few presents around it, advent calendars – including one full of cat treats for George and I – were being opened now, and everyone was fully embracing Christmas. It even smelt like Christmas. That might have been because Claire decided to try to make a Christmas cake, and let's just say . . . it didn't go well. She was not the best baker and even Pickles turned his nose up at the scraps, which was saying something.

Snowball and I were going back to Harold's when George found us.

'I am so fed up,' George huffed.

'Why?' I asked.

'Hana isn't right but she won't admit it. She's tired, and eating all the time, and though I'm not one to comment on her weight, she has definitely put on some pounds.'

'George, it's because of Theo, I know these things,' I said, remembering how tired we all were when Summer was a baby, and how when I'm tired I eat more. And exercise less. It wasn't rocket science.

'We always eat more when we're tired, George,' Snowball said, echoing my thoughts. 'Look, get the show over and if she still doesn't seem to be getting better we'll think of something, but as soon as Theo starts sleeping she'll be back to her perky self, I'm sure.'

'I am trying to be patient but I got cross today because she was too tired to go for a walk. I can't remember the last time we went out together, apart from rehearsals, and I snapped and she snapped back, which she never does.'

'Hey son, give her a bit of space and then check her later. We're going to Harold's so why don't you come with us, he'll be pleased to see you.'

'At least someone will be,' George grumbled. I understood. Young love was hard and true love was hard. I'm pretty much an expert on both.

We were braver now when we approached Barbara's flat and though we usually just walked past, today, we stopped. Because sitting on the doorstep was Barbara, head in her hands.

'Should we see if she's OK?' I asked.

'What, and get chased or worse?' George asked, still in a bad mood.

'Alfie, you go and see. Just stand a bit of a safe distance

away from her,' Snowball said, pushing me with her paw. I thought about it for a minute but then I moved, tentatively, towards her. I stopped a few paces away, and she looked up. I felt a little nervous, but I stood my ground. I could see her face was wet with tears, and she really did look distraught.

'Meow?' I said carefully.

'Oh goodness, it's no good, it's really no good.' She started crying again. Her body was wracked with sobs and I felt bad for her. This wasn't an act, I was pretty sure. I returned to the others.

'I think she's really upset,' I said.

'What do we do?' Snowball asked.

'I think we should get one of the humans,' I suggested. We never, ever turned our backs on someone in need, no matter what they'd done.

'Let's get Harold,' George suggested. He was the closest, and if he couldn't handle it he could call someone who could.

We trotted quickly to Harold's and let ourselves in. He was in his chair.

'Oh there you are, I was wondering,' he said when he spotted Snowball. She started mewing at him and pawing at his legs, as per my instruction.

'Mew, mew, mew,' she said.

'What is it?' he asked. The three of us went to the front door. 'What on earth?'

But he put on his coat and picked up his walking stick. He opened the door and we burst out in the direction of Barbara's flat.

We slowed down, realising that Harold was a bit slower

than us and he was muttering about having to come out in the cold – he didn't like to go out unless he had to. We finally reached Barbara, who was still on the doorstep. Harold looked at the three of us, his face slightly red from the cold.

'Um, hello,' he said. She looked up; her eyes were very red and she had clearly been crying quite hard all this time.

'H-hello,' she stuttered.

'Hey, you'll catch your death out here, why don't you come to my house, where I can make a cuppa and you can tell me what's wrong?'

'But I'm the woman who ruined the show, or at least tried to,' she said.

'To me, you look like someone who is very sad, and that means you come to mine, I'm not going to take no for an answer.'

Barbara resisted for a bit longer but then she stood up and followed him, trying to stop her tears. The three of us followed. I wasn't sure if we were all going to try and find out what was going on, or to protect Harold in case she was still a little unhinged. Probably a combination of both.

When we reached Harold's living room, he gestured to his chair.

'Go and sit by the fire and warm yourself up,' he said. Goodness, Harold had softened in the last few years since we first met him.

'Thank you,' Barbara mumbled.

'I'll go put the kettle on. Tea OK for you?' he asked. She nodded and started crying again.

★ ★ ★

It took a while, because Barbara kept breaking down, but they had a long and in-depth conversation in the end. It was all about loss. Harold understood what it was like to lose a partner (as did I, of course), and he told her that as much as she felt she wouldn't be able to carry on, she would. He really did a good job, I have to say, I was immensely proud of him. He was kind and caring and sweet, nothing like our old Harold – who used to wave his walking stick at George – that was for sure.

'I'm just so lonely,' Barbara said. 'I never lived alone before and I'm here with no friends, and any friends I hoped to have are gone because of my stupid behaviour.'

'Hey, you weren't yourself. And you've done the right thing, getting counselling, not that I ever held with it, but now I can see it's the best thing. It's not going to be OK overnight. And as for friends, well, yes, you did burn some bridges, but bridges can be re-built. And I'm your friend now.' Oh Harold, I thought, I couldn't have done a better job myself.

'The cats are always together aren't they?' she asked suddenly. George raised his (still slightly pink) tail, he clearly wasn't ready to trust her yet.

'Yes, and you know, I didn't think I liked cats before. George used to visit me and I'd tell him to go away but one day I collapsed and he somehow managed to get me help. They are amazing, the cats of Edgar Road – especially these three – and I don't know why anyone wouldn't love cats.'

Again, I couldn't have put it better myself.

'My husband didn't like cats, so I suppose I didn't either. He said they were pointless, not like dogs, but then they were the ones who caught me, weren't they? So, not so pointless, I guess.'

I wasn't sure if that meant she liked us now or not and I tried not to take umbrage that anyone could think cats were pointless.

'They may take a bit of getting used to, but if you want to be friends with us, then you better start liking our cats. They're part of the family,' he chuckled.

'Oh I miss having a family so much.' She started crying again.

I glanced at George, I really needed to get home. Not only was I hungry – Harold was too busy comforting Barbara to give us snacks – but also, this room was so warm I was about to fall asleep. We all went into the kitchen.

'We better go,' I said. 'But Snowball, tell us how this ends, if you can get away later. Or if not, see you at rehearsal.'

'Will do.' She nuzzled me goodbye. 'And George, be patient with Hana, she's worth it,' she said.

He raised his whiskers. 'Seeing how sad Barbara is made me realise when we love someone we do whatever we can to keep hold of them,' he said sadly. It was very true. And some of us weren't lucky enough to hold on to them forever, so when you could, you should.

I had a lovely sleep, I dreamt of Christmas, dinner, all the treats, the happiness, and the show. It was all merging into one. When I woke I did think of Barbara, as she really did seem so upset and I was pretty sure she wasn't acting anymore. But how could we convince the others to let her back in, maybe not to the show, but as a friend? She and Harold seemed to be friends now so maybe he would help her, but it would have been good if she could join the Sunday Lunch Club – I couldn't believe I was thinking that. I was better at forgiveness than I thought.

'Dad,' George said, as I woke up fully.

'Yes, son?'

'I think we should all forgive Barbara. I was thinking how bad I felt when we lost Tiger mum and how sad I was after. I didn't always want to be nice, did I?'

'Neither of us did, lad,' I said.

'So, maybe she should have another chance, although with her it'll be about her hundredth chance.'

'I think you're right. After all, what would Tiger mum do?' We often asked this, because it kept her alive not just in our hearts, but in our lives.

'She'd give her another chance, but she would only let her have one more,' George said. He was right, that was exactly what she would do.

'The thing is, I'm not sure how we get everyone to give her another chance?' I said.

'I don't think we need to, I think Harold will do that,' George said. Interesting, I thought, if he was right then I would be one happy cat.

George was spot on, as it turned out. At rehearsal that evening, Harold climbed on stage, clutching Snowball for confidence, and addressed everyone.

'I know that Barbara messed up. She knows she messed up. But we've had a heart to heart and she is very sorry. She's getting help but you know the best help is friendship. Most of you in this room, especially the cats, have taught me that, and so I'm asking you all to extend the hand of friendship.'

'But she nearly ruined the show,' Vic pointed out.

'Yeah, how do we know we can trust her?' someone else shouted.

'Listen,' Harold said. 'I know she did wrong and she is going to put it right. She doesn't have much money but she is going to donate all her husband's clothes to the shelter, and she is also going to volunteer there to make amends. She really is trying and I think if we give her another chance to be in the show, to be friends with her, we'll find out she really has changed; or gone back to who she was before, which I think is probably more the case.'

'Don't forget the Nativity is about God and what he did for the world. God and Jesus are both all about forgiveness,' Ralph the vicar added.

'We should give her another chance, it is Christmas after all,' Sienna, who was so lovely, said.

'Yeah, even though I was a trouble maker for a bit, everyone gave me another chance,' Tommy said. I had a feeling he was more interested in impressing Sienna than worrying about Barbara. Never mind.

'OK.' Jonathan clapped his hands. 'Let's take a vote. Who votes we give Barbara another chance – bearing in mind that we can keep a close eye on her from now on. Raise your hands.'

'I still won't leave the hall without checking it is all fully locked, but I also think she deserves another go,' Franceska added.

I watched, impressed, as everyone raised their hands until

it was unanimous. Barbara was back in. I saw Jonathan grin as he went over to Claire.

'No need to measure me up for a costume then,' he said with a wink.

Chapter Thirty-Two

'Pickles, stop doing that,' Polly shouted as she scooped Pickles up from where he was trying to eat the pretend Christmas presents.

'Can you keep him with you?' She shoved him into Jonathan's arms, and he had no time to object as Pickles started wriggling. Pickles had a new Christmas collar on – it was decorated with Christmas trees and it made him look very festive, we all thought, although he had even tried to eat that.

It was chaos. It was wonderful. We had finally reached the dress rehearsal and backstage was mad. What we hadn't thought of when we were rehearsing was the fact that when the acts weren't on stage they were out front, watching. However, out front tonight was full of the people we were doing this for. Even Claire was struggling to keep everyone under control, but it didn't matter because we were all excited and raring to go.

The hall had never looked better. The Christmas decorations were all in place, it was lit up beautifully, the curtains hung invitingly across the stage, and the smells of mince pies (not baked by Claire), and gingerbread filled the air.

The Helen Street Shelter patrons had arrived, led by Greg and some of the other volunteers. It was so real now, as they filled the hall. We had done it and it was really happening. I was chock-a-block full of emotion. We were doing it for them.

Tonight was the first time we'd all been in full costume.

The dancers and the singing groups had arrived already dressed, as their costumes had consisted mainly of Christmas jumpers, and the dancers wore Christmas leggings and T-shirts, but those in the Nativity, the children, and us, had costumes to be fitted. The children were dressed as reindeer, and we were dressed as sheep, but more about that later.

'Right, dancers get ready. As it's so cramped back here, when you're finished, go and sit in front of the stage, I think that's best,' Claire directed as she, and her clipboard, started organising the acts. She was pretty good at it, calm but just bossy enough. There was so much noise backstage, everyone was excited.

'We need quiet,' Franceska shouted, clapping her hands together, and everyone began to lower the volume.

There was a hush in the hall as Aleksy and Connie made their way on stage. I had to look so I squeezed through legs to the side of the stage, and pushed my head through the curtain so I could see. Not brilliantly, but I could see a bit.

'Hello, good evening,' Aleksy said shyly, finding his voice.

'We'd like to welcome you to your Christmas show,' Connie said. The crowd clapped.

'We hope you enjoy it, but bear in mind this is our dress rehearsal, so if anything goes wrong, please be kind.' They all laughed. 'And after the show we would love for you to join us for hot drinks and some food,' Aleksy added. 'Right, well, here it is, the Edgar Road Christmas show!'

Everyone clapped as the curtains opened – much to our relief – to reveal the dancers waiting on stage.

I couldn't see much of the show from where I stood but I'd seen most of it before, though having everyone in costume made it even more amazing. The music sounded good, and from what I could see the audience were enjoying themselves. I began to relax, and I saw from Aleksy's face that he did too. It was all going to be more than alright.

By the time the children, who looked adorable as reindeer, mounted the stage with Pickles, the show was in full force. I had to watch this, so again, I snuck round to where I could almost see. They sang and danced enthusiastically but Pickles was trying to get his antlers – possibly to eat – and he ran around in so many circles he ended up falling off the stage.

There was a bit of a commotion, but one of the dancers caught him and put him back on stage. He seemed relatively unharmed as he resumed trying to eat his antlers. The children, professional as ever, kept going and they got the biggest cheer of the night so far.

With the Nativity about to begin, it was all still going well. Snowball, George, Hana, and myself were ready to go. We looked like sheep, and I know this because we all had the same costumes and I saw how the others looked. Even the woolly hats made us more sheep-like. Hana looked the best because she was small and round, but we all looked pretty amazing, I thought. We didn't like dressing up, as a rule, but I was willing to make an exception. It was for a good cause.

'Break a leg,' George said, before we were due to go on.

'Why on earth would we do that?' Snowball asked.

'Oh boy, it's a showbiz term, means good luck,' he hissed. 'But you're not supposed to say good luck as it's bad luck and now I have. Twice. Oh no!'

'Calm down, George, it'll be fine, and how do you know all this anyway?'

347

'I've been in the business longer than any of you,' he said. Of course.

The Nativity was flawless, almost. Mary and Joseph arrived at the Airbnb on a tandem. Mary (Sylvie) had a pillow in her dress and Connie was holding Theo backstage.

'There's no room in my Airbnb. My business is very popular and successful; in fact I consistently get five stars on trip advisor so, no, there's nothing for you, here,' Polly said and everyone laughed. I didn't get it, but it was apparently quite funny.

Before we knew it, it was our turn with the shepherds. I was actually quite nervous as I mounted the stage. My legs were shaking. I gave Snowball a reassuring look as George ran ahead. We all did our sheep impression, George bounding around taking centre stage while we hung back, pretending to eat grass as well as shuffling around a bit. I don't think any of us wanted to steal George's limelight, especially as the audience seemed to be lapping it up. We all became still as the lights dimmed and the song 'While Shepherds Watched Their Flocks by Night' began, sung beautifully by Ralph's choir. Then we were told about the baby Jesus and we set off to meet him after being herded up by Tomasz, who, because he had this sort of head covering on which fell over his face a bit, stepped on my tail.

'Yelp,' I said, not sounding like a sheep at all.

'Sorry,' he whispered as he adjusted his head piece. Apart from that, I thought it was a very authentic representation. And when Peter juggled the toy sheep he only dropped them once, so that was a definite improvement, as he closed our first part.

The choir sang again, and after that a break – or interval, as Aleksy called it – the stage was set and ready for the last part of the Nativity.

When we arrived at the stable where the baby Jesus was born, we all looked on curiously – not sure if sheep did that, but they did in our play. Theo started bawling suddenly, causing us all to jump back, but Sylvie put a dummy in his mouth and that stopped him. Apparently they didn't have dummies in Jesus' time, but as Aleksy said, needs must.

After the finale when Santa Harold came and sat in the armchair, pretended to fall asleep and the children found him there – which was a very sweet scene – he got up and started throwing treats out to the audience, who were all trying to catch them, and then as many people as possible crowded on stage and sang 'We Wish You a Merry Christmas'. It was over too quickly and as the curtain closed, the audience clapped and cheered with gusto. The curtains opened and everyone bowed again. Well, we tried, but it's not easy to bow when you're a cat.

I was exhausted but, for some reason, I couldn't wait until we got to do it again.

'That was brilliant, wasn't it, Dad?' George said, eyes sparkling.

'It was, George, and I now see why you were so keen about stage stuff,' I said.

Backstage was once again chaotic as people tried to change out of costumes and props were tidied up.

'Can I help with the cats?' Barbara asked. I narrowed my eyes. Not likely.

'That'd be great, thank you,' Claire said. Barbara picked

me up and I resisted the urge to jump out of her arms. She had behaved perfectly since the day that we foiled her plan, and Harold was convinced she was a nice lady. She gently took my costume off and then put me down. Wow, that felt better, my fur felt free again.

'There you go, Alfie,' she said, kindly. 'You were all very good sheep.'

Maybe she wasn't all bad after all.

Tommy and Charlie were showing Aleksy the brilliant response they had received on social media after they put some photos and teasers up. Heather was organising the kitchen and making hot drinks for everyone with some of the other Edgar Road singers, while Franceska was in charge of the food. The audience were all chatting happily, having seemed to have really enjoyed themselves. The cast was mixing with all of them, even the younger members. Summer and Martha paraded Pickles around on his lead to charmingly introduce him to everyone. Sienna and Tommy were handing out food, Aleksy and Connie were shaking hands and chatting to people. It was all truly wonderful. Barbara was being particularly helpful and she had kept her word and was volunteering at the shelter now, so she seemed to know quite a few people. Someone called for quiet again, and as we all looked on, a man, who I assumed was from the shelter, took to the stage.

'I just wanted to say,' his voice broke a little. Greg the manager went to join him on stage and he put his arm around the man's shoulder, reassuringly. 'I just want to say that this evening has been something we will never forget.

We are often forgotten and sometimes we even forget ourselves. Because existing is all we can try to do, there's no way we can think about enjoying ourselves.' His voice broke again. Greg patted him reassuringly. My heart felt as if it was breaking a little bit for these forgotten people, and I saw many wiping tears from their eyes, including Jonathan. 'But today, you did something great. Not only are you putting on a show to help us, which we appreciate more than I can ever tell you, but also you invited us to participate. To feel as if we are part of something, part of the community and that is something that almost never happens to us homeless people. So, on behalf of Helen Street Shelter, and all home-less people everywhere, I want to thank you for seeing us, and hearing us, and letting us be a part of something wonderful.'

Everyone clapped and cheered him, and he became the real star of the show.

A litter while later, I noticed a woman I'd never seen before taking photos as Aleksy and Connie approached her. I joined them.

'This will go in this week's paper,' she said. Ah, she was from the local paper. Claire talked about them doing a piece. 'I've got lots of great photos and I know this will be a wonderful Christmas story.' She sounded emotional.

'Brilliant! Did you enjoy the show?' Aleksy asked.

'I loved it. And I think people are going to love the cats as sheep and the adorable reindeer, so as well as a picture of some of the people from the shelter, we'll use those. I assume there's a link to buy tickets and donate?' she asked.

'Oh yes,' Connie said, and smiled. 'Let me get you all the details.'

'Before we go, we wanted to give you some feedback,' Aleksy said when the people from the shelter had left, so it was just us cast. It had been a long night as we stayed for ages, mixing with our guests and the children were worn out from excitement and too much sugar; they were all about to crash and I felt ready to do the same. But we all listened intently. Were they going to say anything about us sheep? I thought we did a good job, but . . . I held my breath.

'You were all brilliant!' Connie announced and we cheered, well, I mewed, but you get the idea.

'And, the shows are all now practically sold out,' Aleksy added, to more cheers.

'Thank you all for your hard work. Honestly, seeing the response tonight, how much it meant to everyone in the audience, makes it feel so worthwhile, more than worthwhile,' Claire added.

'Can we also take a minute to say thank you to the organisers?' Polly said. 'Without Aleksy, Connie, and Claire there would be no show, so please, a round of applause for them.'

I looked around the room. No one mentioned me. No one. But then, I was just happy that my idea had gone so brilliantly. That was recognition enough. Or at least, it seemed it would have to be.

As we headed home, we all felt that we'd done something important tonight and everyone was happy, but also our hearts were filled with thoughts of those who didn't have a home to head to. And that was sad beyond belief.

Chapter
Thirty-Three

In some ways the day was normal. We woke, breakfasted, then we were allowed our advent calendars. The children squealed as they opened their doors and got rewarded with chocolate. George and I waited patiently as Toby and Summer then opened ours and handed us our cat equivalent to chocolate. A very nice treat indeed. It was one of our Christmas traditions I would have been happy to keep going all year.

But the day wasn't normal, because it was opening night. We were all excited, nervous, and ready to go all at the same time. The dress rehearsal had been so special, it gave us a confidence in the show that really pushed us all forward. We had also become far more sure about our ability to make it a success. Even with the small mistakes made, which, by the way, I didn't notice, the audience had loved it and that was what mattered. The best news was that all three shows were now sold out. The local paper had written a piece saying the show was 'full of Christmas spirit' and as a result we had sold all the tickets. Donations had also been coming in. Our house was full of gifts that had been wrapped for the people in the shelter; there were so many that Tomasz was going to collect them with his van and we were going to deliver them after the show was finished, just in time for Christmas.

I had mixed feelings thinking about the show being over. It would be sad in so many ways but also good. We could think properly about Christmas then, which we hadn't had much time for, although the turkey had – thankfully – been ordered. The children had written their letters to Santa and were excited but also tired because there was a lot going on at school on top of the show. Actually, we were all quite tired. We had rehearsed and rehearsed, and now we were coming towards the end. Sad, but happy too. We had a lot to look forward to after the show but I might miss being a sheep sometimes. I would definitely miss the applause.

'We are going to be so worn out when this is all over,' Snowball said.

'I'm already quite exhausted,' Hana replied. Poor thing, she did look weary.

'Hey, maybe after Christmas Theo will start sleeping more,' I chipped in cheerfully.

'We can only hope.' She did sound a little dejected and I hoped George wasn't giving her a hard time, but he was off practising his prancing so I couldn't ask him.

I managed to look out and see that the hall was packed full of people. People who had paid money to come and see us. I knew some of them were friends and family of the cast but still, it made me feel proud and warm inside. It really did make me think of embracing the show business bug, as George said. How he had it after his very brief appearance I will never fully understand, but here, with the lights and the audience and the music, it was intoxicating. Perhaps I *should* have been a showbiz cat!

Barbara was doing funny vocal exercises, which she said would help everyone warm their voices and they were all going along with her. Vic and Heather had fully forgiven her now, which meant the rest of their singing group followed suit.

'Meowwwwwww,' I tried to join in but I couldn't make the right sounds. Everyone laughed.

'Oh Alfie, you are such a funny cat,' Barbara said. I still couldn't quite get used to the fact she seemed to like us now. Trust was hard to give to someone who had tried to injure you more than once, but I was trying.

'We have our own warm up,' George said, to me, Snowball, and Hana.

'We do?'

'Yes, swish our tail, raise our whiskers, stretch our paw and say Mewmewmewmew.'

None of us thought it was doing anything at all, but we humoured him.

And then the curtains opened, the lights came on, the music started and the dancers began their dance.

The first proper night of our Christmas show began.

I decided, after three long shows, that I wasn't actually cut out to be a showbiz cat after all. It was the last show and I was exhausted. It had all gone swimmingly, Pickles didn't fall off the stage but he had lost his antlers a couple of times and somehow managed to get covered in glitter. Theo was sick over Sylvie when she was holding him, but it was only a little bit and he slept brilliantly through two of the shows, which they said meant he would be awake all night.

Barbara sang a bit too loudly in her solo part and in the group songs but no one seemed to mind. I think she was still a bit disappointed to be a wise man as she did make a bit of a meal out of her 'we come bearing gifts' line. Ralph the vicar had already invited her to join his church choir and she'd said she'd love to. We cats were purrfect as well, not a paw out of place. We really were very good sheep, even if I do say so myself. I think everyone, on the whole, did a very good job.

It was time for the last scene of the last paid-for show.

'I have an idea,' George whispered to us as we had now been relieved of our sheep costumes. 'Why don't we go on stage one last time and we can pretend to sleep by the fire and then we can get up and join in with the last song.'

'That is a great idea, George, let's go!' We couldn't persuade Snowball and Hana, who were taking a break and having a rest, but we both went on stage and when the curtain opened we were pretending to be asleep by the fire.

The set was really quite lovely, a fake fire glowed in the hearth, a mantelpiece with stockings hung, and in front of the fire sat a mince pie and a glass of milk. There was a big tree, sparkling with lights and decorations and presents – which were fake and had been rescued a number of times from Pickles' trying to eat them, and an armchair.

Harold was relishing his role as Santa. He mounted the stage saying 'Ho, Ho, Ho,' and swung his sack around to put it down. Then he made a fuss of the mince pie and milk and if he was surprised we were there he didn't show it. Maybe he'd had acting lessons from his new friend Barbara, I thought. He sat down in the chair, and he started snoring, which sounded real and a bit like a freight train. There were some giggles from the audience.

Toby, Henry, Martha, and Summer came on stage in their pyjamas all yawning and stretching, as if they had just woken up.

'Let's see if he's been,' Henry said.

'He has, he has,' Martha said.

'But look, he's still here,' Summer exclaimed.

'Wow, that's amazing,' Toby finished. However, as it turned out. Harold had actually fallen asleep and he kept snoring as Toby and Henry prodded him. The audience laughed as if it was part of the show. I looked at George.

'Let's go wake him,' I suggested. We got up and jumped onto Harold – Santa's – lap, mewing with all our might.

'What the hell?' he shouted, startling awake. The audience laughed again. 'I mean, Ho, Ho, Ho, I've been rumbled.'

As the children and Santa walked to the front of the stage to sing the final song, George and I joined them, and as Harold threw sweets into the audience, I felt quite emotional. Yes, we would be doing it again for the Sunday Lunch Club, but not with everyone, and so, really, this was our last full show. And it had been wonderful. As the audience clapped and cheered, George and I took our bows – which we still couldn't quite master. But, we really were showbiz cats right at that moment.

Aleksy, Connie, and Claire climbed on stage and Greg from the shelter came up with them.

'We haven't got the final figure yet as money was still being donated, but we have raised at least three times as much as we set out to do,' Aleksy said and everyone clapped.

'Thank you for coming to our show, it has been a real pleasure to work on and thank you to the cast who worked so hard, the backstage crew for all their amazing work, and, well, just thank you to everyone for making it such a success,'

Connie said. Aleksy and Connie held hands. Their confidence had grown amazingly since doing this. Smiles were so bright and everyone radiated happiness. It was a moment I never wanted to forget.

'I would like to say, on behalf of Helen Street Shelter, that we cannot thank you enough. Not only did we get to enjoy your wonderful show ourselves, but the money you have raised will make a real difference. This is a wonderful community, and I think this show has proved that beyond a shadow of a doubt,' Greg said. There were more cheers and photos taken. Apparently we would be in the papers again. Honestly, I hope all this fame didn't go to our heads! It probably would though.

'We came to see you,' Nellie said after the final show. The humans all still chatted inside and we had managed to get out for some fresh air and a bit of space.

'You did?' I was touched.

'What a fine show and what fine sheep you were, not that I've ever really seen a sheep,' Elvis said.

'Oh the singing though, that was something else. I loved it. My owners were in the audience but we hid,' Rocky added.

'Because you didn't buy tickets, did you?' George grinned.

'How can we, we're cats?'

'It's thanks to you that this show made it, and now it's finished.' I felt quite emotional.

'We didn't do much, Alfie,' Rocky said.

'You did, you helped us save the show. And Salmon, is he here?'

'Yes but he went straight home, just in case his owners check his camera collar.' We still hadn't figured out how to get that thing off him, so it looked as if he was stuck with it. Thankfully, Salmon was always on his best behaviour anyway. 'Also, he said his owners were talking about bringing him here on Christmas Day when you do your last performance.'

'I'm sad that that's going to be our last show,' George said. 'I'll miss it.'

'Actually, so will I,' Hana said. 'It's been a real experience being a sheep.'

'There's always next year,' Nellie said and I wasn't sure if she was joking.

'I'm not sure I would be able to cope with this every year,' I said.

'Not if we have all the drama as well,' Snowball finished.

I felt reflective as we headed back to our own homes.

'Oh my goodness, Alfie,' Snowball said. 'I think it's snowing.' We looked up as a soft cold snowflake landed on my nose.

'It is, it's snowing! How magical,' I said, running around in circles. It was only a light dusting but it still made me feel even more like Alfie the Christmas cat.

Chapter
Thirty-Four

It was here. Finally. George and I loved every minute of Christmas Day because the excitement never waned. From the children waking up early – they always woke far too early – to going downstairs to see if Santa had been, lunch, family, friends, and of course today we had the added bonus of the show to look forward to. Our last ever performance. I know we felt the last paying performance was the last one but that was because that was the one where we had all the cast. As expected not everyone could make it today. The dance crew were all in different places, as were the school singers, however everyone else would be there – Vic, Heather, and their group were going to be one or two short but Vic was going to double up on the 'Twelve Days of Christmas'; he was days five and seven, or something like that. Ralph had most of his choir. Of course we were all there, and much to Tommy's delight, Sienna would still be the angel; her grandparents were staying for Christmas so they were coming to see it. Tommy's crush on Sienna was so sweet and I kept trying to think of ways to get them together, always the matchmaker. I couldn't help it, it was in my blood.

I snuck outside and saw that although some of the snow had settled, there wasn't much, which was good because it meant everyone could still make it to lunch without getting stuck, or skidding too much. Barbara was eating with us today. George hadn't quite forgiven her yet but I was happy about it.

Harold and her were getting closer and I wondered where that friendship might lead . . . Not yet, because she was still grieving her husband, but maybe one day in the future. Who knew? Maybe next year I would be Alfie the matchmaking cat again.

For now, I just wanted to enjoy my Christmas Day. It had been an exhausting, stressful, wonderful run up to Christmas and it was going to be the best day ever. I did say that every year, but it generally was.

After the children opened their presents, and Claire and Jonathan made us all a delicious breakfast of smoked salmon, George and I went our separate ways. Although we were going to have lunch with Hana, he wanted to wish her Happy Christmas first. Young love; he couldn't wait. I was pleased that he had stopped moaning about her and they seemed to be back on track. Paws crossed. I made my way to the recreation ground to find Nellie, Elvis, Rocky, and Oliver there.

'Merry Christmas,' I said.

'Hey, Happy Christmas, Alfie,' they replied as one.

'How has yours been so far?' I asked.

'Got my usual cat Christmas stocking, can't complain,' Rocky said.

'I got some fish for breakfast,' Nellie said.

'I got this toy mouse on a stick, what do they think I am – a kitten?' Elvis added.

'I got a new cat bed, which looks very comfortable, but I haven't tried it yet,' Oliver finished. We all compared notes and had a lovely catch-up before we returned to our homes for the rest of Christmas.

I was still feeling full of festive spirit. And smoked salmon. It was noisy at home — of course it was, it was Christmas. The children were being wrestled into clothes — they would have happily stayed in their pyjamas all day, but we had lunch to go to and a show to do. Jonathan was about to leave to pick up Clive and Doris; they had coordinated lifts for everyone to the restaurant, which was a bit like organising a military operation, Jonathan said. I thought it sounded as complicated as organising my humans, in actual fact. Or perhaps not quite that complicated! By the time we were all ready to head out, it was beginning to feel as if order was almost restored. As the adults all met outside our house, most carrying presents, the children took it in turns to hold Pickles' lead. We followed them, and although tempted to jump into Theo's pram and get a ride, we all walked. It wasn't snowing, but it was cold and bright.

'Happy Christmas, Alfie,' Snowball said, falling into step with me. Harold wasn't carrying her for once as Marcus had driven him, picking up Barbara and some of the Sunday Lunch Club before meeting us there.

'Happy Christmas my beautiful Snowball,' I replied.

'It's going to be amazing,' she said. Her eyes sparkled with joy and my heart filled with happiness. It was already amazing. I felt like the luckiest cat ever.

Chaos and noise returned as we walked into the restaurant. Hugs and kisses were exchanged and the presents all piled up – out of Pickles' reach, of course. The tables had been put together around the room to fit us all in; there were a lot of us today. We greeted all our friends, old and new, and then snuck into the yard to see Dustbin and Ally.

'Can't you take a day off?' I said, which I pretty much said every Christmas.

'The rodents don't know it's Christmas, so no,' Dustbin replied, but we all laughed.

'We are going to come and see the show later though,' Ally said.

'I'm so excited that you are,' I said. Since we had joined the last scene of the show on a whim, or actually, on George's suggestion, Aleksy declared that we should have been in it all along, so we were going to do the same today. Better late than never, I guessed.

'I'm probably the most professional out of all of us, but they didn't do a terrible job,' George added, joining us.

'I thought you were looking after Hana,' I said.

'She is having a quick rest. The walk here has worn her out,' George replied.

'Are you sure she's OK?' Snowball asked. Hana had made all the shows but otherwise we'd barely seen her.

'She's just tired out. She says after Christmas is over she'll be her old self again.' George didn't sound concerned so I decided not to worry. That was the gift I wanted for Christmas: a worry-free day.

The noise level from inside told us that everyone was finally here. We went back in.

'Secret Santa,' Claire announced. As there were so many of us for lunch, the humans did something called a

Secret Santa, whereby everyone bought one gift for someone else.

'Can we give them out?' Summer asked. Thankfully, Harold had been persuaded not to wear his Santa costume all day, otherwise he might have insisted it was his job.

'Of course, sweetheart.' The children all dove in and started distributing gifts. As chocolates, bath stuff, scarves, and things like that were all opened, everyone declared themselves delighted with their presents. Even Barbara beamed with happiness. We didn't get to participate in present giving.

'I've got something for the cats as well,' Doris said. Oh, maybe we did this year. I felt excited.

'Oh no, not another cat bonnet,' George hissed at me. Ah, I hadn't thought of that. But actually, she had made us Christmas hats – Santa hats – and we had to wear them now. Mine kept slipping down over one of my eyes, which was most irritating, but I didn't want to offend Doris. George said his made his fur itch.

'It's only one day, son,' I assured him as Snowball tried not to laugh at us.

'I wish I had one, I liked wearing antlers,' Pickles said. If George could have given him his, he would have done.

'Pickles, you'll get to wear your antlers again later,' I assured him.

'Yay!' He did a little wriggle with excitement.

'Alfie, George, come here so I can take a picture of you in your hats. Social media will love this,' Tommy said, and took a photo of us with his phone. Apparently we were on our way to becoming Instagram famous, not that I knew what that was.

For me, the best part came next. Christmas dinner. We cats were given turkey and we tucked in. Dustbin and Ally also had some, but out in the yard. Hana seemed to have perked up as she ate with gusto, but then she said she was too full, and she waddled to the corner and lay down. She did look full, I had to say, but we all ate a bit too much at Christmas. Humans and cats alike.

Games were played with the children, the adults, and Tommy and Aleksy organised them. A couple of members of the Sunday Lunch Club fell asleep in their chairs, and I wished I could join them but there was still so much to do and I didn't want to miss a single minute. Some of the adults cleared up, with Franceska and Tomasz in charge, and all in all, it was a huge amount of fun.

'Could I say something?' Barbara asked. George gave me a 'look'.

'Of course, Barbara,' Claire said.

'God, I hope it's not another *Hamlet* monologue,' Jonathan muttered. Claire poked him in the ribs as Matt laughed.

'I would like to say that this has been the most difficult year of my life. And I have behaved badly, unforgivably so. But you all took me in and forgave me. Not only that, but you also invited me to part of this wonderful Christmas. I don't know how I will ever thank you, but know that if anyone ever needs anything, I will be here for you all.' She started crying. I gave George one of my 'be compassionate' looks as Harold went over to Barbara and put his arm around her.

'Do you think they might be a couple?' George asked me.

'I don't know. I think it's probably too soon after losing her husband for her.'

'Just as well, imagine poor Snowball having her as a human step-mum.'

'George, I think she's sincere and nice now,' I chastised.

'Well I still have a pink tail that says otherwise.'

Shortly after that, we were told it was time to go because this Christmas Day we were going to perform our final, final show.

As coats were put on, lifts organised, and presents put in bags to go home we all left and made our way to the hall. And I resolved that although I had worked hard at all my shows, I would give this one my all, as it was the last ever time I would be a sheep.

Chapter
Thirty-Five

It was easier getting ready for this show with fewer people in the backstage area, but we did miss the acts that couldn't be here. While we changed, the Sunday Lunch Club were all chatting to each other with Christmas music playing in the background and Claire making sure they were all alright, which involved waking a few of them up. I could understand – a big lunch made us all sleepy – but we had a show to do. No time to rest yet.

Without the dancers to open, the kids and Pickles opened the show. As they launched into the by now well-known routine, the whole hall erupted with cheers.

By the time we got to the finale I was full of mixed feelings yet again. Happy that we had performed yet another successful show, sad that it was all over for the year and also sad that Christmas Day was coming to a close. The following day we had smaller family gatherings to look forward to, and the older children were going to go and volunteer at the shelter in the evening, which made me so proud of them. I planned to go to give them a paw.

Aleksy and Connie were overjoyed as the final curtain fell, and Tommy was so excited he actually gave Sienna a hug. When I saw them both blushing red, I thought perhaps she had fallen for his charms after all. Then I noticed them holding hands. Maybe I didn't need to matchmake . . . Another teenage romance to look forward to, that was my prediction. And we all liked Sienna, she was such a sweet girl.

At the end of the show there were lots of hugs and congratulations; everyone had enjoyed it more than they imagined. And as mulled wine was handed out and mince pies eaten – although how anyone had any room, I will never know – I flitted around, listening as our guests all seemed to be happy and complimentary about the show and the lovely Christmas they'd had. There was nothing I liked more than seeing happy people. It warmed my heart. It was what Christmas was all about.

I loved Christmas Day, I really did, but I always felt a bit sad when it came to a close. We had spent so long planning for it and working to make it amazing – and it was – but it seemed to go far too quickly. I had to look around and take a snapshot for my memory. The show, the hall which we might not see again – at least not for a while; the Sunday Lunch Club, who were all having the most fun, social time, rather than being on their own; my own families, who were smiling and laughing; my son, who I couldn't have been more proud of; and Snowball, my love. Life was complete . . . I would hold the picture in my mind forever. There was nothing, simply nothing, that could make this day any better.

'Dad, I can't find Hana,' George said in a panic, interrupting my sentimental moment.

'Well she can't be far.' I looked around but couldn't see her either. We had a quick search of the hall – under chairs, in the kitchen, the backstage area – but we couldn't see her at all. Oh no, today of all days I really didn't need another crisis.

'What should we do?' George asked, getting more and more upset.

'Let's go find Connie, make a lot of noise and hopefully she'll find her,' I said.

'Anything we can do to help?' Dustbin and Ally, who had stayed hidden at the back of the stage, came forward.

'Amazing show by the way,' Ally said.

'Just keep your eyes out for Hana,' I said. 'We'll go and get Connie.'

Connie was talking to a group of people when we approached her.

'Meow,' I said.

'MEWMEWMEW,' Snowball shouted.

'YOWL!' George added.

'What is it?' Connie turned and looked at us. 'Where's Hana?'

'MEOW!' We don't know. She started looking.

'Has anyone seen Hana?' she shouted. The hall stopped talking, and started looking for her. Some people didn't know where to look so they just glanced around, puzzled. But there was no sign of her. Hana wasn't the sort of cat to wander off, that much I knew, but she had been tired. I hoped she'd just fallen asleep somewhere, but where? We had looked pretty much everywhere we could think of. Oh, no, poor Hana. It better not be Barbara.

'Have you seen Hana?' Aleksy asked Barbara.

'No I haven't, honestly. I wouldn't do anything to hurt any of your cats,' she said quickly.

'I was asking not accusing,' Aleksy said.

'Hey, we'll find her, son,' Harold said, putting his hand on Aleksy's shoulder. It must have crossed some people's minds that Barbara might have had a relapse, I know it crossed mine.

'Hana, Hana,' Franceska and Sylvie were both shouting. There was still no sign.

We carried on looking, getting more and more frantic. She can't have disappeared into thin air.

'Um, George, Alfie, I think you better come back here,' Dustbin said. 'Backstage.' We followed him. Because the final scene was the Santa scene, the Nativity set had been moved into the area behind the stage. As we approached, we could all hear a noise which sounded strange, alien almost.

'What is it, have you found her?' George asked.

'Um, yes, and you better come,' Ally said. Thank goodness Dustbin and Ally had kept their word and come to see the show, they were pretty good at finding people, as Dustbin had helped me a long time ago when Snowball got lost.

We made enough of a racket to get Connie to follow us yet again, Aleksy with her. I hoped nothing was wrong as Dustbin led George to the stable and the manger where baby Jesus had been lying on a soft blanket – in case Theo turned out to be allergic to hay – not that long ago.

'Oh my,' George said. 'Hana, are you alright?' I couldn't see what was going on but George's eyes were like saucers.

Hana made a small noise but she didn't sound alright. I tried to get nearer, but it wasn't easy.

'Mum, you better come,' Connie shouted, and the adults rushed over. I still couldn't see what had happened as I got pushed further back, panic building in my fur.

'Oh my goodness she's had kittens,' Sylvie said. I looked at George who was staring into the manger and standing very still.

'Kittens?' I thought, what on earth?

'Jonathan,' Claire shouted.

It was crazy for a few minutes.

'Is there a vet here?' Marcus shouted, as he held on to Theo.

'How did this happen?' Jonathan asked Claire. 'I thought you'd had George, you know . . .' He made a scissor sign, but I had no idea what that meant.

'I thought you did,' Claire said, scratching her head.

'And Hana was a house cat so it didn't occur . . .' Sylvie added.

One of our Sunday Lunch Club pushed through; a man who I think went to the Barkers' house.

'I used to be a vet, let me through,' he said.

I sat down. Kittens? I was in total shock. As, it seemed, was George, who still hadn't moved.

'Can we see them?' the children all said as they tried to push through.

'Give them space, darlings, just for now,' Polly said, holding them back.

'Mother and three babies are fine,' the vet declared. I really wanted to see them, so I finally managed to snake my way through legs to where George was standing. Lying in the manger was a very tired Hana, and three kittens who looked like a cross between both of them. I felt absolutely choked up. My kitten had kittens.

'It's a Christmas miracle,' Toby declared.

'Kittens born on Christmas Day, in a manger, like Jesus,' Summer added. 'Can we call one of them Jesus?'

I hoped we could not. Imagine calling him in from outside, that was, if there was a him. I couldn't tell, they were so tiny, so beautiful; it really was a miracle.

'Oh my goodness, George and Hana have become parents,' Claire wiped a tear. 'This is truly miraculous.'

'Amazing that no one noticed the cat was pregnant,' Jonathan said.

'We've been so wrapped up with Theo, I feel so guilty,' Sylvie said, she was crying too, but I hoped they were happy tears. Marcus hugged her.

'All's fine here, you'll need to get them home carefully, make sure they are fed and after Christmas, take them to your own vet for a proper check-up,' the retired vet said. He looked quite nice, for someone who used to like prodding and poking us about, anyway.

'What an end to the best Christmas ever,' someone said as they all toasted Hana and her babies with their sherry or mulled wine.

Franceska was crying and Tomasz had his arm around her, with Aleksy and Tommy close by. Sylvie was holding baby Theo, and Marcus and Connie stood beside her. Polly and Matt had their arms around Henry and Martha. And Claire, Jonathan, Toby and Summer were all huddled together. All our families and our new additions.

George and I stood a little apart as the retired vet cleaned up the kittens and suggested that they should transport Hana and her babies home in the manger, as it seemed safest not to move them.

'There are two boys and a girl,' he declared.

'Can I hold them?' Martha asked.

'Not yet, love, but soon,' Polly assured her. As many people as possible were crowded round the manger. George and I reversed ourselves to an open bit of space, because for now we couldn't get near.

'Are you alright son?' I asked after a minute.

'I'm in shock. Wow, Dad, I'm a dad. An actual dad. I mean . . . I had no idea . . . All this time, Hana was tired and a bit sick and then she put on weight but none of us had a clue.'

'And now you're a dad. To three beautiful kittens – two boys and a girl. Who would have thought it?' I said, still stunned.

'It explains so much. Poor Hana, not knowing,' Snowball said as she joined us.

'Congratulations, George, what a wonderful thing to happen,' Dustbin said.

'Well, I never. I think that a celebration is definitely on the paws,' Salmon said, joining us.

'What is it?' Pickles asked. The humans had somehow dropped his lead in the fuss. I hoped he behaved himself.

'Hana had kittens,' I explained, still unable to fully process it.

'Can I eat them?' Pickles asked.

'NO!' we all shouted at the same time.

Somehow we all ended up back at Sylvie's house; it seemed everyone wanted to check the kittens were alright. Franceska had driven them, with Sylvie in the car, and George had gone along with them. When they'd arrived home, Hana and the kittens had been moved from the manger to Hana's soft cat bed.

'Can we call the girl Holly?' Summer asked,

'Ah, yes that's a lovely name for a girl kitten,' Connie said. Um, I had to say I quite liked it.

'Jesus,' was suggested.

'No, honestly, just no,' Polly said.

'How about Santa?' Franceska suggested.

'Oh, I really like that,' Sylvie said and everyone agreed. 'Santa and Holly and . . .'

George turned to face me and blinked. I understood immediately. I wasn't sure how to convey it but I stepped on Jonathan's foot.

'Not again,' Jonathan said.

'Meow,' I said, trying to paw his trousers. George then joined me. We took a leg each. Matt laughed but Jonathan was trying to shake us off.

'What are they trying to tell you?' Claire asked. Jonathan paused and looked at me. Finally I saw him seem to understand.

'Oh, why don't we call the last kitten Tiger? You know, after that cat that Alfie and George seemed very fond of – the Barkers' cat who died,' he suggested.

'What a lovely idea,' Marcus said. 'Tiger is a great name for a kitten.'

'But wasn't she a girl?' Claire said.

'Yowl.' It doesn't matter, I replied.

'It can be a boy's name too,' Aleksy said.

'Mew,' Hana said, quietly.

'Meow,' George added.

'Purr,' I finished.

Tiger was a very fitting name indeed, and a very fitting tribute. Jonathan was rewarded with a nuzzle.

* * *

'My lad, a dad,' I said to George as we snuck away slightly. 'Who'd have thought it. I really can't wait to see them properly.' Emotion welled up inside me. My boy, my kitten, was a dad. I probably had to stop calling him my kitten now.

'I know you probably want to stay,' I said to George, 'but I'm going to have a last breath of air, just for a minute.' It was our Christmas tradition, to go and speak to Tiger on Christmas night. And despite everything that had happened, it was important for me to do so.

'I'll stay here,' Snowball said, knowing instinctively, as she always did, that I needed to be alone, or alone with my boy.

'I'll come; just for a minute though,' George said.

We sat outside and found the brightest star in the sky.

'I'm a dad, Tiger mum,' George said. 'And we've named one of the kittens after you.' I could barely keep my emotions in.

'George, you will be an amazing dad,' I said. I meant it.

'Wow, it hasn't sunk in yet, a dad. Three kittens, it means—'

'It means you are going to be very busy. I just had you, and you kept me on my paws.' I laughed, but was choked up at the same time.

'Oh, Dad, you are the best dad ever.'

'And now you are going to be too,' I said.

'And you are going to be the best granddad ever,' George said.

'Oh boy, I'm a granddad cat – a grandcat! Wow, I mean . . .'

'You can help me and you will teach those kittens everything you know, like you did me,' George said.

'And we will love them so much, we really will.' I already did. Those tiny bundles of fur who would no doubt keep both George and I on our paws for a good while to come. I nuzzled my boy. He nuzzled me back.

Just as I thought my heart was as full, as full and as big as it could ever be, it suddenly grew once again.

Alfie's Guide to
Helping the Homeless

One of the central themes of this novel was helping the homeless. As I was once a homeless cat myself – I may have mentioned it once or twice – it is a cause very close to my heart. I believe in my fur, my paws and my whiskers that everyone deserves a loving home and it breaks my heart to think that not everyone has one.

We don't talk about Covid-19 in the novel, but it has hit us all hard in many ways. Being homeless at this time must be unbelievably tough, so I cannot stress enough how people that are struggling need extra protection in these times.

But we can make a difference, and I've put this guide together to help you understand how you can do your bit. I'm in no way an expert, being a cat, but I think we can all do something to help if we really put our minds to it.

Donate to homeless charities. There are the larger national ones, as well as those who serve local areas. If you are able to donate, then please do. If you can't give money – and I know that not everyone can, believe me – then donating clothes (perhaps T-shirts in the summer, coats and jumpers in the winter) is also just as important.

Fundraise. If you are unable to donate money, then time is just as — if not more — valuable. Look at ways to help support the charities, and you can get friends and family involved. I believe that charity is a great way of bringing people — and cats — together.

Volunteer. Again, if you have the time, local shelters often need help, and this is a great place to start and really get involved.

Food Banks. There is a greater need than ever for these. If you can just put one or two things in the food bank trolley when you are doing your shopping, that would be amazing. Imagine if everyone did that? And if you are donating to the food bank, remember they may have cats or other pets!

Initiatives. There are many initiatives that you can find online. Here are a few...

Change Please: Helps those experiencing homelessness train to be baristas and earn a living wage.

Second Shot Coffee: Again, using coffee to help the homeless — who would have thought it? It's a cafe in Bethnal Green, London, and they train homeless people up to work there.

Big Issue: Just buying a magazine and having a chat to the vendor can help, so I encourage everyone to buy the Big Issue when they can.

Crisis: Every Christmas, this homeless charity runs an initiative to help people who have nowhere to have a Christmas meal. My family always does this and it's great if you can too or find something similar.

There are also many other homeless charities – too many to mention, although I wish I could thank each and every one of them for all they do. I have a local charity, **Encompass Southwest**, which I support, so my advice would be to see what you can do in your local area to make a difference.

I hate to sound like a lecturing cat, but I do feel we all need to educate ourselves on homelessness. It is sometimes unavoidable – as it was in my case – and it's also very sad. But those who don't have homes are people and that is the thing I worry is forgotten. They are human beings, with their own stories and their own beating hearts. I think that the most important thing is to see them as such, reach out as a fellow human being, even if you feel you don't understand – perhaps that might be the first step to doing so.

Even if you feel you can't do much, doing anything, no matter how small, is so much better than doing nothing. And I thank you all, if you do reach out to help, because that is what will help to make the world – for people and cats alike – a much, much better place.

At Christmastime,
we all need a friend . . .

Alfie and his mischievous kitten
George are back for more adventures –
this time with a puppy in tow!

Can Alfie and George save Christmas on Edgar Road?

Another heart-warming Alfie adventure that is perfect to curl up with this festive season.

It's time for Alfie's first ever holiday!

Alfie and George are back for more adventures – this time taking them a long way from home . . .

One little kitten.
A whole lot of trouble.

The *Sunday Times* Bestseller

ALFIE

& Ge🐾rge

One little
kitten.
A whole lot
of trouble...

RACHEL
WELLS

**The *Sunday Times* bestseller returns –
and this time he has a sidekick!**